THE MAIDEN BELL

THE MAIDEN BELL

John Pilkington

severn
House

This first world edition published in Great Britain 2005 by
SEVERN HOUSE PUBLISHERS LTD of
9–15 High Street, Sutton, Surrey SM1 1DF.
This first world edition published in the USA 2006 by
SEVERN HOUSE PUBLISHERS INC of
595 Madison Avenue, New York, N.Y. 10022.

British Library Cataloguing in Publication Data

Pilkington, John, 1948-
    The maiden bell. - (A Thomas the falconer mystery)
    1.   Thomas the Falconer (Fictitious character) - Fiction
    2.   Great Britain - History - Elizabeth, 1558-1603 - Fiction
    3.   Detective and mystery stories
    I.   Title
    823.9'14 [F]

    ISBN-10: 0-7278-6293-6

Typeset by Palimpsest Book Production Ltd.,
Polmont, Stirlingshire, Scotland.
Printed and bound in Great Britain by
MPG Books Ltd., Bodmin, Cornwall.

One

On a warm August night, its balmy stillness broken only by the hooting of owls, a knot of men moved quietly into Lambourn Wood.

As the trees closed about them they fanned out into a line, treading softly, allowing their eyes to adjust to the gloom. Only when their leader, John Tolworthy, the miller from Uplambourn, felt the ground begin to rise under his feet did he judge that they were deep enough into the wood, which stretched southward to Coppington Hill. He stopped and gave a low whistle. Four of the party readied the nets, while the other men huddled together, striking sparks and quickly putting flame to the torches. Will Ragg the blacksmith then lifted his flame aloft. The other two torch-bearers separated, one moving to either side of the group. They now formed a rough semi-circle, in the centre of which Tolworthy, a big muscular man, stood tense with anticipation. As everyone watched, he unwrapped the clapper from the low-bell, then shook it vigorously.

In an instant there was mayhem. The bell's harsh clang was the signal for all to move forward, shouting and beating the trees with sticks or simply with bare hands. Those with torches waved them to and fro, yelling like madmen. And almost at once, their efforts began to yield results.

The roosting pheasants and woodcock, their slumbers so cruelly broken, seemed to fall out of the trees. Along with screeches of alarm came a frantic beating of wings as the terrified birds flew in all directions. Yet fly where they would, it seemed at every turn there was either a blazing light, a clanging bell or a shouting man barring their way. Some birds flew into branches and crashed to the ground, where nets descended upon them in an instant. Others tried to fly upwards, but their way was blocked by the dense canopy of summer foliage, and they soon met a similar fate. Still others were so unnerved by the din and the dancing lights that they merely dropped to the ground and froze in terror, seemingly unaware of the nets which dropped over them. And all the while the bat-fowlers hurried to and fro, calling for lights here, nets there, shouting in triumph as the catch multiplied.

Finally, it was over. The panting, sweating men gathered around their leader, grins breaking out.

'A goodly catch, Master Miller.' Even Peter Hare, the grey-headed and usually taciturn shepherd, was content.

'Did Faither not tell 'ee 'twas the best time for bat-fowling?' cried a young man with strings of lank hair about his face. Some of the others nodded indulgently. Tolworthy's son Edward was slow-witted, and few folk paid him any mind.

Tolworthy surveyed the nearest of the nets, which heaved with a tangled mass of game-birds. Like others he was bare-chested, the sweat on his skin gleaming in the torch-light.

'Not bad for one night's work,' he allowed.

Ragg the blacksmith was smiling to himself, thinking of the supper he would lay out soon for a certain widow. Peter Hare the shepherd had lapsed into his habitual, quiet manner. The others were young village men, of similar age to Edward Tolworthy. They nodded, eager to get to the business of wringing the birds' necks and parcelling out their catch.

The last member of the group was John Nightingale, the landlord of Lambourn's only inn, the Horns. But as the miller's glance fell upon him, the man stiffened and half-turned to his left, towards the deepest part of the wood.

'Did ye hear that?'

The others were alert, peering beyond the torch-light. But the only sound was that of game-birds struggling in the nets.

Then they heard it, and froze. A high-pitched laugh, almost a giggle, but seemingly made of both malice and mirth.

Edward started like a frightened child, though he was a swarthy seventeen-year-old almost as broad as his father. Embarrassed, the miller placed a hand on the boy's shoulder.

''Tis naught . . .' he began, then fell silent as the voice came again. This time the laughter gave way to a long, musical note, high and shrill, which struck fear into every man present.

'Jesu . . .' one of the village lads swallowed and turned to the others. 'Some wood-spirit we've woken with our racket . . .'

The blacksmith snorted and shook himself. 'Don't talk foolish, boy. There's naught here but beasts . . . mayhap a weasel snapped a coney's neck . . .'

But Nightingale, a thin, hatchet-faced man, and as level-headed as any of this remote Downland village, was unwilling to believe that. 'Never heard a coney sing in such fashion,' he muttered, 'nor any creature that goes on four legs.' He took a torch from the nearest village lad and stepped forward.

'Where are you going?' Ragg asked.

'To take a look,' the innkeeper answered. 'Something isn't right.'

'What d'ye mean?' Tolworthy was frowning as he followed Nightingale's gaze. Beyond the torch-light they could see nothing. But then there came, faintly, a noise of some kind. It was likely no more than a confused pheasant, still flapping about in the undergrowth. But somehow, no man present drew that conclusion.

'Nay – don't 'ee go out there!' The miller's son drew closer to his father, his lip quivering.

'Peace, Edward,' Tolworthy answered, with some irritation.

Hare the shepherd spoke up. 'I've the best eyes for night-time,' he grunted. When the others looked to him he added: 'Naught will satisfy Master Nightingale till he ease his curiosity. You may stay here.'

Feeling somewhat foolish, the miller nodded brusquely. 'Poke about if you must,' he said. 'Meantime we'll do the work we came to do.' Gesturing to the others, he walked to the nearest of the bulging nets and stooped. As Nightingale and Hare walked off through the trees, they heard the crack of the bird's neck as it broke.

The torch's warm yellow gleam was reflected off leaves of beech, hornbeam and ash. Silence closed about them as the two men, walking in step, drew deeper into the wood. The lights from the main party were now only a distant glow behind them. After another minute, Hare stopped.

3

'The ground's steeper,' he muttered. 'We're climbing Coppington Hill – trees are thinning out.'

Nightingale nodded, in no hurry to turn back. A plain but thoughtful man, he was blessed – cursed, some said – with an enquiring mind that bordered on the scholarly.

'There's someone in this wood that mocked us,' he announced. 'I'd like to know who.'

Hare frowned. 'I wish I'd the dogs with me,' he muttered.

Nightingale had raised the torch and was moving it from side to side, but still there was nothing to see but the trunks of trees. He walked a few paces forward, though it seemed now that even he was losing interest in the search. 'Whoever it is I wager they're gone,' he said over his shoulder, unable to keep the disappointment from his voice.

Hare grimaced to himself, took a step and almost fell on his face. 'By the Christ!' he cried and scrambled up, stepping back in alarm. At once Nightingale was beside him.

'What . . . ?' He peered down, holding the torch out to illuminate the obstacle that had tripped his companion. And sharply, both men drew breath.

An old man was sitting up against a tree with his legs apart, arms by his sides, as if resting. Indeed, he might have been asleep, save for the fact that his white head hung forward, revealing the deep gash about which dark blood had congealed; though not before a good deal of it had run down his neck and on to his jerkin.

Nightingale's hand shook, so that the torch flickered. For what seemed like minutes, neither spoke. Their shock was the greater because they both knew the man whose corpse – for by the pallor of his skin, and the way the head lolled, a corpse it was – now lay at their feet. Then they saw the cord, roughly knotted, which passed twice around his body, binding him to the tree. And if either of them had harboured any thoughts of this death being a mere accident, the notion faded quickly.

'Old Will Stubbs . . .' Hare swallowed. 'Near a saint, he was – never had an enemy in the world.'

John Nightingale's voice was unsteady. 'Who'd do such, to the churchwarden? Not to say bind him – and laugh and screech like that?'

4

The other shook his head. From far away, a shout startled them anew, but it was only one of the other bat-fowlers calling. The party was ready to leave.

'Who would do such?' Nightingale repeated softly, as if to himself. 'Who could murder a saint – lest it be a devil?'

Hare started and, scarcely knowing what he did, made the sign of the cross. Then he caught his breath, as if he could call back the gesture, and glanced furtively at Nightingale. But the other gave a shrug, dismissing the matter. The shepherd wasn't the only man on the West Berkshire Downs who cleaved to the old religion.

A more strident sound stirred both of them from their private thoughts; Tolworthy had rung the low-bell. Wordlessly the two backed away from the fearful sight and turned to go.

Some way off, a barn owl screeched at the interlopers who had ruined her night's hunting. But closer to – closer than either John Nightingale or Peter Hare would have dared imagine – another pair of eyes watched from the cover of an ancient, rotted tree-trunk as the two men hurried away.

Two

Thomas and Ned were in trouble.

The Petbury falconers stood in the park, gazing down at a sorry sight: the mangled body of one of their master's new peacocks. The shiny green plumage had lost its lustre, while the preposterously long tail-feathers were broken in several places. Saddest of all, the bird's delicate crown was flattened and bloodied, as was its neck. It did not take a deal of imagination to work out what had happened.

'The work of one of your hawks, I think, Thomas.' Martin the steward, in his customary black doublet and plain hose, stood frowning at his master's Chief Falconer. A hundred yards away, smoke rose slowly from the kitchen fire of the great house, to hang motionless in the morning air. Another hot day, with no breeze to temper it.

Thomas glanced at Ned Hawes, his young helper, who struggled to keep the colour from his face. The boy could no more stop himself looking guilty than the hapless peacock could resurrect itself.

'I can only ask pardon, Master Steward,' Thomas said. ''Twas careless of me to let a young bird stray from the lure.'

It was a lie, and both Thomas and Martin knew it. But it was not in Thomas's nature to let Ned shoulder the blame. The boy had learned much in his first year as prentice to Sir Robert's falconer, and had earned his trust.

Martin growled under his breath, leaning upon his staff of office. Since the winter, the steward's years seemed to sit more heavily upon him. But his mind was still sharp as a scythe.

'I know full well what the gossips will say,' he muttered. 'That your half-wild falcon has done the household a service. One less of these fowls to wake them up with its shrieking.'

6

Thomas kept a straight face, though inwardly he was inclined to laugh, for Martin spoke the truth. On a whim, Sir Robert Vicary had purchased half a dozen peacocks in the spring, and allowed them the run of the Petbury park and gardens. Within a very short time the entire manor, from Lady Margaret herself to the humblest gardener's boy, had grown heartily tired of the great, clumsy birds. Their sharp, keening cries rang out day and night, startling every living thing on the estate. And while the males strutted about displaying their ridiculous fan-tails, the hens pecked at anything: from the scraps Ned had set aside while he went to draw water for the falcons to the bed-sheets the washerwoman had spread on the hedges to dry. When word got round of the deed of one of Thomas's untrained hawks, there would no doubt be much secret rejoicing.

'I swear it will not happen again—' he said, meeting the old steward's eye, but Martin interrupted him.

'Indeed it shall not! Sir Robert is in a poor enough humour as it is, while Lady Margaret is away at Stanbury . . .' He trailed off, his face clouding. 'And I fear she will not return for a good while. The master has sent word she must not travel, now the worst has come.'

Thomas frowned. 'You mean the news we have feared? The plague . . .'

Martin gave a nod. 'The word from London is that the infection is renewed, after last year – yet with even greater vigour. Hundreds dead across all parishes, and it increases daily.' He looked away, beyond the paddock to where sheep dotted the distant Downs. 'I pray it does not travel upriver to Reading, and thence to Newbury, as it did in that dreadful year of sixty-three.'

Thomas nodded, his mind leaping back thirty years, to his boyhood. For his part, Ned was too young to recall such a time; yet the very word 'plague' struck fear into his heart, as it would anyone else's.

'Is there naught we can do by way of prevention, Master Steward?' he asked. His fresh face bore such a mixture of unease and innocence that Martin's own expression softened. But sadly he shook his head.

7

'There is little, except safeguard our borders,' he replied. 'Already I hear many are fleeing the city.' He turned to Thomas. 'Sir Robert asks us to be vigilant, and to turn away any incomers. Not even a poor palliard, though he seem free of infection and ask only for common charity, must be admitted past the gates.'

Like any man might, Thomas was thinking of those closest to him. His daughter, Eleanor, now a fair young woman of eighteen years, had gone as lady's maid with her mistress, Lady Margaret; she at least was safe at Stanbury, the home of the Vicarys' married daughter. Much closer to hand, if not to mind, was his wife Nell, the Petbury cook, believed to be the only woman in Berkshire permitted to rule the kitchens of a great house. After a courtship famous for its stops and starts, the two of them had married in March, to heartfelt rejoicing. At last, folk said, Thomas had taken a new wife, and henceforth would be less bound up in himself; while for her part, Nell would be less heated and spare the kitchen folk her notorious rages. Yet to universal disappointment, neither thing came about: Thomas the falconer, now past his fortieth year, remained as distant as ever; while Nell continued to cuff the scullion when he fell asleep at the spit, and shout at the wenches when they spilled the pottage. Change, if it came, would be slow indeed.

'See now . . .' Martin had recovered his earlier sternness, and was pointing with his staff at the dead peacock. 'You'd best get rid of that. And mind your birds hunt away from the park!'

Thomas signalled his compliance, and gestured to Ned to pick up the peacock. The two of them watched as the old steward trudged back towards the house, then turned to make their own way to the falcons' mews.

Ned was thoughtful. 'You don't think the plague will come up here, on to the Downs?'

For a moment Thomas said nothing, then saw that he was alarming his young helper. 'I think it unlikely,' he said in as light a tone as he could muster. 'The infection seems to flourish strongest in the towns, where folk are crowded together. We have a deal more space about us.'

Ned nodded, seemingly reassured a little, then his boyish face clouded again. 'I owe you, for not telling Master Martin 'twas I loosed the young hawk . . .'

But Thomas's mind was elsewhere, and knowing his moods, Ned quickened his pace and strode ahead. The notion struck him that it was a pity to waste the flesh of a full-grown peacock. He turned, then saw that Thomas's thoughts ran ahead of his.

'If you pluck it, I will take the carcase to the kitchens,' Thomas told him. 'I wager we'll be the toast of Petbury when word gets round. Nell will likely give you a good supper.'

Ned grinned broadly, and tucked the bird tightly under his arm.

An hour later, as the falconers were on the point of walking up to the Ridgeway to exercise their birds, Thomas was summoned to the great hall.

Sir Robert stood by an open window, fanning himself with his hand. It was two hours before noon, yet already the heat indoors was oppressive. But thinking he was about to find himself berated for the loss of the peacock, Thomas was surprised to see another man present, a gentleman in a fashionably garish doublet of deep burgundy set off with gold trim. He quickly put a name to the handsome, dark-bearded face: William Elyot, one of Sir Robert's hawking friends who owned most of the lands south-west of Petbury, on the Lambourn River and beyond. His ancient manor of Bickington bordered on Betterdown, Sir Robert's westernmost tenant farm.

He stopped to make his bow but his master waved him forward, wasting no time with preamble. 'Thomas, my neighbour Master Elyot needs our help.'

Thomas inclined his head politely. Elyot opened his mouth to speak, then hesitated for some reason. Sir Robert, seemingly a little tense, took charge.

'It's a matter of some delicacy. I wish you to ride to Lambourn and see what aid you can give to the constable. His name is . . .' He broke off, turning to Elyot, who said:

'Samuel Hubbard. He is known to you, I think, falconer?'

Thomas signalled assent. Though Chaddleworth-born, he occasionally went to Lambourn, which was three miles to the west of Petbury. Hubbard, a man of considerable girth though of limited wits, was familiar enough to him.

'In what fashion do you wish me to aid the constable, sir . . . ?' he began, but Sir Robert held up a hand. Though the three were alone, with not even a servingman at hand, he lowered his voice.

'A man has been done to death in Lambourn wood, close to the borders of Master Elyot's land. He was found in the night, by some villagers who were out bat-fowling.'

Thomas remained silent.

'The sheriff will not journey here, because of the risk of infection,' Sir Robert went on. 'Nor I fear will the Lord Lieutenant, Lord Norris, be willing to send men to aid us. It seems that we Downland folk are, in this instance, on our own.'

Thomas glanced at Elyot, beginning to understand the reason for his nervousness. Indeed he now appeared considerably agitated.

'Falconer . . . Master Finbow, you are too wise to be unaware of your own reputation hereabouts. This matter needs to be addressed speedily. Lambourn is a small village, somewhat isolated, as you know. The manner of the man's death, not to mention his identity, will unnerve the populace. His name is—' he swallowed and went on: ' . . . was, Stubbs. One of the two churchwardens at St Michael's.'

Now Thomas showed his surprise. A more unlikely victim than the gentle, kindly William Stubbs he could scarce imagine.

'Are they certain it was murder, sir?' he asked, but Elyot was nodding impatiently.

'My thoughts ran as yours do, falconer,' he said. 'Yet there is little doubt. His head was stove in from behind by some sharp weapon, a hatchet or . . .' He gestured distastefully. 'And it seems the body was bound to a tree . . .'

While Thomas digested the information, his master spoke up.

'I touched upon the delicacy of the matter, Thomas . . .' He glanced at Elyot before continuing. 'The fact is, there is unrest in the parish of Lambourn – has been ever since the new rector took up his living. The murder of a churchwarden is likely to cause serious strife, if accusations start to fly . . .'

But, clearly not liking that notion, Elyot cut in sharply.

'I will use all my powers to see that blame is not rashly apportioned, Sir Robert,' he said. 'The matter is, as you say, we two landowners are closest to the nub of these events, and must aid each other in bringing them to peaceful conclusion. Especially as the constable has his hands already full, selecting men for muster duty . . .'

He broke off as Sir Robert bridled slightly. 'Indeed, sir, I am well aware of the county's dilemma in that regard.'

There was a brief silence. It was well known that the great military commander Sir John Norris, from his father Lord Norris's seat at Rycote twenty-five miles away, was raising an army to fight in France – even though Queen Elizabeth's continued support for Henry of Navarre was become less and less popular, especially since the news of the French king's conversion to Catholicism only a month or so back. The men of Berkshire, no less than those of any other county, were understandably reluctant to fight for a foreign monarch whose loyalty to their own Queen was, to say the least, questionable. Hence the plain fact was that in the towns and villages, the men pressed into service were often those who had least choice in the matter: convicted felons, rogues and vagabonds – or perhaps simply those whom the local constables wished to be rid of.

Questions were forming in Thomas's mind. 'Sir, would not Hubbard resent someone from outside the village, with no proper warrant, treading on his toes . . . ?'

Sir Robert smiled. 'No doubt he would, Thomas. I look to my friend here to provide you with the required authority.' But before Elyot could voice his agreement, the knight added: 'Besides, I have reason enough to send you to Lambourn. Master Elyot has a sick hawk that needs expert attention . . . is that not so, sir?'

Elyot nodded, while Thomas sighed inwardly and bowed. With mixed feelings, he acknowledged Sir Robert's instruction to make ready, turned to go and had almost gained the door before his master called to him. He looked round to see Sir Robert glaring.

'That peacock – don't think I have forgotten it!'

Within the hour he was mounted on a gelding from the Petbury stable, and riding beside William Elyot across the Downs to Lambourn.

Descending from Greenhill Down, with the dry, empty grass-lands stretching away on all sides, it seemed to him that Lambourn looked somewhat forlorn in its shallow valley. It was one of the three small villages on the upper reaches of the river: Eastbury, Lambourn itself and, remotest of all, the tiny, windswept hamlet of Uplambourn, which marked the source of the chalk stream. Lambourn, however, boasted a busy enough market on Fridays, and it was indeed upon a Friday that Thomas rode downhill to join the Wantage to Lambourn road, and parted company with Elyot at the bridge. Having promised to attend him later and offer what succour he could to his ailing falcon, he was not sorry to see that gentleman turn aside and ride off downriver to his manor of Bickington. He had said barely a word to Thomas since the two of them had left Petbury.

Thomas crossed the little packhorse bridge and entered the village place, its thatched houses standing in a rough half-circle about the ancient church of St Michael and All Angels. St Michael's always came as something of a surprise: an old Norman church that had been added to time and again until it looked too large for the remote community it served. And above, the imposing square tower, which had been extended upwards to bear the ornate, crenellated bell-tower with its grand corner spires and carriage of four bells. How many evenings, walking homewards along the Ridgeway with a falcon on his wrist, had Thomas paused to hear the peal of those bells at evensong, drifting across the Downs on the breeze? But then, he had a more recent memory of this church, that brought a wry smile to his lips: back in the spring, a pair of wild peregrine falcons had nested in the bell-tower, where their young had hatched. Who else but the most famous falconer in West Berkshire would be summoned, to climb precariously up a long ladder and take the eyases from the nest? And was it not one of those same young birds, which

12

Ned was now training at the lure, that had dared to fall upon Sir Robert's peacock?

He reined in, feeling thirsty after his ride, and the hubbub of the market-day throng rose about him. The sun was past its zenith, yet the market would last most of the day. Booths and stalls were pressed together about the ancient market cross, the cries of sellers mingling with the barking of dogs and the bleating of sheep in the pens. Village folk in plain dress looked round at the tall falconer on his fine mount, who was easily recognized. Some called out a greeting. Thomas smiled in return, dismounted and led the horse to the water-trough. Almost at once, a figure materialized at his side.

'Thomas! Are you come to our Church Ale?'

Thomas looked round, breaking into a smile at sight of the small, untidy-haired man in simple attire who stood before him. He had known Jonas Crouch, Lambourn's busy little parish clerk, for most of his adult life – not least because the man owned a hunting bird of his own, and delighted to sing her praises to any who would listen.

'Jonas . . .' The two men embraced briefly, before Thomas faced his friend with eyebrow raised. 'I knew nothing of any Church Ale. What's the occasion?'

Crouch was surprised. 'You do not know of our plight? I thought all within a ten-mile would have heard!'

At that Thomas naturally thought of the death of the church-warden, and wondered what that tragedy might have to do with the holding of a Church Ale: the old village custom of raising money for some purpose by brewing a special batch of strong ale and selling it at the church. But Crouch was gesturing excitedly towards St Michael's, its bulk louring over the market booths.

'Our tenor bell has cracked, and is taken down. Already the founders are here to cast a new one!'

Thomas glanced at the church, realizing that he had barely noticed the rickety-looking scaffold of lashed poles which stood against one side of the tower. Ropes dangled from the belfry.

'The old bell . . . broken, you say?'

The little clerk nodded. 'The clapper had worn a groove in

13

him long ago. But 'tis my belief he suffered worse damage back in Armada year, when folk tolled him for hours on end.'

'I'm sorry to hear it,' Thomas murmured. 'But when you spoke of your plight, I thought you meant the death of Master Stubbs . . .'

Crouch's face clouded. 'You know of that already? We have striven to keep it quiet.' He glanced about him. From the cheerful demeanour of the market throng on this bright summer's day, it now seemed clear to Thomas that most folk as yet knew nothing of the tragedy.

'My master has sent me to find out what I can and aid Sam Hubbard,' Thomas said quietly, drawing closer to the clerk. 'William Elyot is Sir Robert's neighbour, and he's anxious—'

'He!' Crouch lowered his gaze. 'Aye . . . he will wish the matter soon despatched, I dare say.'

Thomas looked at his old friend in some surprise.

'Will Stubbs was in debt to him . . .' the other went on, then seemed to think better of touching upon that subject. 'It's best you come with me to the church, and present yourself to the rector and the sexton before you go looking for Hubbard. They should be glad of Sir Robert's assistance – indeed, of anyone's.'

Thomas nodded and turned to take up the gelding's rein, seeing the animal had drunk its fill. The two of them skirted the market and made their way round the side of the church. A small crowd of purchasers was gathered about its porch, where the ale-sellers were doing brisk business from a large barrel. But on the east side, by the chancel, Thomas found bustle of a different nature.

The patch of empty ground between the church and the river was a scene of quiet but purposeful activity. Most notice-able was the large pit which had been dug in the ground, more than six feet deep. Sweating labourers were still shovelling earth out. Close by was a half-built, dome-shaped structure of brick, which for a moment Thomas failed to identify. Then he realized that he was looking at the furnace in which metal would be melted down, and the pit in which the new church bell would be cast. A channel had already been cut from the furnace mouth to the bell-pit, down which the white-hot, molten bell-metal would be run to fill the mould beneath.

Like anyone, Thomas knew of the ancient and mysterious art of the bell-founders, though he had never seen one at work. Since the Dissolution, the demand for bells had dwindled, and itinerant founders who had once travelled the length and breadth of Britain in search of monasteries and churches in need of a new casting were fewer in number. Nowadays bells were often cast at the large town foundries and shipped upriver or transported overland. Yet the journey across the Downs to Lambourn would be great indeed, and hence someone had come to break up the old bell, melt it down and cast a new one on the spot, as was the old practice. Somehow when the need arose, the founders always knew; and one would soon appear, as sure as the sun rose in the east.

Thomas turned to Crouch, still at his side.

'Who is the founder?'

'Goodchild,' the other answered, and pointed out an imposing figure in somewhat tattered artisan's dress, who had the air of an Old Testament prophet about him. His face was tanned as old leather, while his grey hair and beard hung long. 'That's Master Simon. His wife and youngest son travel with him and aid him in his work. There's young Edmund.'

Thomas saw a slim lad of eighteen or nineteen, alert and agile, who seemed to be supervising the digging of the pit. About to ask another question of Jonas Crouch, he was startled by a loud shout from behind.

'Master Clerk!'

He turned to see a figure in dusty black clothes striding towards them, and tensed immediately. Richard Starling, the vicar of St Michael's, had that effect on most folk. A zealous, prickly man of more than fifty years, he was a bachelor who lived only for the work of the God whom he knew beyond all doubt to be a Puritan. His arrival in Lambourn less than a year back had sent shock waves through the sleepy Downland village.

'By your leave, sir . . .' Crouch assumed a deferential manner that, Thomas knew, was his friend's method of dealing with the man. Indeed, with Starling little else but unquestioning obedience would serve.

'The hour appointed for our meeting is past,' the rector snapped, ignoring Thomas and fixing the little churchwarden with piercing, crow-black eyes. His long, storm-grey hair was swept back severely behind his ears. The man wore no surplice – indeed, it was said as a young parish priest he had been suspended for his refusal to wear anything which to those of his persuasion smacked of popery. 'The sexton is already here,' he added, 'and we await you.'

Crouch met his gaze. 'I was on my way,' he answered. 'But Master Finbow's arrival has put another complexion on . . . on our trouble.' He indicated Thomas, who made his bow. When Starling merely stared, he gave his station and explained the reason for his presence.

There was a silence. Voices rose from around the furnace, where there seemed to be some dispute among the bricklayers. But a deep voice – Simon Goodchild's, Thomas surmised – quietened them at once.

Starling was breathing steadily, but Thomas sensed suppressed excitement, even anger behind his words. 'The loss of our elder churchwarden is an ecclesiastical matter,' he said. 'Your master need not concern himself in this.'

Gently Thomas explained that it was at the request of William Elyot that Sir Robert wished him to render assistance. But at once Starling threw his chest out like one of the Petbury peacocks.

'Indeed – I would expect such, from . . .' He broke off, biting back words which he clearly thought better of uttering before Thomas. In a quieter voice he added: 'The bishop will be informed, and his authority is enough. We need no others meddling in our affairs, especially in such a time of grief.'

Thomas was thinking how glad he would be to convey those sentiments to Sir Robert, and find himself relieved of all involvement in the matter. But before he could summon some words of reply the rector had turned on his heel and was striding off. For his part, Crouch could do naught but throw an apologetic look at Thomas and follow. But as he went, he spoke over his shoulder in a tone of some urgency.

'We'll speak later . . . you may find Hubbard in the Horns. The landlord Nightingale is the one who found Stubbs's body!'

Then he was gone, quickening his pace to trot after the rapidly retreating form of the rector.

Thomas sighed, then, realizing that he had been given a good enough reason to enter the inn, brightened somewhat and went to slake his thirst.

Three

It being market day, the Horns was packed to the doorway. Outside, several ageing shepherds, too feeble now to work, sat on benches in the sunshine and eyed Thomas as he walked past. As he forced his way inside, the melodious sound of a small harp, skilfully played, drew his eyes to a corner. There sat Dickon, the blind harper, plucking sweet airs from his instrument as he had done for as long as most could remember. His fine tenor voice rose, and others joined in with the song.

Thomas called for a mug. The harassed drawer Nicholas, who had served here for years, managed a grin. 'You shall have beer as soon as I've time to rinse a mug for ye, falconer!' he cried, wiping the sweat from his ruddy face. Thomas smiled his thanks, then asked where Master Nightingale was. The man waved a hand. 'In the parlour . . .'

He pushed his way past the row of kegs, stooping as he entered a low doorway at the rear. A party of men and women were at table within, nearing the end of what looked like a substantial dinner. Another group stood drinking by the open casement, trying to get the benefit of what breeze there was. One of them looked round as Thomas entered, and recognized him at once.

'Falconer . . .' John Nightingale came forward to greet him. 'You do us a rare honour.'

Thomas took the outstretched hand, detecting a little irony in the man's clear grey eyes. The landlord of the Horns, he well knew, was perhaps the most sharp-witted man in Lambourn. 'I would have speech with you, John,' he said. 'If you can spare a little time.'

Nightingale regarded him for a moment, then put his mug

down and gestured Thomas to an oak bench that stood against the far wall. As they sat Thomas glanced around, then broached the matter head-on. Quietly he explained his business, ending with the fact that he had learned that it was Nightingale who had found the body of William Stubbs.

'Not I,' the landlord answered after a moment. 'Peter Hare, the shepherd from Betterdown, found him. I but held the torch. We stayed not long enough to look much about us.'

'Long enough to see the gash on the churchwarden's head, I heard,' Thomas said. 'And the rope which—' But then he blinked, as the other cut in sharply.

'Rope?' he echoed. 'I saw no rope. Who says so?'

Thomas watched him carefully. 'Master Elyot says so. At least, that is what he told my master.'

'He is mistaken.' Nightingale's tone was firm. ''Tis my belief Stubbs tripped and cracked his head on a tree. He was past his seventy years.'

Seeing Thomas's gaze upon him, the man looked away suddenly. 'But I'm no surgeon – I know not how he died. It was full dark, and we were unmanned by the sight . . . a man's mind may play tricks with him at such a time.'

Still Thomas said nothing, until finally the landlord's composure broke. 'What matters it to you?' he demanded. 'The churchwarden will be buried tomorrow – let him rest easy in the earth. We are all come to dust in the end – he was a good man, who had lived a long and a pious life.'

And as if to signal an end to their discourse, he made as if to rise. Whereupon Thomas spoke up softly.

'Who has come to you, and bade you change your tale?'

Nightingale sat down again.

'Was it Elyot?' Thomas continued, keeping his eyes fixed on the other's. 'I know he wishes to smooth this matter over . . .'

But Nightingale's face had hardened. 'I'm but an innkeeper,' he said. 'If you are come to drink, you are welcome. As to the other business, I cannot aid you further. Now, I've customers to attend.'

And deliberately he got up and walked over to join the group by the window, picking up his own mug as he went. Almost at once laughter rang out, and several folk glanced towards

19

Thomas. It seemed as though the landlord had made some joke at his expense.

Wordlessly he got up and made his way out of the parlour. But as he left he caught John Nightingale's eye, conveying the signal that as far as Thomas was concerned this was not the end of the matter. While he was not particularly concerned at being the butt of someone's humour, he disliked being taken for a fool. How, he might have asked, could a man who had fallen and died from a cracked skull then sit himself up against a tree and bind himself to it?

After taking a quick mug and listening to the blind harper's song, Thomas left the Horns a short time later. Outside, he drew in a draught of sweet Downland air and walked towards the post where he had tethered the gelding. But almost at once someone hailed him. He looked up to see the unmistakable figure of Samuel Hubbard, constable of Lambourn village, bearing down upon him.

'Master Finbow!' Hubbard puffed towards him, drenched with sweat in the midday heat. The man's belly hung so low over his belt, he had almost to hold it before him. 'I hear from the clerk you been seeking me out!'

Thomas sighed inwardly. 'Master Constable . . . indeed, I would value your help,' he muttered, chiding himself for uttering a lie, and a feeble one at that. Then for the third time since arriving here he stated his business, without acquainting Hubbard of his conversation with John Nightingale. The substance of that, he sensed, might best be kept for Sir Robert's ears.

The constable was subdued. 'I've little to do with the death in yon woods,' he said after a moment. 'Rector bade me leave it to the church . . .' He glared suddenly. 'I've more'n enough on my shoulders already – you'd quail just to hear me tell of it! Picking men to fight for Norris, and keeping the peace . . .' He leaned closer, breathing beer fumes into Thomas's face. 'Now there's plague in London, and I'm supposed to issue orders against the infection – what am I, a conjuror?'

Thomas managed a sympathetic smile. 'Travellers are rare this far upriver, surely?'

Hubbard snorted. 'There's the bell-founder for a start,' he countered, with a look of distaste. 'Acts like he's a law to himself, and his boy's no better. As for the wife, she don't speak. Struck dumb, they say.'

Thomas raised an eyebrow.

'See now . . .' The man's broad face darkened suddenly. 'I don't want you ruffling feathers here. If you want to render me a service, you can help keep order at Stubbs's funeral tomorrow. There's some bad feeling in this village, since he forbade the death knell.'

Thomas was taken aback. 'You mean, the rector . . . ?'

'Who else but he?' Hubbard turned aside and spat heavily. 'Starling . . . he and his new-fashioned Bishops' Rules . . . no tolling the bell – and no hand-bells to be rung, neither! What sort of a funeral will't be, without bells?'

Thomas considered as he untied the gelding's reins. 'I will help. And in return, have I your leave to move about and make a show of asking questions, that I may tell my master I have done all I can?'

Hubbard grunted. 'If you will. Though from what I hear, there's naught much to discover. Stubbs was old, and getting feeble . . . kept more to hisself, this past year.' He looked away. 'There's many will weep when they hear the news, for he was a good neighbour, and a true friend.'

Thomas nodded, and couldn't help adding: 'Who deserves justice, surely?'

But the constable's chest heaved, and Thomas almost stepped back as the fellow doubled up and gave a great sneeze. Wrinkling his nose, he sniffed loudly. 'What's that?'

'No matter.' Thomas turned to take his leave, then paused. 'Do you happen to know who else was bat-fowling last night, when they found Master Stubbs?'

Hubbard pointed with his chin towards the blacksmith's forge which stood across the market place, beside the old track leading westwards to distant Baydon.

'Ask Will Ragg,' he answered. 'He was one.'

And, rotating his considerable bulk, the man took himself off.

Thomas thought for a moment before deciding to postpone

visiting the blacksmith. Since it now seemed he was going to be here on the morrow for Stubbs's funeral, at which the entire village would be present, he might have a better chance to make enquiries then. He led the gelding round the edge of the market to the riverside, mounted and prepared to ride homewards. Aside from Nightingale's obvious evasion, which for the present he could not fathom, two other thoughts had struck him. One was that for a small village where gossip was normally rife, no one seemed in any great hurry to spread the news of the loss of a much-loved churchwarden. The second was that the funeral was to follow hard upon the death . . . but then, in summer that was often the case. He was still musing on the matter when he remembered the other reason for his being here. Crossing the bridge, he turned right and rode the mile along the river's bank, to Bickington Manor.

The sprawling greystone house was set upon a slope above the river, with a walled park in front and outbuildings behind. On the north and east, the ground rose to the treeless Downs beyond. Two hundred yards upstream, with the manor in view ahead of him, Thomas had ridden past the run-down small-holding of Henry Howes, the sexton of St Michael's, a man he seldom saw but whose presence was always felt in Lambourn. A humble, conscientious man, he tolled the bell on most occasions, and busied himself about the church. Folk often wondered how he found time to farm his little plot of land; by the look of the place, the church was the winner in the struggle, and the farmstead the loser.

Passing through Bickington's park and paddock, he skirted the house and dismounted in the stable yard. A groom took his horse and said he would take him to Master William, but instead Thomas asked if he might first see the Master's falcon. And it was here some minutes later, as he was standing at the mews of willow hurdles looking the bird over, that Elyot came out to him.

The man's manner was somewhat more friendly than it had been on their ride earlier that day. He had also changed his clothing for more homely attire. Not without pride, he

22

untied the ageing falcon and placed her on his wrist so that Thomas might examine her.

'I named her Artemis,' Elyot said. 'After the moon-goddess. I pray you can heal the canker within her mouth, Master Finbow. My wife, no less than I, is most troubled to see her in distress.'

Thomas stroked the falcon's wing-feathers, murmuring softly to her. Then he eased open the bird's large beak and looked inside her mouth. Artemis jerked in alarm and began to rouse, but swiftly Thomas let go and soothed her. 'She is troubled with the Frounce, sir,' he said. 'It's like a canker . . . if you will follow my instruction, I think you may heal her readily enough.'

Elyot showed his relief. 'I am in your debt, Master Finbow. Whatever you advise, it shall be done.'

Having a notion of what he might expect to find here, Thomas had put a few things in a pack before he left Petbury. Now he took a tiny, blue-glass bottle from his jerkin.

'*Aqua fortis*, thinned with spring-water,' he said. 'Some say the Frounce may be eased merely by washing the falcon's mouth with lemon juice, but this remedy is best. You take a little stick with a cloth tied about the end, no bigger than a pea, dip it into the liquor, and apply it to the sore.'

Elyot stared. 'But she would not permit such. She will bate with the pain . . .'

Thomas nodded. 'You must have someone wrap her in a strong clout and hold her firmly beneath his arm. Then while another forces her beak open, he may apply the liquor.'

Elyot hesitated. 'Will you do it now, if I help?' But when Thomas showed his surprise, the gentleman smiled.

'You think I am loath to soil my hands, falconer? Then you do not know me. When I inherited Bickington it was a tumble-down place. While the lawyers reckoned and argued over their fees, being short of servants with strong backs I was fain to do much of the work myself.'

Thomas inclined his head. 'I will be glad to be your hawk-farrier, sir,' he said. 'Especially to such a fine old lady as Artemis.'

So together the two men set to work. And within the half

hour, when it was done and the falcon left alone to recover with a little water beside her, a grateful William Elyot was steering Thomas towards the house for a late dinner and a mug of the manor's own fresh-brewed beer.

He had not been inside Bickington before, and its opulence surprised him. The great hall, though smaller than Sir Robert's, was sumptuously furnished and hung with Turkish carpets. A minstrel gallery ran the length of the far wall. Thomas sat somewhat ill-at-ease before the great gold-and-glass salt, to take his meal of bread and jellied eels, with a dish of sallett and watercress. Meanwhile his host sat close by, talking of their work. And though he had done little more than hold the bird while Thomas had treated the falcon, there was no doubting the man's pride in their success.

A side door opened suddenly, and Thomas rose to make his bow as Jane Elyot entered the room, flanked by two young maids. The lady of the house was small and slender, dressed in a fine blue and green gown over a snow-white kirtle. Her red hair, dyed in imitation of the Queen's, looked garish above the thin face painted with ceruse.

Elyot rose and was about to present their guest, but his wife looked at once upon Thomas and favoured him with a smile.

'I have heard what you did, falconer,' she said. 'And am come to add my thanks to those of my husband.'

Before Thomas could reply she turned to dismiss the maids, who went out at once. There was a short silence. Elyot took a farthingale-stool from the wall and placed it near the table, where wine and silver cups were set. But Mistress Jane remained on her feet.

'I would have my husband reward you,' she continued, her eyes still upon Thomas's. 'Not only for treating our dear Artemis, but for aiding him in the other matter, of which I know he has spoken to you.'

Thomas inclined his head, but a tension was stealing over him. For some reason the memory of John Nightingale's lie flew into his mind; and at once he was on the alert.

But Elyot intervened. 'I was about to talk of that matter with Master Finbow,' he said, somewhat coolly.

24

Jane Elyot turned to face him. 'Only now? Have you done naught as yet but speak of hawks?'

A sickly smile spread over Elyot's face. 'Any guest at Bickington is allowed time to eat and drink before talking business,' he said.

There was a moment, before his wife seemed to relent. Turning to go out, she threw Thomas a parting smile and said: 'Your tireless service to Sir Robert is well known, falconer. I trust you will show the same loyalty to his friends.'

And quickly she was gone. Thomas glanced at Elyot, who motioned him to take his seat again. Thomas did so, now feeling decidedly uncomfortable, especially when the other man drew his own stool closer and sat, looking intently at him.

'My wife speaks, of course, of the churchwarden's death,' he said. 'I would ask what progress you made, in the village.'

Thomas hesitated. He had remembered Jonas Crouch's statement, hastily made, about Elyot's being a creditor of the late William Stubbs, and his suspicions were now multiplying by the minute.

'I confess I discovered little, sir,' he began, trying not to sound too guarded. 'The funeral will take place tomorrow, though as yet the news of the death is spreading somewhat slower than I would expect.' When Elyot made no reply, he added in a casual tone: 'I did speak with one of those who found the body – Nightingale, the innkeeper. Though he seemed somewhat unwilling to speak of the details . . . it was dark, and he and the man with him were afraid. I have yet to encounter the other – Hare, the shepherd. Mayhap he will be more forthcoming.'

Having obeyed his instinct to say nothing of Nightingale's denial that Stubbs was bound to a tree, as Elyot had told that morning, Thomas waited. But to his surprise, the man merely nodded eagerly.

'It was Hare who first told me of the matter, early this morning,' he said. 'By all means speak with him – speak with anyone. That clod Hubbard is fit for naught but stuffing his fat belly. I want the killer found swiftly, before tongues start wagging – which they will in any case . . .' He broke off, frowning suddenly.

'They do already, sir,' Thomas murmured, feeling bold enough to touch upon the matter. 'For one thing, I hear Master Stubbs owed money to someone . . .'

Elyot looked sharply at him. Unflinchingly Thomas met his gaze, and said nothing. But whatever reaction he had expected, it was not the one that followed. For the man suddenly threw his head back and gave a shout of laughter.

'So that is how your mind moves!' he cried. 'I was told you were an accomplished intelligencer.'

Thomas sat up, thinking he had overstepped himself and was to be upbraided – if not now, by Sir Robert when he learned of the matter. He opened his mouth, but at once Elyot stayed him.

'Nay, Finbow . . .' He shook his head. 'You will learn soon enough of the Statute Merchant I held upon Stubbs. Since he is dead and cannot pay, his property will pass to me – such as it is. He was a poor man, who owed me a mere ten pounds. I was glad to lend it, for he had the highest motives . . . not least, that he might make a contribution of his own to the casting of the new church bell.'

Thomas blinked and tried to form some words of apology, but William Elyot stayed him again. 'I had no more intention of pressing that debt than Stubbs had of calling in those loans he made, to folk even poorer than himself,' he said. 'The more you learn of that old man, the more you will understand why folk dubbed him Lambourn's own saint.'

And signalling that their discourse was at an end, he rose and gestured Thomas towards the door.

But as they made their exit a slim, dark-haired man in this thirties appeared from a side passage, and made his bow to Elyot. With barely a glance at Thomas, he drew close to his master and spoke urgently in an undertone. While waiting some-what awkwardly to be dismissed, Thomas observed the man he guessed to be Elyot's steward, Ralph Stainbank by name. Stainbank was not a native of the county, but one whom Elyot had brought with him from London when he took over Bickington. An overbearing, hollow-eyed fellow, he was not well-liked in Lambourn, though since he seldom left the confines of the manor it scarcely mattered – at least, not to him.

Finding Stainbank's eyes suddenly upon him, Thomas looked away; whereupon Elyot, who had been staring at the floor while listening intently to his steward, seemed to recollect himself. 'Master Finbow . . .' he fumbled for his purse, opened it and drew out a gold angel, 'please take this for your pains. Along with my gratitude and that of my wife. Now God speed you back to Petbury. We will speak again, and soon.'

Thomas voiced his thanks, took the coin and made his bow. As he turned to take his leave, he felt Stainbank's eyes fixed upon the back of his head. Nor did he truly relax until he was mounted and riding back up the river once again towards Lambourn bridge.

Four

Thomas had intended to ride on to the Downs and make his way back to Petbury, where his work awaited him. Though Ned had proved himself fully capable of tending Sir Robert's falcons, he disliked leaving the boy on his own for long. But his instinct made him halt at the bridge, then cross it and ride into Lambourn once again. A little more time spent with Jonas Crouch would, he believed, help him gain a better picture of the events surrounding Stubbs's death, which seemed to grow more murky by the hour.

Afternoon was drawing on, and the market crowd had thinned. Dismounting, he led the horse round to the east side of the church once more, expecting to see the same flurry of building work that he had found that morning. But the digging of the bell-pit seemed to have been completed. Two or three planks had been placed across the deep hole, perhaps to stop some late night reveller falling in. The brick furnace, though still unfinished, had also been abandoned. There was no one about, save a stooped figure in a canvas jerkin and an old threadbare hat, who appeared to be surveying the builders' rubble.

'Master Howes, is't not?' Thomas dropped the gelding's rein and walked forward, his hand raised in greeting.

Henry Howes was an unlikely sexton: a man with a deep-lined, sunburned face that spoke of the farmer rather than the churchman. He had always looked old, folk said; though he was barely past forty, his hair and beard were grizzled, his shoulders bent from years of toil. He had lost a son to the war against the Spanish, and a wife to some unnamed sickness. Work was all he had; so long as it filled the hours from sunrise to sunset, he declared himself content. Though a less

28

contented-looking man, Thomas always thought, would be difficult to find.

'Who's that?' Disturbed from his reverie, Howes looked up sharply and squinted into the sun, which was behind Thomas. Then recognition dawned, and he nodded a cautious greeting. 'Master Finbow . . . I heard you were about. How may I aid you?'

Thomas smiled. 'I would not trouble such a busy man as you, Master Sexton. I'm looking for my friend Crouch.'

'Inside, last I saw of him, at some discourse about the morrow.' Howes nodded towards the church. 'There is much to do . . .' He broke off, peering at Thomas. 'Then, I think you already know of our loss?'

Thomas nodded. 'It was sad news.'

Howes said nothing, but looked away. There was a tenseness about the man, as if he wished to be elsewhere. Feeling he was intruding, Thomas was about to take his leave when there came the click of a latch behind him. In the south-east corner of the church, where the chancel wall met the little south-facing annexe of St Mary's chapel, was an old priest's doorway, a hangover from older times. Thomas turned as the narrow door opened, and a stout man with a bald pate and brown side-locks squeezed himself through it. The fellow appeared in something of a hurry, but seeing Thomas, he checked his stride at once.

Henry Howes addressed him. 'Are you finished within? I wish to prepare the nave.'

John Wilmott, Lambourn's other – for the present its only – churchwarden, glanced from the sexton to Thomas and back. 'We are done,' he said somewhat irritably, and fixed his eyes again upon Thomas. 'Falconer? What do you want here?'

Thomas paused for a moment. 'I though all were welcome at St Michael's,' he answered mildly. 'Rather, that was always so in times past.'

Wilmott bristled. 'True believers are always welcome,' he retorted. 'I do not recall seeing you at worship here.'

'I think you know my church is St Andrew's in Chaddleworth,' Thomas said, maintaining his mildness of tone.

'Though as I recall, you were quick enough to call upon my services when those falcons were nesting in the belfry.'

There was a cough, and it came from Henry Howes. 'The falconer comes looking for Jonas,' he said.

'He's gone to his accounts,' the churchwarden said, with a bland look at Thomas. 'You may seek him at his home. Now if you please, church business will not wait.'

Thomas eyed him, and walked off to collect his horse.

He found Jonas Crouch in the garden of his small cottage on the west side of the village. To his surprise, the little clerk was busy feeding his goshawk. His greeting was warm and, finding himself welcome, Thomas was glad to stand in the late-afternoon sunshine and admire the man's bird. The big grey-brown hawk with its richly speckled chest sat atop a bow perch, pecking hungrily at the scraps Crouch had thrown down.

'I sought you at the church,' Thomas said with straight face, 'and was told you were busy at your accounts.'

Crouch smiled. 'It serves as an excuse to attend to my Clement. I bought him at our November fair of St Clements, and so named him.'

Thomas smiled in return. 'A good enough reason!'

'Shall we drink to it?' The other asked. 'There's a jug of sack within that begs to be tasted.'

They sat on a home-made bench in the garden and watched the sun sink behind the far hills that marked the border with Wiltshire. But when Thomas told his friend a little of what had passed that day, Crouch's manner altered. He took a drink, then said: 'Thomas, I am troubled, and I fear there's none here to whom I can unburden myself. You I trust, and I know you will keep my confidence.'

After a moment, Thomas nodded.

'St Michael's . . .' Crouch lowered his eyes, as if it pained him to speak of it. 'St Michael's is not the haven of peace it once was. A house of joy, where all could find succour . . . rather it is become a place of conflict.'

Thomas raised his eyebrows. 'Reverend Starling . . . ?'

But the other shook his head vigorously. 'Nay – he is always blamed, yet he is not the ogre folk have dubbed him. Yes, he

30

is a strict man, even an angry one. Who would not be, who feels as deeply as he does . . . fired with righteousness ever since he heard the great Thomas Cartwright lecture in Cambridge, more than twenty years ago? Yet he had taken part in prophesyings, and was almost stripped of his vestments, even before that.' He sighed. 'Men like Starling loathe not merely papists, but the slow progress our Queen makes to reverse the wickedness done by her sister, Queen Mary – he lives only to further the Puritan cause. And so, you may imagine how he suffers when two of his friends – the separatists, Greenwood and Barrow – were hanged not four months back, for writings which the Crown calls seditious.'

He broke off with a frown. 'You have seen that he wears no surplice. Many times I have begged him to wear one, that folk of this parish may grow accustomed more slowly to the changes he makes here . . . yet to go slowly is not his way.' He shook his head once again. '*Malleus improborum* some have named him – "the hammer of the wicked". He seethes like a boiling pot, yet it is the rage of one who wishes to do right, and has not enough time in which to do it!'

Thomas took a moment to digest what his friend had said. 'You say you are troubled . . .'

Crouch looked up. 'Howes, and Wilmott,' he said quietly. 'The one I believe is in fear for his life. The other hated Will Stubbs to distraction.'

Thomas drew breath. 'Enough to kill him?'

Crouch looked shocked, and shook his head. 'Nay, I cannot believe such . . .' He struggled with the notion. 'I *will* not believe it!'

'Tell me what you can,' Thomas urged. 'Surely you wish that Will Stubbs's murderer be found, and brought to book for his crime?'

The clerk bit his lip. 'You are certain it was murder?'

'It appears so.'

'Then indeed, such wickedness must be punished.'

Thomas hesitated. 'You said Howes is in fear for his life – what makes you say so?'

Crouch was looking increasingly ill-at-ease. He took a pull from his stoneware cup, then said: 'He has never been a contented man, Thomas; that much is well-known. Yet for a while now, he has seemed to me like one always on watch . . . nervous as a hare, and so bowed with worry, he can scare hold his head up.'

Thomas nodded. 'I have seen the poor state of his farm . . . mayhap he is heavily indebted?'

'That is no secret,' Crouch said. 'Yet he has always had debts . . . He once told me he worked two hours a day for himself, six hours for God, and another six for his creditors.'

'Who might they be?' Thomas asked – whereupon the answer came at once. 'William Elyot . . . ?'

Crouch shrugged. 'Very likely. Elyot has loaned money to many a poor man in Lambourn. Yet that in itself would not account for Henry's manner.' He frowned to himself. 'More puzzling to me, a week or two back he had a spring in his step, as if his troubles had somehow diminished. Yet of late he is grown more careworn and more nervous than ever.'

Thomas frowned. 'What of John Wilmott?' he asked. 'Why do you say he hated Stubbs?'

Crouch winced. 'That is more difficult to speak of,' he replied. 'For it a matter of plain sin. The sin of covetousness – rather I will say, jealousy.'

Thomas looked blank. 'He was jealous of his fellow church-warden? That kindly old man?'

Crouch nodded. 'Precisely because he was such a kindly old man,' he murmured. 'Lambourn's own saint . . .' the last words were spoken low, as if to himself. Then he looked up at Thomas. 'I have watched John Wilmott's manner change with the years. At first he felt as others do – that Will Stubbs could do no wrong. Always helping folk, always giving thanks for his lot, devoted to the church and its works – the man seemed to need nothing else in life but to serve God in any way he might. But slowly, Wilmott began to see that it was Stubbs folk admired; him they looked to, and not Wilmott – he never had the other's easy way with folk, nor his humble manner. They measured him against that old man – and then John began to measure himself. Once he realized he could never fill Stubbs's shoes, he began to resent it. In the end, I believe he grew to hate the very ground Stubbs stood upon, though he hid it well enough. And if Stubbs noticed, he never let on. Yet to do murder?' He looked away, and repeated himself. 'I cannot believe such.'

'Who else noticed?' Thomas asked. 'Apart from you?'

Crouch shrugged. 'I cannot say. Certainly not the rector – he pays little mind to any of us. Sexton, warden and clerk – we will never be good enough servants of the church, for him. What man could?'

Thomas sighed. 'From what you say, St Michael's indeed sounds a place of strife.'

'And it never ceases,' Crouch added unhappily. 'Will Stubbs cruelly slain . . . and now the bell-founders have stopped work until the matter of their price is addressed!'

Thomas frowned slightly. 'Is it not usual to agree a fee *before* work commences?'

Crouch nodded. 'Indeed – but no one told Simon Goodchild that he was expected to carve an inscription upon the new bell when it is made. A phrase from the good book, and the year of casting, mayhap the rector's name – a penny a letter is usual, in these matters. The whole amounts to a matter of a couple of shillings, yet Starling refuses to let us pay it. Says to do God's work is honour enough, and the founder should be grateful for what he gets.'

It was Thomas's turn to shake his head. 'Small wonder there's unrest . . .'

Crouch lifted his cup and drained it. 'Think yourself fortunate you can ride back to Petbury, and your own birds,' he said, and managed a smile. 'How's that new wife of yours?'

Thomas emptied his own cup. 'She is well . . . and it's time I went home.' He stood up. 'Till tomorrow, Jonas. I have promised Hubbard I will help at the burying.'

The little clerk gazed at the goshawk, still busy at his supper, and his face clouded. 'How that will fadge, without the passing-bell to send poor Will on his way, I do not know.'

It was past sunset when Thomas arrived back at Petbury. Ned had gone to his bed; he now slept in the stables with the grooms, and went home to Chaddleworth on Sundays. Having

33

looked in on the falcons and found them well fed and watered, Thomas went to his cottage and found Nell seated before an unlit fire, fast asleep. She started as he came in, and looked round in alarm.

'I ask pardon for waking you,' he said, and went to her. She stood up, yawning, and leaned against him. As always, her hair and workaday clothing smelled of the kitchens.

'I must go back to the house. They dine late . . . Sir John Norris is come.'

Thomas was surprised. 'Sir Robert doubted the Norrises would travel, with the infection spreading . . .'

'Lord Norris, perhaps, for he feels his age,' Nell answered. 'Yet his sons fear naught. Sir John is making a tour of the county recruiting stations. They say he means to leave for Brittany before Michaelmas.'

She leaned upwards, and kissed him. 'Ned expected you at suppertime, to share a roast peacock. What kept you away?'

He sighed. 'I'll tell you, when we have more time.' Then he too found himself yawning. 'As for the morrow, I must leave for Lambourn once again.' He gave a wry smile. 'I seem to have got myself appointed marshal at a funeral.'

The next morning, Lambourn seethed – not merely with the press of folk from the village, from Uplambourn and from Eastbury, but with an outpouring of emotion, such as Thomas had not seen here in years.

He felt it as he crossed the bridge and dismounted. The market booths were gone. Instead villagers in their best clothes, with as much show of mourning black as poor folk could muster, thronged the square. A few were tearful, but other faces looked, to Thomas's eyes, taut with anger. Some people held branches of bay or rosemary, others carried sprigs of yew. Voices were low, but collectively the hubbub was like that of a rumble of thunder that speaks of the approaching storm.

The press about the church was tightest and, fearing for the high-spirited gelding which quickly grew nervous of the crowd, Thomas led it away, seeking a quiet place to tether the animal. But such looked difficult to find, until he thought of the old almshouses which stood north of the church, built long ago for the poorest folk of the village. Soon he had left the churchyard behind and rounded the long stone building, finding a haven of tranquillity in the small patch of sunny garden at the rear. He tied the horse to a bush, looking round to see if there were anyone to watch over him. But the almshouse folk too were seemingly all gone to lay William Stubbs to rest.

He was on the point of walking away when a woman's voice called to him. He turned to see a somewhat stout, matronly figure peering at him from the end doorway. Shielding his eyes from the harsh sunlight, he smiled a greeting.

'May I leave my mount here, mistress?' he asked. 'There's nowhere else I can find that's so quiet.'

The woman left the doorway and walked down the short path towards him; and the closer she came, the more her smile widened. She wore a low-cut chestnut gown and a cheap red periwig. The white-lead foundation on her face was painted over with patches of vermilion, as if she were the frequenter of some city alehouse rather than a Downland village.

'You are welcome, master, though it be somewhat early,' she said. 'I have seen ye before, have I not?'

Thomas blinked, taking in the woman's smile as well as her dress and posture; then the truth dawned.

'Nay . . .' he began awkwardly. 'I am not come to seek ye out . . . not to say that you wrong me in any fashion, I mean . . .'

The woman's smile broadened yet further. 'No need to be abashed, sir. Ye have heard of sweet Sarah Caldwell, and come a coney-hunting. Will you step inside?'

'Nay, mistress . . .' He shook his head, managing a weak smile. 'I spoke the truth when I said I was but looking for a place to tether the horse.'

Sarah Caldwell stared at him for a further moment, then her smile vanished. 'Do I look like a horse-holder?' she demanded. Her chest heaved with indignation.

Not like any I've seen, Thomas thought, but maintained his smile and answered: 'I ask your pardon. I will pay for his keep, if you will let me leave him here.'

She considered. It occurred to Thomas that never before had he known a village trull do business from church property. Then he thought of London's Bankside, where he had once spent an unpleasant few days as prisoner in a trugging-house, and remembered that all those establishments stood on the Bishop of Winchester's land, and paid His Grace a goodly sum in rent.

'Sixpence.' Mistress Caldwell's voice cut his reverie short.

'Sixpence?' he echoed, becoming indignant in turn. 'I asked merely to leave him – not that you serve him as a customer!'

At once he regretted his coarseness, but the woman was not in the least dismayed. 'Threepence, then,' she countered. 'And if you return not before noon, I'll water him for you.'

Thomas found a smile spreading across his face. 'I should have marked you as a shrewd woman of business,' he said wryly, and felt for his purse.

Sarah Caldwell took the money, and grew more at ease. 'Who have I the honour to address?' she asked. But when Thomas gave his name, a wary look came into her large brown eyes. 'You're the one took the eyases from the tower last spring.'

He nodded.

'You won't speak of what passed between us – I mean, with the church folk?' She was anxious now. 'Reverend Starling is merciless, and I'm but a poor widow who will need a roof over her come wintertime.'

Thomas smiled and shook his head, then walked away towards the churchyard.

To his relief, the funeral passed peacefully enough; though not without its moment of excitement.

Richard Starling, he had to admit, conducted the rites with passion, whatever his own feelings for Will Stubbs may have been. By the time the black-draped coffin was borne to the graveside, there was not a man nor woman present who had not been touched by the service. The throng surged about the grave in the sunshine, filling the small churchyard and beyond. As Stubbs's body was committed, there was a loud chorus of keening and lamentation from the women, sounds which had

36

not changed in England for a thousand years. A shower of garlands and wild flowers fell upon the coffin.

Thomas stood apart beside a silent Samuel Hubbard, whose eyes roved across the crowd as if he expected trouble any minute. He could see the churchmen – Henry Howes, John Wilmott and Jonas Crouch – in their suits of black drugget, standing close to Starling as he intoned the last words: *Ashes to ashes, dust to dust . . .*

Then something happened that was not entirely unexpected. From somewhere in the thick of the crowd came the loud clanging of a hand-bell.

Hubbard stiffened and peered in the direction of the sound. Glancing about, Thomas saw other heads turning. Then he looked at once at the rector. To his surprise, Starling gave no sign that he had even heard the bell being rung – clearly an act of brazen rebellion, since his forbidding of such customs was so well known. Instead the man kept his gaze fixed upon the coffin, now resting in the bottom of the grave, as with his right hand he made the sign of blessing. Then he merely turned, nodded to the sexton to do his work, and walked away.

The bell rang again, and again. Thomas found his heart was pounding. Beside him the bulky Hubbard was blowing like a plough-horse. But if the constable had expected a near riot, he was mistaken. For the rector, on this occasion, had bowed to the collective feeling of this ancient Downland village as it laid one of its inhabitants to rest, and had let the passing-bell ring. Now it ceased, and a silence fell. Folk made way for Starling as he walked erect and dignified through the press of mourners, and disappeared inside the church.

For a moment, nobody moved. Then Henry Howes stepped forward, spade in hand, and stood ready. Beside him Jonas Crouch bent, took a handful of earth and threw it into the grave. Then he turned to go, and at last others began to follow. Slowly, with heads bowed, the villagers moved away and left their sexton to do the burying. The sense of release was almost palpable, and many began to weep openly – as if they had at last been given permission to grieve in their own way, and not in the manner imposed upon them by this stern rector that few liked, and even fewer could fathom.

37

But Thomas stood motionless while the crowd disappeared, and his eyes filled, for memories had welled up unbidden: of the funeral of his first wife, Mary, in Chaddleworth churchyard, and eight-year-old Eleanor standing still and silent beside him. It had been ten years.

Finally he too left the churchyard. But then for some reason he glanced back, and saw that apart from the sexton there was yet another figure beside the grave, standing bowed, as if unwilling to leave: John Wilmott.

As Thomas stared the man suddenly raised his head, met his eyes, and quickly looked away.

Five

Thomas wandered through the village, looking for Jonas Crouch. It appeared to him as though the custom of feasting and drinking that normally followed a burial was not being observed, for he saw no sign of it. Folk stood talking quietly in groups, or drifted away. If the wake too had been discouraged by Richard Starling, he guessed it would have been even harder to bear than his refusal to toll the passing-bell. Though since that prohibition at least had been defied, perhaps discreet imbibing was taking place after all, behind certain doors.

Samuel Hubbard had disappeared, and there was no sign either of the parish clerk. Aware that he might not be well received at such a time, Thomas nevertheless made his way to the blacksmith's, girding himself up for a task he did not relish. But on reaching the open-fronted building, he found a workaday atmosphere within. The heat of the forge hit him, a withering blast that made the sweat run from his pores. There came a low hiss of air and, peering inside, he saw a boy in a dirty, waist-open shirt working the ancient bellows.

'Is the smith here?' he called, allowing his eyes to adjust to the comparative gloom. The boy looked round in surprise.

'Gone to the burying, like everyone else!'

Thomas nodded and was about to leave when a voice behind him growled: 'That don't mean we can't do business. Be civil to the customer, can't ye?'

He turned to find himself face to face with the swarthy, round-shouldered blacksmith. 'Master Ragg?'

Ragg looked surprised. 'You . . . what d'ye want here?'

Thomas began to state his name and station, but the man cut him short. 'I know who ye are. I asked what business you have with me.'

39

Thomas took a breath, and told him. The other listened, then said: 'I can tell ye naught of the churchwarden's death. I did not look upon his body. Others bore it away.'

'Who were they?'

'John Tolworthy the miller, and Peter Hare, and a couple of the younger men.' He squinted up at Thomas. 'What good will come now, of raking over those coals? He is laid in his grave. Let him rest.'

Thomas said nothing, but watched the man's face closely. Yet he saw no sign of unease, or of evasion. He knew Ragg's reputation as a straight-talking man, and relaxed somewhat.

'I ask pardon for troubling you on this day, of all days,' he said finally. 'I am charged by my master with finding out what I can of the death . . .'

Ragg snorted, but his hostility did not seem to be aimed at Thomas. 'Your master . . . I wager he's naught better to do than find chaff to talk over at suppertime. But he sends you to do the sifting for him!'

Thomas put on a wry smile, and nodded. 'Though the harvest be bare, thus far.'

He stood aside, to allow the blacksmith to pass into the body of his shop. Unbuttoning what was no doubt his best jerkin, the man walked to the furnace, peered at it and muttered something to his boy. Then he turned back to Thomas.

'I fear I cannot make your task any easier, falconer. You'd best ask the others – John Nightingale, and Tolworthy . . .' He broke off, looking sombre. 'Though it was a goodly night for bat-fowling, I see now it was an evil one, nonetheless.'

Thomas blinked. 'Evil . . . ?'

Ragg eyed him. 'I'm not easily afeared,' he muttered. 'Yet there was someone else in that wood. We all heard it . . . someone laughing, only not like any voice I've heard.'

And despite the heat, the man almost shivered at the memory. Then, seeing Thomas's eyes upon him, he drew himself up sharply, and repeated: 'Ask Tolworthy. Though you'll have to go to Uplambourn Mill – from what I see, he hasn't come in for the burying.'

Then he turned his back and began issuing orders to his

prentice, leaving Thomas in little doubt that the conversation was ended.

He walked back to the almshouses to recover the gelding. There was no sign of Mistress Caldwell, but he was pleasantly surprised to see an empty pail beside the horse. It seemed the woman was as good as her word. Within minutes he had mounted, left the village and was riding along the narrow path which climbed steadily up on to the Western Downs.

The tiny, isolated hamlet of Uplambourn was nothing more than a cluster of poor cottages, some of them abandoned and now little more than ruins. But dominating the grassy skyline, where larks and plovers flew in great numbers, was the windmill in which John Tolworthy and his family lived and worked, as generations of his forebears had done before him.

Thomas dismounted, letting the gelding's reins trail so that he might browse, and watched the mill's great sails turning slowly in the breeze. There was a sudden whirr of wings, and a partridge shot up not five yards away.

A low storehouse stood beside the square-built wooden mill. Looking round, he saw a heavily built young man had emerged from it and was lumbering towards him. At first he did not recognize the boy, then realization dawned.

'Edward, is it? Must be years since I've set eyes on you . . . now you're full grown.'

But Edward Tolworthy stopped some distance away. 'Faither's too busy to come to mustering!'

Thomas raised his brow. 'Mustering? I know naught of that . . .'

'We're mill folk – got to feed 'er!' The lad pointed towards the mill as though it were some ravenous beast.

Thomas made no reply. He was recalling something of Edward's life history . . . how the boy was said to have been damaged at his birth, and had always been slower than other village children, who mocked him mercilessly. As soon as he was big enough, his father put him to work. Now Edward seldom left Uplambourn, and always with another member of his large family.

There came a shout, and Thomas was somewhat relieved

41

to see John Tolworthy himself appear from the mill's entrance. With a nod to Edward, he approached and made his greeting.

Tolworthy was surprisingly agile for a heavy man. He waved Edward away, then quickly steered Thomas into the storehouse, where sacks of flour lined the walls. Thomas was startled when the other thrust his broad face close.

'You're Sir Robert Vicary's man.'

Thomas nodded. 'His falconer . . .'

'He sent you here, did he?'

Thomas hesitated. 'In a manner of speaking – he and Master Elyot wish me to uncover what I can of Will Stubbs's death . . .'

Tolworthy stared, but began to relax somewhat. After a moment Thomas went on: 'You were one of those brought the churchwarden's body in, or so I am told. You saw the condition of it . . .'

The miller paused before answering. 'It was pitch dark, and we had only three or four torches. I saw little before we wrapped him up, best as we could in a couple of shirts.'

Thomas frowned slightly. 'You must have seen his head was split open . . .'

'Aye. Poor old cove must have taken some tumble.'

At that, Thomas lost patience. 'Next you will tell me there was no rope binding him – that before he died, he thought he would sit up against a tree to make it look tidier!'

But Tolworthy was clearly taken aback. 'You'd best ask John Nightingale and Peter Hare,' he muttered. ''Twas they found Stubbs. He were lying flat on the ground when I first set eyes on 'ee.'

Thomas took a breath. 'Are you certain?'

The man nodded. His earlier tenseness seemed to be evaporating. 'What's that you say about a rope?'

The man's puzzlement was genuine. Thomas too began to relax. 'I ask pardon for my sharpness of speech,' he said. 'I have asked Master Nightingale already, and he too would tell me little.'

The miller gave a shrug. 'It's not the sort of memory a man wants to dwell upon.'

Thomas nodded. 'Did you know Master Stubbs well?'

42

'Well enough,' the other answered. 'Though I seldom go down to Lambourn . . .' Looking somewhat uncomfortable, he added: 'I've paid my fines, when I missed Sunday worship, though it hurt me sore to do it. And I know what some will say – I should have come to the burying, and paid my due respects. Well, I'm a man with time for little else but his work, and I might remind them of such. They'd bleat soon enough if they couldn't get flour to bake their bread!'

He turned towards the doorway. But as the two of them stepped outside into the sunshine, Thomas was surprised when the man said: 'It's a warm day. Will ye take a drink of cider before you ride on?'

He smiled. 'Gladly.'

They stood close to the mill's huge sails, which sighed as they rotated overhead. Voices floated through an open window from within, which, together with the sound of the old gears creaking, spoke of the Tolworthy family's constant task of tending what was more a machine than a home. The younger children seemed shy of strangers and kept out of sight, though the miller's tall, bony wife Ann was civil enough. She brought the mugs of lukewarm cider – the last of an old brew, by the taste of it – then left the two men outside. Thomas watched Edward Tolworthy emerge from the door carrying a sack on each shoulder, and trudge towards the store. As he went he threw a baleful glance at Thomas before moving out of sight.

'Your eldest boy has grown mightily since I last saw him.'

The miller nodded briefly. Without wishing to pain the man, Thomas persisted. 'Was he with you, at the bat-fowling?'

Tolworthy faced him. 'Sounds to me as if you know it already.' Then as if to put an end to the tale, he said: 'There was me and Edward, Hare, Nightingale and Will Ragg, and a couple of young lads who drink in the Horns. We'd done our fowling, and were bagging our catch. Then . . .' he hesitated, 'there was a noise in the wood, so Hare and Nightingale went to take a look. That's when they found Stubbs. They called us, and we brought his body back to Lambourn. We woke up the rector, and took it to the church, and that's all I can tell.'

Thomas nodded. 'This noise – you heard it too?'

43

The miller looked as if he regretted mentioning it.

'I can't swear to it. There was birds flapping about in the nets, and owls calling – yes, 'twas likely an owl.'

'Yet Hare and Nightingale went to look?'

'He's a man who likes to poke about.' He drained his mug, and stared ahead.

'Ragg told me what kind of a sound it was,' Thomas said quietly. 'Laughter, the likes of which he had never heard. He said it was an evil night . . .'

John Tolworthy had stiffened. 'I told ye, falconer – I can't say for certain what I heard.' Then, as Edward emerged from the storehouse and started towards them, the miller suddenly reached out and caught Thomas by the arm.

'And don't you go asking the boy! He takes fright at the sight of his own face in a pond!'

Thomas eyed the man, ignoring the power of his grasp. 'I mean no harm to you or your folk, Master Miller,' he said. 'But I believe Stubbs was murdered, and that someone wishes to conceal the matter. Who do you think that might be?'

The other dropped his hand, and stepped back. The strength seemed to have drained from his body. 'Murder?' he echoed softly. 'Nay . . . it cannot be.'

Thomas said nothing.

'It cannot!' The miller repeated, and Thomas saw fear in his eyes. He swallowed, then said with an effort: 'There's none I know of would do that – save it were something less than human.' He paused, and half to himself added: 'And there's some who'll tell you they've seen such on these Downs – ask Mary Pegg!'

Thomas looked blank. The name was unfamiliar to him. He opened his mouth, but Tolworthy had already turned away, and was calling to Edward. The boy seemed to respond to something in his father's voice, and threw a scared look at him before hurrying off round the side of the mill.

'Who's Mary Pegg?' Thomas asked.

The miller hesitated, then pointed due westward, across the hamlet below to the empty Downs beyond. 'The old warrener's place,' he said. Then deliberately he held his hand out.

Thomas sighed, drained his mug and handed it over. 'I thank

44

you,' he said. But the man walked off around the side of the mill. A door banged. Then there was only the skylarks calling, and the soft creak of the old sails turning in the wind.

Thomas's curiosity was aroused, for he hardly ever came to this part of the Downs. He left Uplambourn and rode westwards through the long grass, climbing steadily, until all signs of human habitation were lost to sight. The hills, the colour of old straw, stretched away to distant Wiltshire. Birds of the open heath flew about calling to one another, then dipped in alarm as a pair of buzzards sailed into view overhead. But Thomas paid them no mind, for the miller's words had stirred a memory. The old warrener's place . . . he recalled that there had once been vast rabbit-warrens in this area, enough to tempt some men to dwell here and scrape a living from trapping the creatures. But the last warrener had been too industrious, and the rabbits had dwindled in numbers, so that he had abandoned the site and taken his family elsewhere. Now, it appeared that someone else occupied the remote cottage: one Mary Pegg . . .

There could be several reasons why a woman might wish to dwell alone – if alone she was – this far from the village, and none of them were very much to his liking. He was turning the matter over as he urged the gelding up a long slope; then when he reached the top, he drew rein in some surprise.

In a shallow dip ahead of him stood a low house of wattles and mud, its eaves sagging almost to the ground. The roof was made of turves, which had reseeded themselves so that grass grew high upon the ridge, blending into the hills around. From any distance it would have been possible to miss the place altogether; save that there were pens on two sides, and a tiny hut where animals might be kept. In front of the house someone had wrought a garden of sorts, though what might grow in the poor chalky soil up here, Thomas could scarce imagine.

He remained for a while, sitting the horse, pondering the strangeness of the place. Then with a start he realized that someone had been standing motionless before the cottage, apparently staring at him, for as long as he had been there.

He eased the mount forwards and rode slowly towards what

he now saw was a doorway, though the only door was an old sheepskin tied to the lintel. As he drew closer, he saw to his surprise that the garden was not only well tended, but green with a profusion of vegetables and herbs. A covered rain-tub stood by the wall of the cottage, which now appeared the most forlorn habitation he had ever seen.

The figure materialized into a woman in patched workaday clothes and a rough straw hat, which she took off and used to shield her eyes as she regarded her visitor. Thomas drew rein and gave good-day, but the woman did not reply. To his relief, she was far from the disease-ridden crone he had half expected. In fact her age was probably less than forty years, and her skin, though burned dark by sun and wind, smooth and wholesome. The eyes were clear blue, and rather unsettling in the way they peered unblinkingly at him.

He tried again. 'Your pardon if I startled you,' he said. 'Might you be Mistress Pegg . . . ?'

'What do you want of me?' The voice was cracked and hoarse, as if the woman were unused to regular speech.

Thomas took her words as invitation enough to dismount, but as he did so, the woman noted his tall frame, and the good Petbury horse with its fine harness, and flinched away.

'I mean no harm,' Thomas murmured. But Mary Pegg reached out and took a hazel staff which was leaning against the doorway.

'Come no closer,' she said. 'If you're after charms and remedies, I sell naught but herbs, and only at market. You should 'a caught me yesterday, in Lambourn.'

He smiled. 'I was there yesterday, and I'm sorry I did miss you.' When no reply came he went on: 'I would guess it's a goodly long walk to Lambourn from here . . .'

'No more than four mile, straight.' She was growing edgy, and backed towards the door. 'I asked what you want of me.'

He hesitated, for he had no true reason for seeking her out, or none he could admit to. To begin asking vague questions about things seen on the Downs – things less than human, as Tolworthy had put it – now seemed absurd.

'Forgive me for startling you, mistress,' he said in a gentle

46

voice. 'I was but curious to see your house . . . I recall the warreners left here long ago.'

But for some reason Mary Pegg's attention wavered. She cocked an ear to one side, though keeping her eyes fixed on Thomas. There was a moment's silence. He listened, but could hear nothing . . . then came a scratching from inside the house. The sheepskin curtain lifted slightly, and a pair of small eyes peered at him from ground level. As he watched, the slim, grey-black body of a polecat slid into view.

'Wesht!' Mary Pegg hissed, and the animal vanished.

She turned to face Thomas again, but he had already caught up the gelding's rein. 'Your pardon, mistress,' he said, not unkindly. 'I see you do not like to have strangers here.'

Mary Pegg gave him an odd look. 'I was not plain with ye,' she said suddenly. 'I was never at Lambourn yesterday. Took sick in my stomach.'

He nodded politely and heaved himself into the saddle. Then, half-raising his hand in farewell, he swung the gelding and cantered off the way he had come.

At the crest of the low ridge he slowed and allowed himself a long look behind at Mary Pegg's house; but as he expected, she was gone.

She was not the first such woman he had known of, living alone and isolated with only animals for company. And his instinct told him there was no wickedness about her. Yet as he urged the horse forward, he wondered why she had wished to volunteer the information that she had not been at market, unless she had something to hide. What that might be, he could not imagine.

He was back in Lambourn late in the afternoon, and to his relief the first face he saw was that of Jonas Crouch.

There were few people about, and the funeral atmosphere seemed to have evaporated in the heat. He dismounted in front of the Horns, where the same row of old shepherds, who seemed not to have moved since the day before, regarded him with unblinking curiosity. But his attention was caught by Crouch's manner, for the man appeared agitated.

Without preamble he led the way across the square, past the

47

market cross towards the bridge. Here on the east side of the village he stopped before the end cottage nearest the river.

'This was Will Stubbs's house.'

Thomas looked, seeing nothing amiss. The house was small and somewhat ill-kept, though no worse than would be imagined when its occupant had been over seventy years of age, and lived alone. Then he saw the door was ajar.

'Someone has been in,' Crouch said quietly. 'I think last night. Wilmott came here after the funeral – said the place has been disturbed.'

'Where's Hubbard?' Thomas asked suddenly.

His friend shrugged. 'Once he saw there was not likely to be trouble, even with the bell and all . . .' He broke off, and sighed. 'I would guess he's drunk, and sleeping it off.'

Thomas raised an eyebrow. 'Have you the authority . . . ?'

Crouch shrugged, and led the way inside.

The house had been more than disturbed – ransacked was the word that came to mind. The single downstairs room was scattered with the old man's possessions, few as they were. There was little furniture, and all of it poor quality – save for a stout oak chest which had been forced open, its lid gaping. Looking inside, Thomas found a few papers, some shards of a broken pot and an ancient leather pouch. But when he lifted the flap, it was empty save for a small fragment of wood. He examined the shard, noting its age, and decided it was a bit of hardwood, broken off some old stick of furniture. Though it was not ash, nor oak . . . dismissing the object, he replaced it in the pouch and dropped it back in the chest.

He turned to Crouch. 'I heard he loaned a little money to poor folk. But surely no house-breaker would have thought this prize worth the risk. A churchwarden's wage . . . ?'

The clerk was standing in the middle of the room, looking stunned. 'Who would wish such wickedness upon that man?' he asked. 'Murdered, you claim . . . and now burgled?' He shook his head.

Thomas walked to the narrow stair in the corner and climbed up. But there was nothing in the low sleeping loft, save a pallet and a few items of plain clothing. He descended again, to see Crouch by the doorway squinting at some papers.

'Old church business,' the clerk said. 'Nothing untoward . . .' He looked round. Thomas was examining the fireplace and its crumbling chimney breast. He found a loose brick and drew it out, but there was nothing in the recess behind. He stooped, peered up the chimney, then straightened again.

'If Master Stubbs truly had no secrets,' he muttered, 'then he must have been a rare fellow indeed.'

Crouch frowned slightly. 'What secrets would he have? He needed nothing more in his life than to serve the church.'

'So I have been hearing, from the moment I first arrived here,' Thomas answered. Seeing the look of discomfort on his friend's face, he sighed. 'You must make allowances for me, Jonas, if I think less of humankind than you. Mayhap I have seen too much wickedness. I have yet to meet a true saint.'

Crouch thought for a moment, then said: 'Will would have been the first to say he had his failings, like any other mortal man. He measured himself differently, that is all.'

Thomas nodded and stretched his limbs, stiff from his ride. 'It's likely I'm plucking at straws. I rode far out on the Downs today on a fool's errand, merely because the miller at Uplambourn pointed me that way.'

But at that, Crouch was suddenly alert.

'Pointed you . . . where? Was it by chance to Mary Pegg's?'

Thomas showed his surprise. 'It was . . . what made you ask?'

The little clerk hesitated, then said: 'I would have told you sooner: she was seen, close to Lambourn wood, on the night Will died.'

Six

They closed the door of William Stubbs's house and stood outside. In the west, the first clouds for more than a week had appeared, drifting in from the Downs.

Despite Thomas's questions, Crouch could add little to what he had said. Mary Pegg the hermit, who hardly ever came to the village except to bring her herbs to market, had been seen on the night the bat-fowlers found Will Stubbs's body, by some late drinkers leaving the Horns. She was walking hurriedly up the Ramsbury path, which bordered Lambourn wood.

'Then she did lie to me,' Thomas said. Briefly he told his friend what had passed earlier, on the Downs.

Crouch wore a sombre look. 'You'd best tell your master,' he said, 'and I will tell mine. The rector, that is.'

'I will,' Thomas answered. 'Though it's hard to believe that woman, strange though she be, would harm anyone – let alone commit murder. What had she to gain?'

The clerk shook his head. 'Whoever came into Will's house and caused such mayhem – what had he to gain?'

They were about to part when a voice hailed them. Turning, they saw Samuel Hubbard puffing towards them. Thomas heaved a sigh. The man was tousle-haired and indeed looked as if he had just been woken up.

'You!' the constable was pointing at him. 'You said you'd help me keep order, then you take yourself off somewhere – what've you been about?'

Thomas opened his mouth, but the other jerked a thumb over his shoulder. 'I need you now, over the church. There's some brabble afoot.'

Crouch looked alarmed. 'What sort of brabble?'

'Best come and see for yourself,' Hubbard retorted, then swung his enormous bulk and waddled off. With a glance at each other, the two men followed.

They rounded the south-east corner of the church, to find a small crowd gathered about the bell-pit and furnace. Voices were raised, though quite who was at the centre of the dispute it was difficult to judge. Heads turned quickly as Hubbard arrived, followed by Thomas and Crouch. And at once a black-garbed figure detached itself from the group and strode towards them. 'Master Constable!'

Richard Starling was trembling with rage, his eyes bulging. The constable stopped, puffing in the face of the man's onslaught.

'This is hallowed ground!' Starling roared. 'And I will not have indiscipline! This rabble . . .' He waved a hand to indicate Goodchild the bell-founder, who was standing near to the pit. Beside him was his son, Edmund, with head bowed. Other men, bricklayers and labourers, stood about looking uncomfortable. And there was a middle-aged woman Thomas had not seen before, slight of figure, standing apart in silence. As he gazed she met his eyes, and lowered them at once. He guessed that this was Alice Goodchild, and only now remembered what Hubbard had told him, about her being unable to speak.

Hubbard was trying to get a word in, without success; for the rector was in the full flow of righteous passion. And even Thomas had to admit that it was an impressive sight.

'This rabble,' he resumed, 'have flouted my authority since the moment they arrived! I am the rector of St Michael and All Angels, and the church is their paymaster! They are here to submit their craft to the will of God – not to make demands, but to cast a new bell as ordered, then be on their way!'

He turned to indicate Simon Goodchild, who was regarding him in stony silence. 'Don't think I am unaware that fifty years back that man's forebears and their ilk wandered the lanes of Catholic England seeking monasteries to cast bells for,' he said in a scathing tone. 'Why, as a boy, he probably served the forces of popery himself! Now he seeks to foist his savage ways upon me, and I will not have it!'

51

He drew breath, and at last Hubbard managed to speak. 'But, Master Rector – what is it he's done?'

'Done?' The rector echoed. He paused, seemingly aware at last of his parish clerk, standing meekly aside.

He turned back to Hubbard. 'I'll tell you what he has done. Having already wrung more money out of the church for inscribing letters inside the bell, he now has the nerve to ask me what name I have chosen for it, when it is cast. Then he dares to ask me about the consecration – and what steps I will take to prevent demons entering the mould!' He broke off, as if words were inadequate. 'Such pagan ways belong to a dark age – out of which I, and others, strive to lead the people of this land. And yet when I bid the man look to his own business and leave God's to me, he threatens to stop work again!'

Hubbard blinked and wet his dry lips. 'But, Master Starling, as I see it, 'tis not an arrestable offence . . .'

'No?' The rector's hand shot out, but the finger was aimed not at the founder. Instead he pointed to young Edmund. 'Then mayhap affray will serve – and on church property! Ask him!'

The other men looked, and saw the reason for Edmund Goodchild's demeanour. The young man was holding a hand to his face, and from a distance there looked to be blood upon it.

Here was something closer to Hubbard's territory. With obvious relief he gestured to Thomas, and the two of them approached the Goodchilds.

Simon Goodchild did not move and, being a head taller than the constable, he was able to look down his long nose at him. At close quarters, his dignified bearing resembled even more that of some ancient prophet. Thomas, being closer in height to the bell-founder, looked him in the eye as he drew near. But he saw no malice there, nor even arrogance – rather a passive acceptance of matters which, though tedious, had to be dealt with.

'What happened to 'ee, boy?' Hubbard was peering at Edmund Goodchild, who at last raised his head. Someone had clearly given the lad a bloody nose, and a bruise on his cheek for good measure.

'Fighting in a churchyard – shame on ye!' Hubbard snorted,

summoning a little righteous indignation of his own. 'Who else was party to'n – and where is he?'

The boy did not answer. Thomas glanced from Edmund to his parents, and at the other men – villagers hired by the founder to assist him, as was the usual custom. None of them looked guilty; rather, they appeared baffled by the uproar, which now seemed to have small enough basis. The father still showed no emotion. But the mother . . .

Now Thomas's sympathy was aroused, for Alice Goodchild was obviously distressed. Her small, sunburned face bore care-lines that spoke of a lifetime of struggle. Her eyes were busy, darting everywhere, the mouth twitching, though no sound came forth. She wore the simple garb of a field-worker, but her apron was stiff, and stained deep red-brown. Thomas realized the cause of it, as his gaze wandered to a nearby heap of soft clay. It had been brought from downriver, to fashion the core and cope – the inner and outer halves of the bell-mould – that he now saw filled the huge pit close by.

'I asked who fought with ye,' the constable said, glaring from Edmund to his father and back. 'You refuse to answer, I'll put ye in the lock-up till, er . . .' He broke off, and Thomas had to conceal a smile. Lambourn had no lock-up; only a lean-to behind Hubbard's house, where he normally stored his jugs of cider. 'Till ye make full and true confession of your crime!' he finished.

One or two of the village men snickered, then quickly had to look away. For the rector's wrath had not abated.

'For pity's sake, man – flog him, and have done with it!' he snapped, prompting several reactions; but the strongest came from Alice Goodchild. To everyone's surprise she gave a whimper, hurried forward and dropped to one knee before Richard Starling.

For a moment nobody spoke. The rector was dismayed, though his frown merely changed from one of anger to one of embarrassment. 'Mistress . . . will you kindly let go!' He reached out and took the woman's hand, which had gripped the edge of his thin gown. 'I understand a mother's grief. If the boy would but offer some explanation, mayhap . . .'

'I will!' All heads turned, for Edmund Goodchild, his face

53

livid with shame, had thrust himself forward. Wiping blood from his nose and mouth with a sleeve, the boy stood up to the constable. And there was defiance as well as courage in his eyes.

'I'm no informer!' he said. 'I got into a bit of trouble and took a blow or two – 'twas naught of importance, and it's settled. A matter between two people – is that a felony now?'

Hubbard swallowed. 'How do I know the other bain't hurt worse?' he asked. 'You might have broke his head, for all I know.'

'You have my word the other took no injury,' Edmund replied. After a moment, he added: 'And as to the accusations levelled by Master Starling . . .'

There was a stirring of unease. Thomas sensed the rector's anger welling up again, and steeled himself for another outburst. But Edmund stood his ground.

'My father is the best founder in all of southern England,' he said stoutly. 'You may see bells he has made in churches from Kent to Gloucestershire – and there are none finer, anywhere! He but asks that you let him serve his craft, which takes a lifetime to learn . . .' The boy seemed to be controlling some well of emotion. With an effort, he finished: 'We, his family, ask only that we be allowed to toil alongside him, and work to make this bell as fine as any – for it shall be a maiden bell!'

There was a silence. Early-evening drinkers on the other side of the village could be heard outside the Horns. From the river nearby, mallards clucked in chorus.

For once, Starling seemed lost for words. And at last, as if he had waited to choose his moment, Simon Goodchild stepped forward. Bending slightly, he took his wife by the arm and drew her to her feet. Then, not without pride, he placed a hand upon his son's shoulder. Edmund did not look at him, but lowered his gaze.

'I was told you were a stern man,' the bell-founder said. 'Yet I have observed how you strive to serve a higher master – the one we all serve, in our own ways.'

The voice was deep and the accent seemed to bear traces of a dozen counties of England, and perhaps beyond. Meeting

Starling's eye, the man continued: 'Violence was done here, and since I am the father I take the blame, and ask your pardon. Nothing like it shall happen again.'

Starling took a deep breath. 'There will be no blasphemous ceremonies here,' he said. 'My consecration service shall be enough.'

The founder nodded.

'And . . .' The rector hesitated, then said: 'Let the boy's injuries be punishment enough.'

The founder nodded again, and on all sides there was relief. Starling made as if to turn away, then frowned slightly and said: 'I heard some time ago, of one of your calling, who cast a maiden peal in a village in Sussex . . . four bells so finely made, they needed no tuning. No filing or chipping, to sound the hum or strike notes . . . they were raised untouched from the mould to the tower, and sang as sweetly from the first time they were rung as they do today.'

Simon Goodchild gave a slight smile. 'I have been in Sussex,' he allowed. 'Yet I cannot swear the bells you speak of were cast by me, unless you name the village.'

But Starling's manner had altered so much that the Lambourn men struggled to conceal their surprise. Was this truly their firebrand of a rector, the arch-Puritan, who deemed everything was vanity except complete and constant obeisance to God?

'I do not need to name it,' he said quietly. 'I believe the bells were cast by you.' He glanced towards the bell-pit. 'And our new tenor bell, you say, will be a maiden bell.'

Then he did walk away. And without a word the artisans began to pick up their hammers and trowels, and return to their tasks. Hubbard too walked off; as did Jonas Crouch, who followed the rector round the side of the church. Soon only Thomas and the Goodchilds remained.

They did not move, but stood in silence waiting for him to go. A moment passed. Keeping expression from his face, Thomas glanced at Simon, then at Alice. Seldom, he realized, had he seen such a close family. They seemed to have no need of words; instead it seemed to him that thoughts passed between them like invisible threads. And after a moment, as

55

if some unseen signal had been given, Alice and Edmund both turned and went away: the boy to join the builders of the furnace, which now looked almost complete. His mother, however, walked off towards the river.

Still Simon Goodchild stood, immovable as a statue. And now Thomas read something else in the man's gaze: a wariness, and behind it a formidable intellect. It would be mighty difficult, he thought, to know what this man was thinking.

Then the moment passed, and the man seemed to relax. With a half-apologetic gesture, and a smile that conveyed his need to look to his work, he turned away.

Thomas walked back to the square to collect the horse. Though he wished for nothing more than to get home to Petbury, he remembered that it was Saturday, the Sabbath eve. Tomorrow his master would likely have need of his services, and perhaps he would be spared another journey to Lambourn. He must tell Sir Robert what had passed, and let him decide how to proceed. But riding over the Lambourn bridge, he halted on the far side, feeling the weight of the charge that had been laid upon him. Some hours of daylight yet remained, and there was one he had yet to speak with, before he could tell Sir Robert he had done all he should.

With an air of resignation, he turned the gelding to his right, and rode downriver towards Bickington.

The Downs glowed in the soft evening light as, this time, he climbed the hill above the old manor and skirted it. He had passed Henry Howes's farmstead a few minutes ago, but seen no sign of the sexton. The grass was lush here, on the north slope of the valley; fine grazing land. Howes's modest acreage, populated by a few scrawny cattle and sheep, soon gave on to Bickington land. Elyot's pasture stretched away past the manor, down to the river and beyond, where Cleeve Hill could be seen to the south and, further west, the borders of Lambourn wood.

But Thomas was not heading for Bickington, and the notion afforded him some relief. One visit to William Elyot's was enough, he felt, to meet his master's instruction. Instead he rode a further mile, until the thatched roofs of Betterdown

Farm showed below him. Reining in, he gazed into the distance, across the sheep-dotted Downs. Somewhere up here, he knew, was the fold used by Peter Hare, the shepherd.

He turned the gelding and let him walk uphill, scanning the treeless landscape until at last he saw the little square of willow hurdles, dark against the grass. And mercifully luck was with him, for a small herd of sheep was moving towards the fold, harried by two black dogs which darted about, nipping at their heels. At the rear walked a slow-moving figure, dark against the skyline.

Not wishing to startle the animals, Thomas slowed his mount as he drew closer. He sensed that the shepherd had seen him, though the man continued his work without looking round. Finally he halted, watching Hare gather the last of the ewes into the fold before closing it up. Only then did the man turn and whistle sharply to his dogs, which flew to his side and lay motionless in the long grass, eyeing the newcomer.

Thomas gave his greeting, but Peter Hare merely nodded in return. Reaching down, he took a leather costrel from his belt, uncorked it in leisurely fashion and drank. Then deliberately he replaced the stopper and stood waiting. Seeing clearly enough how unwelcome he was, Thomas dismounted nevertheless and walked a few paces towards the shepherd. Hare drew a sleeve of his old linen smock across the nose, then scratched his grey head and squinted into the distance.

'I would have speech with you, master,' Thomas said, and began to make his explanation. But the man cut him short.

'I owe naught to ye, falconer, nor allegiance to any of Sir Robert Vicary's folk.'

Thomas considered. 'You herd sheep for Giles Ingle,' he said. 'He's one of Sir Robert's tenants.'

Hare said nothing. One of the dogs growled, very low.

Thomas tried again. 'I was told it was you and John Nightingale who found the churchwarden's body,' he said.

Hare gave a short nod.

'My master wishes to know the condition—' Thomas began, but again he was interrupted.

'His head was split like a chestnut,' Hare said harshly. 'Blood everywhere – that a good enough picture for ye?'

Thomas caught his eye and held it. 'What of the rope?'

For a moment, Hare's gaze seemed to waver. 'What rope's that?'

'The rope that bound him to the tree.'

Hare looked puzzled. 'Tree? He was lying on the ground, where he fell.'

Thomas took a long breath. He was tired from riding, as he was from talking to people – more in one day, he thought ruefully, than he normally spoke with in a week. The notion almost made him laugh; save that, above all else, he was tired of being lied to.

'Whoever bribed Nightingale to change his tale has got to you too,' he said.

At that a scowl appeared on Hare's leathery face. And at once both dogs stood up, ears erect.

'You ought to think a mite harder before you go accusing folk of lying, falconer,' he muttered.

But to the shepherd's surprise, Thomas relaxed visibly.

'You have given me all the answer I need,' he said.

'I've told ye naught!' Hare retorted.

'It's you who should think harder, about the consequences of giving false testimony,' Thomas told him, and stepped back to take up the gelding's reins. Indifferent to the business of the two men, the animal was leisurely cropping grass.

'This bain't no inquest – and you're no magistrate!' Hare snapped. 'Naught but a falconer, who's too high and mighty for his own good!'

Thomas stood beside the horse and patted his sleek neck. 'I will speak with my master,' he said. 'And if there is an inquest, you might well find yourself called.'

Hare ran a hand across his brow. 'See now – you stumble on a sight like that of a night-time, ye don't know—'

But Thomas had placed his boot in the stirrup, and this time it was he who cut the other short.

'I do know,' he said, 'for I've heard it already from others. It was dark, you were afraid . . .' Seating himself in the saddle, he looked down at the shepherd. 'You haven't mentioned the laughter – an owl, wasn't it?'

Hare stood watching him in silence, but unease showed in

58

his eyes. Finally he dropped his gaze, turned to his dogs and gave his low whistle. Then without another word he trudged away downhill.

Thomas watched him go, then urged the gelding in the other direction, towards home.

Twilight was falling when he rode into the stable at Petbury and handed the horse over to a groom. As he walked out of the yard he glanced towards the great house, where lights blazed from several windows. Then he recalled that Sir John Norris was likely still here, and sighed; Nell would be at her work until late. From the gardens, one of Sir Robert's peacocks was letting out a fearful shriek.

He walked up the slope to the falcons' mews, and found all of them quiet upon their perches, well-fed and watered. Then, he had expected nothing less; Ned was becoming used to being left alone to tend Sir Robert's birds. The thought troubled him. Once again, Thomas was roaming the Downs like some honorary constable, charged with investigating a murder. It was never a role he had sought, and of late – since he had married – he had been surprised to find himself wishing he might be elsewhere. He and Nell . . . just the two of them, making a new life somewhere, with a house and a bit of garden and enough work to keep them busy . . .

He drew a sharp breath and frowned. What of Eleanor? What of Ned, and Martin, and Sir Robert and Lady Margaret, all of whom in their own ways relied upon him? This is the foolishness that comes upon men when they reach their middle years, he thought; where else would you go – you who were born and bred here on the Downs, and know every hill and gully?

Still berating himself, he walked to the cottage, lifted the latch and stepped inside, half-hoping Nell would be asleep before the fire. But there was no fire, and the place was dark.

Seven

On the Sabbath morning, Thomas woke to find that the cloud had thickened to a grey-white blanket across the entire Western Downs. It was oppressive, heavy August weather, with no wind to bring relief. Having looked first to the falcons, he waited until the Petbury household had left the chapel, then went to seek an audience with Sir Robert.

His master received him alone in his morning chamber, where a small fire burned. As he entered and made his bow, he saw that the knight was tearing up papers, and feeding them one by one to the flames. 'Thomas . . .' Sir Robert's smile was warm. 'I have been called away. I leave tomorrow morning.'

Thomas showed his alarm. 'Sir – surely you will not journey at this time? The infection . . .'

'I must.' Sir Robert threw the last document into the fire, then sat watching it blaze. 'The Queen makes her customary summer Progress, this time to Cowdray in Sussex. She has asked Sir John Norris to attend her there before he leaves for France. He wishes me to go with him, as a loyal knight of the shire.'

He turned to meet Thomas's eye. 'Up here on the Downs, we see little of Europe's strife – of England's strife, come to that. Yet the world moves on, with or without us. How many people know that yet another great Spanish fleet would have sailed against us this summer, save only that unfavourable weather stopped it? How close might England have come to invasion once again, five years after the Armada, had the wind merely changed direction?' He shook his head. 'It chills my blood to think upon it.'

Thomas said nothing.

'The Queen is now in her sixtieth year,' Sir Robert said.

Turning his stool from the fire, he grew brisk. 'Nigh on sixty, yet they say she has yet the strength of a woman half her age! She does state business all day, dances half a dozen galliards every night, and is still debating at the supper table when all but her hardiest courtiers have fallen into a doze . . . how could any man fail to rally to her call?'

Then, Sir Robert changed tack. 'Hence, you see I must leave you to play the rummager, if only to set Master Elyot's mind to rest. I know you will do all you can to bring light to the matter of the churchwarden's death.'

Thomas nodded and, having ordered his thoughts, drew breath and told his master what had transpired over the past two days. By the time he had finished, Sir Robert was on his feet and pacing, his indoor shoes making swishing sounds in the fresh-strewn rushes.

'I like not the sound of it,' he said with a frown, halting to face Thomas. 'There should be an inquest, yet there is no coroner near . . . nor will Bishop Coldwell travel from Salisbury, if Starling hoped for support from that quarter. I would ask Sir John Norris to act, save that he is deaf to all matters except his militia . . .' He frowned suddenly. 'Today is muster day in Lambourn, when those who are picked to serve the Crown must present themselves, and receive their orders.'

Thomas sighed inwardly, guessing what was coming.

'Perhaps if you rode over there again . . .' His master glanced at him, adding casually: 'Or do you have other business?'

'None that cannot wait, sir,' he answered. And, having wished his master God speed and a safe journey, he found himself dismissed.

He reached Lambourn before midday, to find the village square host to a very different kind of gathering than that occasioned by William Stubbs's funeral.

There was a small crowd, but it was made up chiefly of onlookers. At its centre were half a dozen bored-looking men in homespun garb, with staves and pitchforks on their shoulders to serve as weapons. Two wore old corselets, making

61

them look somewhat ridiculous as they stood sweating in the heat. This body, Thomas guessed, constituted Lambourn's muster roll – or rather, Hubbard's attempt to fill the village's quota for military recruitment.

Having tethered the horse, he made his way across the square. He recognized most of the men: villagers of questionable character whom the constable would no doubt be relieved to send away. Small wonder, he thought, that the Queen's army had such a poor reputation. It was well known that not only was Elizabeth loath to equip her troops properly, she hardly ever bothered to pay them. Hence, since most were pressed into service, and sickness, malnutrition and general discontent were rife, the desertion rate was inevitably high. Some of these fellows, he guessed – assuming they even got as far as France – would be back before harvest-time was over.

Will Ragg the blacksmith was standing near the edge of the crowd, so Thomas walked over and gave him greeting. With a wry look, the man waved a hand towards the militiamen. 'First sight this lot get of the enemy, they'll turn tail and run.'

'I can't say I would blame them,' Thomas answered. 'No man but a fool wishes to fight, unless he has to.'

The smith looked sharply at him. 'That sounded like it came from the heart . . . have you shouldered a pike yourself?'

Thomas gave a short nod. But the next moment the other leaned closer and said: 'I've thought a little about our discourse yesterday.' When Thomas raised an eyebrow he added in a low voice: 'I will confess I grow more unsettled, the longer I dwell upon the matter.'

'I, too,' Thomas said after a moment.

Ragg looked uneasy. 'Does your master mean to call for an inquest?'

Thomas shrugged slightly. 'Would that trouble you?'

The other hesitated. 'Did you speak with Tolworthy?'

Thomas nodded. 'Among others – including the shepherd.'

Ragg said nothing.

'He lied to me,' Thomas said abruptly, having decided in that moment to test the blacksmith's honesty. 'As did Nightingale, the day before.' He paused, then: 'I mean, about the rope.'

Ragg's puzzlement seemed genuine. 'What rope?'

Thomas looked round. The militiamen were becoming restless, for no one seemed to have arrived to take charge of them. There was a general milling about, and some muttering.

He spoke in a low voice. 'Hare told Master Elyot, who in turn told my master, that Stubbs was bound to a tree when they first found him. Yet when they guided the rest of you back to the body, Stubbs was lying on the ground.'

Ragg nodded. 'That was how I first saw him.'

'And now,' Thomas continued, 'both finders are swearing there was never any rope, and that the old man must have slipped and broken his head.' He paused. 'I had not chance to view the body, yet I have heard enough to know their testimony is false. Had the old man fallen as they said, the injury would likely have been at his front. But the back of his head was split – by a weapon of some kind.'

Ragg was frowning. 'You must know how it was for us. We were unnerved by . . . by the noises we heard. When Nightingale and Hare came running and said they had found Will Stubbs dead, we were in turmoil. I cannot be certain what words passed, before they led the rest of us to the body. They talked between themselves, but they were ahead, and I heard not what was said.' He thought for a moment. 'This much I know: Nightingale was beside the body when we came up. I thought Stubbs was lying on the ground . . . indeed, I would swear it.'

After a moment, Thomas nodded. 'I do not doubt your word, Master Ragg. And I'm more certain than ever that someone got to those men soon after, to make them change their story. So now it's as if there never was a rope, and the old man's death an accident, when it seems clear to me he was attacked from behind, and killed.'

Ragg swallowed. 'Then, what's to be done?'

Thomas was about to make reply when a voice from nearby hailed him. He looked round to see Jonas Crouch approaching.

The little clerk greeted both men somewhat absently, then gestured quickly towards the militiamen. 'They won't wait much longer,' he muttered. 'Sam Hubbard keeps the musterbook, and he isn't here. Seems there's no answer from his house either.' He wrinkled his nose. 'Drunk again . . .'

Ragg frowned. 'That's not like him – he's particular about his recruiting.'

Crouch shrugged. 'He wasn't at this morning's service – what's more, they say the muster roll isn't filled. Hubbard was supposed to give out the last names today, so he could close the book.'

All three men's glances strayed to the south of the village, and the row of cottages which backed on to Lambourn wood. Hubbard's stood at the opposite end of the row from William Stubbs's house.

'Have they knocked loud enough?' Thomas asked. 'He must be the heaviest sleeper in Lambourn.'

Ragg glanced round. It looked as if the village militia were on the point of dismissing themselves and heading for the inn. 'I'll go,' he said with a sigh. 'I'm nearest we have to a deputy, anyway.' He walked off towards Hubbard's cottage. Left alone, Thomas and Crouch exchanged looks.

'Have you spoken with the rector, about what we found yesterday?' Thomas asked quietly.

His friend nodded. 'He bade me look to my duties, and not indulge in speculation – though it seems to me, my duty is to my Maker and my conscience, as well as to the truth.' He drew a sharp breath. 'And I believe things are passing between my brethren at St Michael's from which I am excluded!'

Thomas frowned. 'What kind of things?'

'The rector and John Wilmott . . . they talk low together, then when I arrive their mouths close like traps!'

At that moment there came a shout from some distance away. Both men looked round to see Will Ragg standing outside Hubbard's house. The door was still closed, but the man was gesturing wildly. At once, the two hurried towards him. A few bystanders had also noticed the blacksmith's manner, and started in the same direction.

The look on Ragg's face was enough. Without a word Thomas and Crouch followed him round the side of the house, through a little side gate into Hubbard's orchard.

If the constable was respected for anything, it was the quality of his apples. He had never married, but as a young man he had inherited a dilapidated old house with a bit of land behind it, along with a dozen apple trees. Now the house may have gone to rack and ruin, but the orchard was the pride of the village, and a source of the best cider in the Lambourn valley. And it was here the blacksmith had found him.

The other men entered the garden, to stop dead in their tracks. For the fat constable's body was wedged by the neck, hanging in a fork of one of his own trees, his stockinged feet barely a foot from the ground.

Necessity at times affords men rapid promotion; which is how Will Ragg the blacksmith found himself acting constable.

Showing more authority than some expected, the man ordered the house and garden out of bounds. Then he gathered together men he believed he could trust – which now included Thomas as well as Jonas Crouch. It also included the landlord of the Horns, John Nightingale.

Nightingale arrived and took in the grisly sight without a word, but on meeting Thomas's eye he looked away at once. Turning to Ragg, he asked if word had been sent to the rector.

Crouch was standing near, staring in horror at the hanged man. 'I will go to him,' he said, and left the garden at once.

It took four strong men to lift the constable's body so that his head could be detached from the tree's fork. Finally he was laid on the grass, and a coverlet fetched from the house to put over him. Then having asked a couple of men to guard the body, Ragg called the others to him.

'Seems to me we'd best get a message to Elyot,' he said in a dry voice. 'He's nearest . . .'

Nightingale was edgy. 'It's a matter for the High Sheriff,' he objected.

'The sheriff will not travel, for fear of the infection,' Thomas said. 'And my master leaves for Sussex tomorrow . . . there's no other authority save Elyot.'

The gate creaked open, and all heads snapped round. Richard Starling, followed by Crouch and John Wilmott, had entered the garden. As the others watched, the rector approached the body of Samuel Hubbard, knelt beside it and lifted the cover. There was a moment while he uttered some words of prayer. Finally he replaced the cloth and stood up.

'Master Blacksmith . . .' Will Ragg flinched as Starling approached him. 'I understand you have assumed the mantle of constable . . .'

Ragg nodded. 'Until some other be sworn to office, rector . . .'

But Starling's gaze was not hostile. 'Indeed – but for the present, the good will of the village rests upon you.' He looked around at the other men. 'Lambourn is isolated because of the infection,' he said. 'Hence we stand alone, and we must face our troubles together.' He paused. 'This garden must be sealed, until I have performed the proper service. It is a mortal sin for a man to take his own life.'

There were intakes of breath from all those present.

'Nay, sir – he would not do such!' Ragg was aghast.

The rector had already assumed his habitually frosty demeanour. 'How else would you account for the manner of his death?' Then he turned sharply, as Thomas spoke.

'In one other way at least, sir,' he said. 'That he was murdered.'

Some men gasped. Ragg swallowed, looking increasingly helpless. 'See now, falconer, that's not what—'

'I ask you to think on it, master Will,' Thomas interrupted, and pointed to the offending apple tree. 'How might a man of the constable's weight get himself off the ground and into that fork? There is naught nearby that he could have stood upon.'

Starling glared at him. 'By the same token, what mortal man could lift someone of that size, and place him there against his will?'

'If there were more than one—' Thomas countered, but the other cut him short.

'I would remind you, Thomas Finbow, that your opinion is not being sought. I have already given you to know that you intrude here, as you did upon our grief yesterday . . .' He trailed off, as if feeling this exchange was unseemly for one of his station. The others were staring from the rector to Thomas and back.

'Your pardon sir,' Thomas answered, maintaining a neutral tone. 'I wish merely to see justice done – as indeed does my master, Sir Robert, who charged me to come here and offer assistance. But if I intrude, then I will leave.'

Starling hesitated, then turned abruptly. For John Wilmott the churchwarden, who had not uttered a word since entering the garden, was bold enough to lay a hand on his sleeve.

'Send the fellow away, sir,' he said coldly.

Thomas stiffened and met Wilmott's stare, which was one of unbridled hostility.

'He is know on the West Downs as a meddler, too proud for one of his humble calling,' the man went on. 'He is often lax in his duties – especially to the church!'

Thomas took a deep breath. 'I know not what I have done to provoke you, Master Wilmott,' he said. 'But I dare say others may have a better opinion of me.'

'Indeed – I, for one!'

Everyone looked round in surprise. For it was Jonas Crouch, the mildest man in Lambourn, whose only known fault was spending time with his goshawk instead of on church business, who had spoken. More, the little clerk was quivering with anger.

'Thomas is a deal better known to some of us here,' he told Starling, darting a swift look at Wilmott. 'He has always strived to expose wickedness. Some have cause to be grateful for what he has done over the years. We should give thanks that he is come to aid us. Many would shun a village where two good and honest men have been slain in the space of a few days!'

There was a silence. Thomas stared at the ground, moved by his friend's spirited defence. Some of the villagers looked almost ready to laugh at the clerk's outburst.

But Starling spoke. 'I will consider your words, friend Jonas,' he said. 'As I will yours . . .' This with a brief nod at Wilmott. 'In the meantime . . .' He frowned to himself. 'In the meantime let the constable's body be taken to the church – yet there will be no hasty burial. Until I am convinced that the man did not take his own life, he may not lie in consecrated ground.'

He turned to Thomas. 'If you truly desire to serve, you may assist Master Ragg in his duties . . . I wish no further disorder, when the constable's death is bruited. We will pray for his soul to-night and every night, until he is laid to rest.'

And with a final nod to Will Ragg, the rector made his way from the late Samuel Hubbard's garden. Crouch, however, did not follow Starling out as Wilmott did. Instead when they had gone he glanced at Thomas, who threw him a brief smile.

The tension had eased, and the other Lambourn men gathered about Ragg – save for John Nightingale, who had watched the proceedings with a somewhat sardonic expression.

'I've an inn to keep, Will,' the landlord said. 'And I do wonder why you thought to call me here.'

Ragg eyed him. 'Mayhap because I know how much you like to poke about,' he replied.

Nightingale said nothing, but moved away towards the gate. Then suddenly Jonas Crouch spoke up.

'I knew there was something else . . . with all the coil, I forgot to tell it.' When the others looked to him he added:

'Henry Howes hasn't come in, and on the Sabbath too. That's never been known – not once!'

Ragg wore a look of exasperation. 'For pity's sake, Jonas, don't we have enough matters to think on?'

But Thomas was alert. 'Does Master Starling know?' he asked, whereupon the clerk nodded quickly.

'And Wilmott – he had to toll the morning bell himself. From what I hear, nobody's set eyes on Henry since yesterday.'

Thomas looked at Ragg with unconcealed relief, for at last here was something he could do. 'My mount is tethered close by,' he said. 'I could ride to Elyot's and tell him what has happened, and on the way I could look in at Howes's farm . . .'

Equally relieved, Ragg nodded. 'That would be a help to me, Master Finbow . . . Thomas . . .'

Thomas nodded at him and turned to leave, but at once Jonas Crouch was at his side.

'I'm coming with you.'

In the clammy midday heat they rode downriver, through herds of sheep that had wandered down from higher ground, as if the heavy cloud meant rain. But there was no rain on this gloomy Sabbath, refreshing as it would have been. Thomas rode the gelding at a slow pace, so that Crouch on a borrowed mare could keep pace.

68

They spoke little to one another. Thomas was glad to get away from the village and order his thoughts, in view of recent events. He sensed that Crouch harboured similar feelings, for the clerk seemed to relish the ride. In a short time, following the path along the river's north bank, they had left Lambourn and reached the ford, where the village path crossed from the other side and became a mere track leading north to the Downs. Howes's farmstead lay ahead.

Thomas slowed to a walk and allowed his friend to draw alongside him.

'Henry has never missed a Sabbath,' Crouch said with a frown. 'Even in sickness he would not do so – unless it were so severe he could not walk . . .' He turned to Thomas. 'I fear something is badly wrong.'

Thomas drew rein and dismounted before a home-made gate of old saplings, which he pulled open. As he led his mount through, he squinted towards the house. The door was open, but no one appeared. Crouch followed him and dismounted in turn.

'Henry has a bullhound,' he said. 'Yet I see no sign of it.'

Thomas's eyes were busy as he approached the thatched farmhouse. To the left was an open byre, but it was empty. The only livestock in sight were three or four chickens, pecking listlessly at the dry earth.

'Henry Howes!' Crouch called in as loud a voice as he could manage. 'It's Jonas – are you here?'

No answer. Thomas walked to the door and stepped on to the threshold. Then he turned and beckoned Crouch to follow him inside.

It took only seconds to ascertain that the house was empty. The fireplace was cold, as was the cauldron of pottage that hung on a chain above it. Howes's simple straw pallet against the wall was also cold, suggesting to Thomas that it had not been slept on the previous night.

The man's tools and simple possessions lay about the single room, looking forlorn. Crouch had gone outside and walked around the house. Now he reappeared, and shook his head. The place was eerily quiet. Finally, when they had opened a chest and found naught inside it but a few pieces of linen, Thomas faced his friend.

'He's gone away, taking only what he needed.'

The little clerk was looking very unhappy. 'He would never leave here! His life is the church and his farm, and naught else.' Then he saw the look in Thomas's eye, and started. 'I see what you think! Hubbard's dead, and Henry's gone . . . can you truly believe he would have aught to do with such a deed?'

Thomas looked away, and walked outside.

Eight

Having agreed to take one last, cursory look, the two of them separated and wandered about Howes's farmstead. Expecting it to be a fruitless search, Thomas was surprised when he heard Crouch call to him from the rear of the byre. He rounded the tumbledown structure to see the other man pointing to a bulky shape on the ground. As he drew closer, he saw immediately that one question at least had been answered: what had become of the sexton's dog. The big bullhound was lying dead in a pool of blood.

'Lord above . . .' Crouch was aghast. 'What further wickedness is this?'

Thomas knelt down to make an examination. There was a trace of blood about the dog's jaws, suggesting that it had been engaged in a tussle of some kind – whether with man or animal, it was impossible to tell. But one thing was plain enough: the deep wound in its side, which had penetrated the hound's vitals, could only be the work of a human.

He stood up. 'Someone spiked the poor creature,' he muttered. 'With a poniard, I'd say.'

Crouch was shaking his head. 'But why? He was an old dog . . . could barely move faster than Henry – and Henry would never have harmed him!' He stared at his friend. 'What in God's name has happened here?'

Thomas gazed uphill, towards the Downs. Crows were wheeling in the distance. A hundred yards away Howes's little herd of red-brown cattle still grazed.

'I recall what we spoke of in your garden, Jonas,' he said at last. 'About the sexton's manner, of late . . . I wonder how well you truly knew him.'

'Knew him?' Crouch echoed. 'You speak in the past – do you think he is dead?'

'Nay,' Thomas answered, 'I think he's a fugitive.'

When Crouch made no reply, he went on: 'I will wager from the look of his corpse that Sam Hubbard died sometime last night. Howes was at the church yesterday but not this morning, and his bed has not been slept in. Hence—'

'And the dog?' Crouch interrupted, his brow creasing. 'How do you account for that?'

Thomas shrugged. 'A man may be driven to desperate acts, when he is on the run.'

'No – I will not let you say such!' The clerk was near to tears. 'I admit I was worried for Henry . . . I told you his behaviour was strange. But he is a good man! He and the constable were never close friends, that is common knowledge – yet they had no quarrel that I know of. And even if they had . . .' He looked away. 'I prefer to believe the rector after all – that Hubbard killed himself. Though why, I cannot know.'

Thomas's gaze was sympathetic. 'You may be right – and it would ease my heart to find myself proved wrong,' he said. 'But it seems a mighty coincidence, wouldn't you say? The question remains: why has Howes fled? And who killed the dog?'

Crouch had no answer, but stood biting his lip. With a sigh Thomas left him, and went looking for a spade.

An hour later, having buried the unfortunate bullhound without ceremony, the two men rode on to Bickington Manor and sought an audience with William Elyot.

This time Thomas was not conducted to the great hall; nor was he treated like a welcome guest. Instead of Elyot it was his steward, the unsmiling Ralph Stainbank, who received them in a small rear chamber. The room was sparsely furnished, save for shelves of ledgers and a table piled with documents.

'My master is out hawking,' Stainbank said, with a bland look at Thomas. 'No doubt he wishes to see if your bird-doctoring is as effective as you claim.'

Thomas ignored the sarcasm in the man's voice. 'We have come from Lambourn, to bring dreadful news,' he said. 'The constable Samuel Hubbard is dead – hanged in a tree.'

He watched the steward's face closely. But the man's shocked expression appeared genuine. 'Hanged . . . how is that possible?'

'He was found this morning,' Crouch said. 'The rector has been informed, and awaits your master's pleasure. Master Elyot is the nearest landowner, and the only justice within reach.'

Stainbank looked unsure of himself. 'Of course . . . as soon as he returns, I will inform him. And Mistress Jane . . .' He hesitated, then asked in a voice of distaste: 'Does anyone know how this happened?'

'The rector believes the constable hanged himself,' Thomas answered, before Crouch could speak. 'Yet . . .' he took a breath, then added, 'others have made bold to disagree.'

Stainbank swallowed. 'You mean, murder is suspected?' The man was thoughtful. His fingers strayed nervously to the sleeve of his blue silk doublet, and began picking at it.

'There is another matter,' Thomas said after a moment. At his side he felt Crouch stiffen, but went on: 'We passed by Henry Howes's farm on our way. The place is deserted.'

A puzzled look appeared on Stainbank's smooth features. 'Yes . . . ?'

Thomas maintained a neutral tone. 'It appears to me that the man has left . . . I might even say, he has fled.'

Stainbank stared at him, then his eyes widened. 'You imply that the two matters are connected.'

Thomas shrugged slightly. Though relieved at having reported everything, he felt decidedly uncomfortable, not least because he was aware how much he had hurt Crouch's feelings. As if to confirm it, his friend spoke up.

'There is no proof of that,' he said quietly. 'The sexton did not appear for this morning's service, it is true, and we found no sign of him at his home. More, his dog has been brutally killed . . .'

But seeing Stainbank's expression, the little clerk trailed off. Barely registering the death of Howes's dog as worthy of a mention, the steward was all eagerness.

'Then it is obvious!' he cried. 'You villagers may be unaware how many times my master has voiced his suspicions about Henry Howes . . . that idle scatterbrain, who lets his farm fall into decay, and has not a charitable word for anyone – even his neighbours.' His eyes darted from one man to the other. 'He was ever a close fellow . . . not to be trusted – I said such from the moment I came to dwell here.'

Thomas was searching for some swift reply, for he sensed Crouch's growing anger. And it would not do, he felt, to express it here.

'Let us not judge the man in haste, Master Steward,' he began. 'Whatever his faults, he was a churchman and a—'

'And an honest one,' Crouch broke in. 'Who has had a hard life, and always strived to do his best . . .'

'Indeed, Master Clerk . . .' Thomas half-turned to his friend, silently imploring him to restraint. With an effort, Crouch fell silent.

'Nay, falconer – you are too charitable in your defence of the man. As are you, Master Crouch.' Stainbank's eagerness had not abated a jot and, watching him, Thomas was hard pressed to account for it. But he sensed that Stainbank had a streak of cruelty; perhaps he was the kind who liked to witness a flogging, or worse . . . Mastering his growing distaste for the fellow, he said: 'We will not stay longer. We rode here to tell Master Elyot what has occurred. If you will excuse us . . .'

Stainbank nodded, growing more brisk by the minute. 'My master will wish me to thank you. Please tell the rector that we will act properly . . . a search must be mounted, of course – and swiftly.'

Thomas inclined his head, and after a moment Crouch followed suit. The two made their farewells, and left the manor.

Outside the stables, as they untied the horses, Thomas opened his mouth to speak, then saw the look on his friend's face, and thought better of it.

They parted at the bridge, having ridden back in almost total silence. Crouch would return to the church and seek the rector out, while Thomas was only too glad to turn his mount towards Petbury.

Mercifully the thick cloud was at last beginning to move east-wards, and patches of blue sky appeared, lifting his spirits

74

somewhat. Reaching the manor by mid-afternoon, he at once sought an audience with Sir Robert. But Martin the steward was preoccupied with their master's preparations to leave for Sussex on the morrow, and stayed him, saying Sir Robert was with his guests and would not see anyone. When Thomas told him the grim news from Lambourn, however, the old man promised to convey it.

With some relief he went at last to the falcons' mews and busied himself with his work. It being the Sabbath, Ned Hawes was home in Chaddleworth helping his father, and there was much to do. Having looked all the birds over, Thomas began taking them out in pairs for exercise, two upon the gauntlet at once. It was not his normal practice unless necessity called, and few falconers had the skill for it. But with his handling, the hooded falcons remained docile even when so close together, something they normally disliked. He was able to fly all of them on the hill above the house, allowing each to soar and take a few small birds, which he bagged up. Then, having swept out the mews and watered his charges, he walked down to the kitchens.

But the place was filled with activity, and Nell too was busy. Quickly she came to him, telling him they would have no chance to be together that day. He had small need to show his disappointment, for she understood it well enough.

'Tomorrow,' she said, taking his hand and pressing it, 'they will have gone, and the house will be quiet.'

He managed a wry smile. 'Tomorrow I will likely have to go to Lambourn again.'

She frowned as he told her of the death of Hubbard, and the apparent flight of Henry Howes. But when he mentioned William Elyot, she was surprised.

'But he's here, with Sir Robert. Did you not know?'

'Nay – his steward told me he was out hawking . . .' He frowned in turn. 'If so, his bird has not been placed in our mews – I know it well, and would have seen it.'

'I know naught of that,' Nell said. 'Save he came some hours ago. He has been walking with the master and Sir John Norris in the gardens, and now stays to supper.'

After a moment, Thomas nodded. 'Then he knows already,

for Martin will have told what has happened.' And leaving Nell to her duties he went back to the cottage, to sit brooding on the day's events. He barely heard the Petbury peacocks as they began their evening chorus.

He was still deep in thought as the sun dipped behind Greenhill Down. Having roused himself at last, he was bending to light the fire when a servant came to summon him to the house.

The great hall was ablaze with gold; from the light of the dying sun through the west window, and from many candles. Servants stood about attentively. At the sumptuously laid table sat Sir Robert and his guest Sir John Norris; a dark-haired, fiery man with a bushy beard and a commanding eye, every inch the military commander. On Sir Robert's other side was the dapper figure of William Elyot, who looked to be enjoying himself. Perhaps he had imbibed too freely of Sir Robert's wine, Thomas thought, as he made his bow and came forward.

'Thomas . . .' Sir Robert grew businesslike. 'We have heard the gist of your news. Will you speak further?'

He told the details of Hubbard's death, and the rector's reaction to it. Then he spoke of what he and Crouch had discovered at Howes's farm, their taking the news to Ralph Stainbank, and the conversation that followed.

Startled, Elyot put down his cup. 'Why was I not told at once?' he asked. Before Thomas could reply, he turned to Sir Robert. 'Your pardon, sir – I had best ride home before it grows dark.' Seeing Norris's eye upon him, he added: 'Unless you wish to take charge of the matter, Sir John . . . ?'

Norris exchanged glances with Sir Robert. 'As you know, sir, we leave at first light,' he said drily. 'Hence, it seems the upholding of the law here on the Western Downs will rest upon you. I know you will order matters as you think fit.'

There was a short silence, and Thomas sensed that both his master and Norris felt as he did: that Elyot had neither the rank nor the authority to dispense justice as they would. More uncomfortably, Thomas was unable to give voice to his private feelings about the man. If anything, his earlier suspicions, though allayed by the conversation with Elyot at

76

Bickington, had been aroused anew by his recent exchange with Ralph Stainbank. Though he would have been at a loss to say why.

But Elyot was on his feet, making his farewell. After some final words with Sir Robert, he hurried from the table and left the hall.

Thomas found Norris's eye upon him. 'Falconer . . .' the knight smiled through his thick beard, 'I have been hearing of your exploits as hawk-doctor. Though I am also becoming aware of your other qualities.'

Thomas inclined his head politely. And now Sir Robert spoke. 'I have often had cause to lay burdens upon Thomas which would be too great for most of his station, Sir John. Now I fear we do so again.' He paused. 'The blacksmith, Ragg; a plain fellow, and an honest one, but . . .' He hesitated. 'Our good friend Master Elyot will need all the good men he can find, to seek out this murderer.'

Norris said nothing, but his silence seemed to convey agreement. Sir Robert eyed Thomas. 'For it is a murderer he must seek, is it not? You were loath to dwell upon it, but I see you do not believe Samuel Hubbard took his own life, as Master Starling does.'

Thomas sighed. 'No, sir, I do not.'

'And I am in similar mind to you, that the sexton's flight casts a deal of suspicion upon him. He must be found, if only to give an account of himself.'

Norris looked squarely at Thomas. 'I am unable to give you a warrant, falconer,' he said, 'nor indeed to endow you with any true authority. You are not of the parish of Lambourn, nor are you even entitled to bear arms, save what any man may need to defend himself.' Sensing what was coming, Thomas sought to keep expression from his face.

'Yet it would please many of us,' Norris continued, 'and I may speak now of my father, the Lord Lieutenant, to see this matter delved into and brought to some conclusion; especially at this troublesome time.' Having said all he wished to, the knight sat back and took a drink from his silver cup.

Sir Robert spoke up. 'I know you have work enough here, Thomas. Yet Ned shapes up well, and once again he must

77

mind the birds in your absence. At least he will not have to serve hawking parties, for the time being.'

'I will do what I can, sir,' Thomas said. And taking his master's nod of approval for dismissal, he made his bow and left the hall.

The morning was fair, and Thomas was at the mews when Ned arrived. As he gave him his instructions, the boy's normally cheerful expression soon disappeared.

'So you're playing intelligencer again,' he muttered. 'I thought as much.'

'Not of my choosing,' Thomas replied.

'It never is, is it?' Ned said. Over recent months, Thomas had grown aware that the boy's manner had become at times less deferential, even rebellious. He narrowed his eyes.

'Got a burr in your breeches this morning, have you?'

Ned flinched. 'I am not overburdened, if that's how your mind moves.' He hesitated. 'I do not wish to see your life in danger again.'

Thomas exhaled. 'Is that all?'

Ned looked taken aback. 'Do you not think folk fret about you? Eleanor, for one, and Nell of course . . .'

'I am obliged to you, Master Ned,' Thomas said drily. 'But what would help me rest easy would be the sure knowledge that you are carrying out your duties properly.'

Ned opened his mouth, then quickly closed it. He could only watch as Thomas stalked off, to disappear round the wall of the stable yard.

In less than an hour, he was in Lambourn again – to find himself caught up in a momentous event: the time had come for the casting of the new bell.

His first intimation that excitement was afoot came when he entered the square, which was deserted. But as he dismounted he heard a loud hubbub of voices from the vicinity of the church. Having tethered the gelding he walked over, and found an excited crowd gathered about the bell-pit. And it looked for the moment as if the death of Samuel Hubbard – let alone that of William Stubbs – had been all but forgotten.

Since Thomas's last visit on Saturday, the site had changed significantly. Drawing closer, he peered down into the pit at the bell-mould – or rather that part of it which was visible: the cope, a great dome made of unfired clay mixed with sand and horsehair. The whole was skilfully shaped with the curved wooden profiles that bell-founders carried with them, called 'sweeps'. Beneath the cope was the inner core, and between the two a narrow, almost magical space which, after being filled with molten metal and cooled, would become the new bell for St Michael and All Angels.

Overseeing the proceedings from a distance was the rector himself, Richard Starling. Beside him stood his churchwarden, John Wilmott. Their attention however was elsewhere, and Thomas now saw that the main focus of attention was the furnace. Not only was it complete, but it was lit – in fact it roared and smoked, and he could feel the heat from a dozen yards off.

Simon Goodchild the founder, assisted by his son and a couple of helpers, was feeding the furnace. Close by was a heap of scrap metal, gathered from the population of Lambourn and its surrounds as was the usual custom: old copper kettles and pots, a few pewter mugs and what looked like shards of the old bell, broken up for remelting. The villagers watched with great interest as Goodchild selected pieces of scrap and passed them to Edmund, who shoved them into the glowing inferno at ground level, pushing them home with an iron rod. The channel from the furnace to the bell-pit was blocked with a slab of stone. But when enough metal had been heated to a liquid, the obstacle would be removed and the mix allowed to run into the mould. Two men in thick leather aprons stood by holding long shafts which ended in flat blades – the 'slices' which would guide the dangerous flow along its course.

A voice at Thomas's elbow made him start. 'Three parts copper to one of tin makes the best bell-metal. It don't take much heat to melt it.'

He turned to Will Ragg, and smiled briefly. 'I would guess your kind of work is closer to this than anyone's.'

Ragg shook his head. 'Founders are a mystery apart . . . though many have had to turn their hands to casting cannons in these times, to earn their keep. Master Goodchild is one of a dying breed.' He pointed. 'See that? Some pious soul's given their precious silver tankard to throw into the furnace. They say it improves the bell's tone – makes it silvery.'

Thomas was intrigued. 'And does it?'

The other shook his head again. 'Naught makes the tone, save yon founder's skill.'

They watched Goodchild and his son at their work. Thomas wished to speak with Ragg about yesterday's events, but clearly this was not the time. Villagers of all ages were milling round, excited by what was about to happen. So in an undertone he asked the other if he had spoken with Jonas Crouch since he and Thomas had left for Bickington.

Ragg nodded, and said: 'I've called a meeting for midday, in the Horns. You can put your halfpenny-worth in then. There's . . . there's things you may not know.' He looked away briefly. 'And Elyot has sent word – he started a search of his lands at first light. If he don't find Howes he wants to widen it, from here outwards, even to the county borders . . .' The blacksmith broke off, looking unhappy with the burden that had been thrust upon him. But the next moment he gave Thomas a nudge, and pointed with his chin towards Starling and Wilmott.

'They've taken it calmly enough. I can't fathom it . . . a churchwarden dead, and the sexton on the run, suspected of murder? Though I for one can't believe he did such.' He eyed Thomas. 'Can you?'

Thomas hesitated. 'I barely knew the man . . .' he began, then, seeing the look that came over Ragg's face, he fell silent. Soon after that, the blacksmith turned and walked off.

Since to wait until the midday meeting seemed the best course, Thomas stayed to watch the casting. Though it was a Monday morning, many folk seem to have been excused from their labours – or excused themselves. And who would blame them? he thought; for the chance to watch the near-miraculous creation of a new bell for their church came perhaps once in a lifetime.

As if at a signal, a hush fell. In his sonorous voice, Simon Goodchild ordered folk to stand back, but still they pressed forward as far as they dared, to watch the furnace breached, and the glowing, hissing mass of molten bell-metal begin its journey.

It was a remarkable sight. Along with the rest, Thomas watched the luminous river of metal guided along its course, until the mould was filled; a process that seemed to take hours, though it was little more than one. Finally when Simon Goodchild seemed content, the channel was blocked again, and labourers hurried to shovel earth over the cope, filling the pit to ground level and tamping it down. Then the furnace was sealed and left to cool, and the founder and his son stood aside, talking low. After a while Edmund moved off to speak with the helpers. Some of the village folk hung around, then, as there was nothing more to see, most began to drift away.

Thomas watched the rector and his churchwarden walk off towards the church entrance. There had been no sign of Jonas Crouch all morning. He was thinking of going to seek him out, when Alice Goodchild appeared from the far end of the yard, nearest the river. With small, quick steps she walked to her husband, who bent low . . . and Thomas stiffened, staring intently at them.

He was some way off, and could hear nothing; but he could have sworn that he saw Alice's mouth open. As if to confirm his suspicion her husband at once uttered some sharp word of reply, then looked round as if afraid they had been overheard. Thomas quickly directed his gaze elsewhere, and the founder, apparently satisfied, turned back to his wife. Taking her arm, he steered her away.

But he was too late; for in that moment Thomas had seen that Alice Goodchild's dumbness was a sham. Why then, if she could speak, did she choose to pretend otherwise?

Nine

The Horns was filled to the doorway. Folk stood pressed against the walls of the taproom, the luckiest being those close to the open casements, as the midday heat grew stifling. Will Ragg, a man used to greater temperatures, sat stolidly in the centre of the room; beside him was John Nightingale. As Thomas pushed his way in, he saw Jonas Crouch standing near the window to his left, and at once made his way towards him.

Crouch's face bore a strained expression, but he managed a smile. 'I know not what this council will achieve – but then there's naught else for entertainment, now the bell's been cast.'

Thomas smiled in turn, relieved to find that his friend appeared to bear no further rancour towards him; but then, that was not Crouch's way. 'I watched the casting,' he said. 'A wondrous process . . .' Then he lowered his voice. 'I learned something else, too.'

But at that moment there was a stir from the doorway. All heads turned, and a silence fell as the rector came in, followed by his churchwarden, John Wilmott.

Starling cast an imperious glance about the room. At first, seeing he would be addressing his usual congregation, he looked as if he was about to adopt his sermon voice. But instead his gaze fell upon the blacksmith, and he kept silent.

Thomas was thinking over Ragg's words, earlier that morning: *there are things you may not know*. He glanced round at the faces of the Lambourn men: hardy, weather-beaten folk who lived by and off the land, who seldom went further than their own village. They all knew each other, and no doubt guarded many a secret among themselves. Small wonder they were prey to suspicions of every kind – not to say old hostilities . . . he found himself frowning as he examined individual faces. Was there truly a murderer here in this room? He caught one or two odd glances, then realized they were directed at him. He sighed inwardly; of course, he thought, I am an outsider: the falconer from Petbury, who took the eyases down from the bell-tower. Then his gaze fell upon someone he had not expected to see: John Tolworthy, the miller from Uplambourn. The man was sitting near to Nightingale the land-lord, though as far as Thomas could see neither was paying any attention to the other.

At last the silence was broken, as Ragg rose to speak. 'Ye all know why we gather here this day,' he said. 'Sam Hubbard is dead . . .' He paused, seeing the rector's eye upon him, then continued: 'And I have come to see, 'tis likely he was murdered.'

There was a collective gasp, followed by expressions of disbelief. Thomas saw Starling's face darken in anger. But before the rector could speak, Ragg held up a meaty hand.

''Tis true, some say he took his own life,' he went on. 'And bad though that be, it would be the easiest way to think – save that our rector has told, such a man may not be buried in hallowed ground. I for one knew Hubbard as well as any of ye – and I deem it an insult to his memory not to see him rest in the churchyard, where he belongs by right.'

There were murmurs of agreement, and looks flew about thick and fast. Thomas caught Crouch's eye, and saw his friend was troubled.

'What swayed me, though,' Ragg said, raising his voice above the muttering that rose, 'was what our parish clerk told me yesternight.' He glanced at Crouch. 'For he and the falconer there . . .' he indicated Thomas, and all heads turned to look at him, ' . . . rode downriver, and what they found has caused me much dismay.' With an effort, he announced: 'Henry Howes the sexton has fled, and is deemed a fugitive.'

At that, the dam burst. Expressions of amazement gave way to anger. Thomas saw Starling was about to intervene, but again Ragg beat him to it. 'Yet I, for one,' he said loudly, 'do not think he is the one should be accused!'

'Why is that, Master Blacksmith?' came a sharp voice from near the entrance. All turned to see William Elyot, dressed in smart riding clothes, standing just inside the door. Because of the hubbub, only those nearest had noticed his arrival. With the gentleman were Ralph Stainbank and a burly manservant, clearly there in case of trouble. For the atmosphere inside the inn had indeed grown tense.

Ragg blinked, but stood his ground. 'Because like most men here, sir, I have known the sexton all my life . . . He has his faults, but I cannot think him a murderer.'

'Yet no sooner had the constable been found dead than Howes fled his farm,' Elyot threw back. 'Left his livestock to wander free – he even killed his dog!'

Voices rose again, and now at last Starling spoke up. Thomas, watching closely, saw that the rector had gone pale with anger. 'Master Elyot – could you not have brought this matter first to me?'

A silence fell, as Elyot turned to face him. 'Indeed, sir – I would have done so, had I found you at home. Do you truly think this assembly a fit place for a gentleman?'

Starling gasped. 'This is my flock, sir!' he almost shouted. 'Where else should I be, when evil threatens our community, but here among them?'

'A noble sentiment.' Elyot smiled, and few could fail to discern the sarcasm in is tone. 'Meanwhile, the fugitive is further away . . . Has any man here thought to organize a search?'

Ragg, somewhat out of his depth, kept silent. Thomas was watching Elyot, but the man seemed not to have noticed his presence. Before anyone could answer, he spoke again.

'When the news was brought to me – somewhat tardily, I might add – I returned home and ordered my steward to organize a mounted party at once. There was little time to accomplish much yesternight, and so we were out at first light this morning. We have already scoured my lands to the borders, without finding any sign of Howes. Hence, it is obvious that the search must be widened – and in every direction.' He paused. 'Unless anyone has a better plan?'

Thomas was surprised. William Elyot looked like a different man from the one who had seemed ill-at-ease in Sir Robert's company – and as different again from the one who had appeared so relaxed at his home, when they tended his falcon. Never before had he seen the gentleman exude such authority.

But Starling had rallied himself, and spoke in a voice of thunder. 'Master Elyot – be good enough to hear me!'

The silence that now fell was profound; as if the village folk were truly in church, hearing their rector deliver one of his famously forbidding sermons.

'If my sexton is indeed fled – something of which I am as yet unconvinced – then of course he must be found and brought to account for himself. In that matter, as our nearest landowner and Master of Bickington, we naturally look to you and your servants.' He paused, then said more softly: 'Yet I say again, you ought to have spoken first with me. There are matters that should perhaps be aired between us.'

Elyot was looking impatient. 'Well – then let us go and look to them,' he answered. But to his irritation, Will Ragg spoke up again. And Thomas almost smiled, for despite his discomfort, the blacksmith still felt himself to be acting constable, and he would have his say.

'Sirs . . .' he looked first at Elyot, then at Starling, 'a search must indeed be raised. Yet I ask you to remember certain matters. The danger of pestilence, for one . . .' Seeing the looks that appeared on some villagers' faces, he took encouragement. 'Is it wise to have men riding about hither and thither at this time? Might it not be best to narrow the search to places where we who know the sexton think him likely to be found?'

Richard Starling seized the opportunity. 'Well spoken! There must be no disorder – and I for one will not permit mob rule in my parish!' He faced Elyot again. 'Might I suggest, sir, that you and I, together with the constable and the church officials, gather now in St Michael's and decide how to proceed?'

There was a short silence. Now that they came to consider the matter, few folk liked the notion of scurrying about the Downs searching for a fugitive. Leave it to the law, some began to whisper; there had been enough excitement of late . . .

Elyot nodded curtly, and made as if to go out. Stainbank, close by the door, was already turning to leave. But just as the atmosphere was lightening, a voice rose unexpectedly from the centre of the room. Heads turned towards the landlord, John Nightingale.

'Sir . . .' he called, in a somewhat strained voice, 'might I and certain others – principal men of Lambourn – be permitted to attend you? I think you will find it worthwhile to hear us.'

Elyot hesitated, then indicated assent. Starling showed his disapproval, but merely signalled to Jonas Crouch to follow him out. The meeting was over, and its outcome was clear enough: the gentry intended to order matters their own way, and not entrust it to a village council. Well then, most said – let them. And why not take a mug, while we're here . . .

Crouch turned to Thomas. 'You should come along – you are Sir Robert's man.' He gave a wry smile. 'And since your master has seen to it that you are well mounted as usual, I expect you will be called upon to join the search.'

Thomas made a wry face and began pushing his way out. As he left the inn, he heard men calling for the drawer. If talking was thirsty work, he reflected, listening was sometimes just as taxing.

It was a tense meeting, in the high-ceilinged vestry in the south transept of the church. And at first, Thomas thought his entrance was about to be refused by Richard Starling, whose temper had not improved. But William Elyot disagreed.

'The falconer is charged by his master, my good friend Sir Robert Vicary, to assist in the matter,' he said smoothly. 'I would value his sharp eyes, not to say his knowledge of the country, in our search.'

So Thomas stood by, along with Crouch and John Wilmott, who had not yet uttered a word. Stainbank also waited, behind his master, who along with Starling occupied the only chairs, uncomfortable-looking oak seats with no cushioning. In a close group, as if huddled together for comfort, stood the village men – Will Ragg, John Nightingale and one other, the miller, John Tolworthy.

Yet Thomas had no time to observe Tolworthy's demeanour, nor to wonder at his presence here, for Elyot was burning to take charge. And to Thomas's mind, that gentleman's enthusiasm for hunting down Henry Howes matched the eagerness that his steward Stainbank had displayed yesterday for casting blame upon the man. What might occasion such hostility – apart from a distaste for the way their humble neighbour neglected his farmstead – he did not know.

'Master Ragg – ' Elyot's tone was businesslike – 'can you get yourself a horse, and ride with us?'

'I can sir,' Ragg said stiffly. 'Yet I would speak of—'

'And I too would speak,' Starling said sharply.

Elyot turned to him and inclined his head ironically. 'Master Rector – we hang upon your every word.'

'I am glad to hear it, sir,' Starling retorted. 'For there are some matters that appear to have escaped your notice. One is that Henry Howes was a servant of my church . . . I would seek the bishop's word before acting in haste.'

Elyot bridled impatiently, but the rector continued: 'Yet I fear His Grace is unwilling to travel in these pestilent times . . . hence we are driven to fall upon our own resources.'

Now others were beginning to feel the same impatience as Elyot, aware of Starling's liking for the sound of his own voice. Ragg opened his mouth, but unexpectedly John Nightingale stayed him. 'Sirs . . . if you please, there are things you should hear, before you mount your search.'

Starling and Elyot both looked sharply at the man, but something in his expression caught their attention. The innkeeper was not one to waste folk's time. When the rector nodded his approval, he spoke up.

'There is one place we believe – Master Ragg and others, including myself, that is – you should search first.' He hesitated, then: 'The home of Mistress Pegg, out upon the west Downs beyond Uplambourn . . . the house, and the land about it.'

Starling was taken aback. 'That ragged woman, who comes to sell her herbs? What can she have to do with this?'

For answer, Nightingale turned to John Tolworthy, who had been standing motionless. Now, recalling his meeting with the man but two days before, Thomas saw the miller's discomfort. Indeed, if anything he looked afraid.

'Master Tolworthy – ' Starling fixed him with a dry expression – 'it's seldom you honour us with your presence in

Lambourn – unless, from what I hear, it be for a night's bat-fowling.'

But Tolworthy did not meet the rector's gaze. Instead he looked directly at William Elyot. 'Sir . . . there's things been seen upon the Downs, up where my home is, and beyond . . . I am afeared to speak of it, yet after what's happened, I must.'

Elyot nodded. 'Tell us, Master Miller.'

Tolworthy's mouth was dry. He gave a cough, then said: 'My children have seen something of late . . . tall and pale, and loping about the Downs . . . it does shriek, sir.'

In the silence that fell, a chill crept up the neck of every man present. Thomas felt it, and knew the others did too.

'I paid no mind at first,' the miller went on. 'Until I saw it myself. My wife was with me, and she saw it too. It does seem . . . it's not human, sir!' he blurted.

'What do you mean, man?' Starling's voice was sharp as steel, yet there was anxiety in his eyes. 'I'll hear no old tales of hobgoblins, or any other blasphemy!'

'Nay, sir . . .' Tolworthy shook his head. 'I do not say what it be – indeed, I know not. I only tell what I have seen – and from a distance at that. Yet my children lie awake in their beds for fear, and I sleep with a dagger in my bolster . . .' He glanced at John Nightingale. 'Others have heard the sound – laughter, and shrieking . . . all of us did, in Lambourn wood on the night we found Will Stubbs's body!'

Thomas looked sharply about the room, scanning faces. The unsettling news, he felt certain, came as a shock to everyone present – save Nightingale, who now spoke in his turn.

'It is true, there was some such sound in the wood that night,' he said in a cautious tone. 'Though could be it was no more than an owl . . .'

Tolworthy looked hard at him. 'You did not think so at the time,' he said. 'Mayhap like me you preferred to talk yourself into believing such later. After you found Stubbs.'

But Nightingale remained impassive. 'I cannot say for certain what I heard, John – any more than you can.' He turned to Elyot. 'Yet, since Mary Pegg herself was seen near the wood on that night—'

'And she has long been a cunning-woman, and a whore to

88

boot!' It was Stainbank who spoke, taking everyone by surprise. When all eyes fell upon him, he looked to his master and added: 'Your pardon, sir, but I am in agreement with these men. The woman Pegg lives as an outcast by her own choice, for none has sent her there that I know of. What better place for a fugitive to hide than that remote warrener's hut?'

Elyot nodded. 'It is a place to begin, at least . . .' He faced Starling. 'Like you, sir, I set little store in sightings of elves and sprites, and whatever else may spring from old Downland tales. Yet the matter bears investigation, does it not?'

For the first time, Starling looked unsure of himself. As if for support, he glanced at John Wilmott. But the churchwarden merely lowered his gaze, as if unwilling to be drawn on the matter. Finally, the rector turned to Elyot.

'Well sir,' he said shortly, 'it seems we must bend to your will, and allow you to conduct your searches. Though how all these matters – in particular, tales of shrieking figures loping across the Downs – hang together, I cannot fathom.'

'Nor I, sir.' Elyot had risen, with a nod towards Stainbank. 'I will of course inform you of any discovery. Now, with your leave . . .' And with a glance that included Thomas as well as his own servants, the Master of Bickington left the vestry.

As he followed the man out, Thomas exchanged glances with Jonas Crouch, but saw only a helpless look on his friend's face. Behind them came Tolworthy and Ragg, and lastly Nightingale, also eager to take their leave.

Outside in the sunlit yard, Elyot gathered them together. It seemed he himself had had enough of hard riding for one day, and Thomas's heart sank as he learned that Ralph Stainbank would lead the search party.

Within the hour they had all found mounts, and were riding north-westwards, up the narrowing river towards Uplambourn: Thomas, Will Ragg, Stainbank and Elyot's other close-mouthed servant from Bickington, whose name was quickly given as Hugh Bedell. Tolworthy would travel with them as far as his mill, then leave the party to journey on alone. He had done his duty, he said, by reporting the strange sightings on the West Downs; and clearly he had no wish to investigate further.

*　　*　　*

Thomas expected it to be a sombre party, given the company in which he found himself. And indeed no man spoke during the short ride to Uplambourn, where John Tolworthy took his leave. With a brief nod at Ragg and an even briefer one to Stainbank, the miller turned his old black horse aside and ambled towards the mill. At sight of the familiar sails on the skyline, it seemed to Thomas that the man had grown in stature; as if he belonged here, and nowhere else.

They were now four, who skirted the little hamlet and turned westwards across the grassy Downs, with a fair breeze in their faces. As the mill's sails disappeared behind them, their leader Ralph Stainbank slowed his big chestnut horse to a walk, seemingly in no great hurry. And it was then that Will Ragg, riding a poor dappled mount borrowed from one of his customers, drew alongside him.

'What did you mean, naming Mary Pegg a whore?' he asked bluntly.

Stainbank turned to him and raised an eyebrow. 'Come, Master Ragg,' he said, and a sardonic smile began to curl about his mouth. 'A woman living alone out here – a little wild perhaps, but not too ugly . . . what else would she be?'

Ragg bristled. 'She's fey, and wary of company,' he replied. 'And it's no secret her knowledge of herbs and remedies has helped many a Downland woman in trouble. That don't mean she sells her own favours.'

Stainbank's smile remained in place. 'You are gallant to defend her. Then, your knowledge of such folk is greater than mine. How fares Mistress Caldwell? I have not called upon her for some weeks.'

Thomas and Hugh Bedell, who had not spoken since they left Lambourn, were riding behind. Both heard the question, and the tone of it, and exchanged glances. For Ragg's shoulders had thickened like a bullock's.

'I'll thank you not to speak of her in that way,' he said in a low voice.

But Stainbank's smile grew broader. 'What way is that? Do I give offence, in singing the praises of one of the best trulls in West Berkshire?' When Ragg made no reply, the steward sighed theatrically and went on: 'What nights I could speak of in her bed – a woman of great warmth, I've always said so. And no little imagination . . .'

Ragg jerked the rein and drew the startled horse to an abrupt halt. 'You'd best watch your mouth, Stainbank,' he snapped. 'Else I might bloody it for ye.'

Stainbank's smile faded, as he too drew his mount to a halt. 'That would be most unwise,' he said.

A tense silence fell as the two faced each other. Bedell's eyes darted from one man to the other, though it was clear whom, as Elyot's servant, he would have to defend. Thomas for his part was caught between two camps.

'Master Stainbank,' he said mildly. 'We are almost upon the old warrener's house . . . beyond that slope, as I recall. What orders do you have for our conduct?'

Stainbank hesitated, and only now seemed to recollect his position. For Thomas's Master, Sir Robert, was a knight of the shire, and of greater rank than William Elyot. His falconer's reporting of this unseemly exchange would do the steward little credit.

'Conduct?' he echoed. 'We will search the place, is all . . .'

But his glance fell upon Bedell, who was now pointing directly ahead. All of them followed his gaze, and saw the figure of Mary Pegg, or rather the top half of her, standing in the long grass on the crest of the slope. As each man stared she turned and ran, disappearing rapidly from view.

The tension was broken. Without another word, Stainbank shook the reins and urged his horse uphill. The others followed close behind.

91

Ten

They descended the slope in no great haste, the grass-covered roof of the little house ahead of them. There was no sign of its occupant, but that surprised no one. She has likely barred herself within, Thomas thought, then recalled that the place had no door but an old sheep's hide. He sighed; this visit was not of his choosing, and now that he was come here once again, he liked it less and less.

Stainbank assumed a brusque manner as he neared the cottage. Carelessly, or perhaps deliberately, he walked his horse through the garden, trampling plants in the process. Then he halted and called out Mary Pegg's name. There was no answer.

Thomas drew alongside Will Ragg, who sat his mount some yards away. 'I had not known you and Mistress Caldwell were friends,' he said quietly.

Ragg kept his eyes on the house. 'I've asked her to marry me,' he said. When Thomas said nothing, he added sharply: 'She is a goodly soul, who has been driven to her condition by naught but poverty. Her husband died of a sickness; Caldwell was my friend – he would wish me to wed Sarah, as soon as I do myself. Then I can make a life for her . . .' He looked squarely at Thomas. 'And if you think badly of me like that stuffed fowl there – ' this with a jerk of his head towards Stainbank – 'I'll deal with you the same way!'

But Thomas shook his head and, seeing the expression on his face, Ragg relented. 'Your pardon . . .' he muttered.

'Mary Pegg! I am steward to William Elyot, of the manor of Bickington!' Stainbank's voice cut through the warm afternoon air. 'Come outside and give account of yourself!'

Still there was only silence. Larks called from the Downs.

92

In the distance a partridge took flight, and Thomas wondered idly if Ned had exercised the falcons.

Stainbank dismounted and walked the few yards to the doorway. But at that moment the flap lifted abruptly and he halted, then involuntarily stepped back. For the Mary Pegg who suddenly appeared was not the frightened recluse they had expected. Instead, she came out fighting.

'Get back! This is my 'ouse!' The hoarse voice was as Thomas remembered it, but the tone was shrill. The woman wore a coarse apron over little more than rags, and her hair was loose, giving her the look of some half-wild creature. In both hands she wielded a stout billet, swinging it before her. More alarmingly, tucked into the length of twine which served her as a belt was an old butcher's knife, rusty but whetted along its edge, which glinted in the sun.

Stainbank blanched visibly, but with the other men's eyes upon him, he had to act. 'Stay, woman!' he shouted, in a voice that was half an octave too high. 'I am here by order of my master, and the vicar of Lambourn, to search your house. We seek a fugitive!'

'There's none here but me!' Mary Pegg spat. 'And I do harbour no one! Get ye gone!'

'You'll not harm me!' Stainbank retorted. 'Else the constable here will arrest you, and we will take you back to Lambourn to be tried.'

Thomas and Ragg exchanged looks. The notion that this poor woman should be dragged across the Downs tied behind a horse pleased neither of them.

Nor, it seemed, did it please the bull-headed Hugh Bedell. To Thomas's surprise the bulky man, who had been sitting his horse some distance away, got down and walked past Stainbank, to within a few feet of Mary Pegg. 'Come, mistress ...' he said in a gruff voice that spoke of too much indulgence in cheap smoking weed. 'No man here thinks you would wish to shelter a murderer. Let us but look within the house, and then we may depart.'

She gave no answer, but remained half-crouching, facing them like a beast at bay. Then, to everyone's surprise, she looked suddenly at Thomas, hefted the weapon into her left

93

hand, and pointed. 'He . . . the tall one. Let him come, and none else!'

Thomas stared at Mary Pegg, then met her eye, and saw . . . what? Fear, naturally enough, and anger – and something else he could not fathom. After a moment he threw a questioning glance at Stainbank.

The steward's face was pale with rage and shame; having seemingly lost his authority – first to a servant, and now to Sir Robert Vicary's falconer – he struggled to recover it in some way. But seeing the look on the others' faces, he had little choice but to relent.

'Very well . . .' Haughtily he gestured to Thomas, who dismounted. Ragg did so too, and took the reins of Thomas's horse to hold with his own. All three men watched as the falconer walked slowly forward to stand before Mary Pegg. This close, he towered over her. But seemingly the woman had judged him, and decided he bore her no harm. Lowering the cudgel, she stood aside and allowed him to enter her house.

The smell hit him first: a feral scent of wild animals. Then as his eyes adjusted to the gloom – for though there was a window, the house was so cluttered that little light came in – he saw the eyes. Half a dozen pairs of eyes regarded him from what he now saw were small cages made of bent withies. Gradually he made out the occupants: foxes, weasels and the polecat he had seen the last time he was here. Between them they set up a chorus of spitting and snarling which would have driven him back, save for the fact that the creatures were confined. Then he looked closer, and understood: for each one was lame, injured or deformed in some way. Mary Pegg, he felt, would not have caged any animal unless it were for the good. She was indeed a healing-woman – though her charges, it appeared, were more often animal than human.

As for rest of the dwelling, he need do no more than cast his eyes around once: an open hearth with a cooking pot, a crude pallet, and little else but rows of jars and old bottles. No doubt they contained the home-brewed medicines for which this wise-woman had become known.

He came out into the sunshine and straightened up. Since

94

the inside of the house was so low, he had been bent almost double. He threw a glance at Stainbank, and shook his head.

There was a moment's silence. Bedell had moved off and brought his horse closer to Ragg's. The two of them stood waiting, as did Mary Pegg. Her eyes darted from Thomas to Stainbank and back.

The steward's gaze scanned the untidy garden, then fell upon the crude little hut of wattle and thatch which stood a dozen yards away. 'What's in there?' he demanded.

Mary Pegg glared at him. 'Firewood, and withies, and a cadge for drying herbs.'

He hesitated, then took another tack. 'You were seen four days ago close to Lambourn wood, after dark. What business had you there?'

She tensed visibly. 'I weren't. I never goes in, 'cept on market day.'

Stainbank took a step closer. 'Don't lie to me – you were seen! Could anyone mistake your wretched appearance?'

The other men stiffened. All of them had by now concluded that coming here was a fruitless exercise, as well as a distasteful one. Further, there was much about Stainbank's conduct that Thomas and Will Ragg disliked more and more. And it was Ragg who now voiced his feelings.

'There's naught for us here. I'm for riding on – now.'

Stainbank swung round irritably. 'I lead this party, and I will say when we leave!'

Ragg opened his mouth to reply, but never uttered a word. For a sound that none of them expected came suddenly from somewhere, muffled yet shrill: a high-pitched laugh, followed by a yelping that ended on a single high note, then died away.

To a man, they froze. Ragg swallowed, and turned to Thomas. 'In the wood, that night . . .'tis the same voice . . .'

The others were equally unnerved. Stainbank was at a complete loss, while Bedell whirled about, looking in all directions as far as the horizon. Quickly he pointed to the little hut. 'It came from there . . .'

But Thomas watched Mary Pegg. At sound of the voice she had started, then looked deliberately in the opposite direction from the hut. Now she gave a low groan, and turned to face Stainbank.

'See, master . . .' her tone was suddenly humble, 'there's naught to fear, and naught here for you. I do swear it . . . Will ye not take my word, and go?'

'Your word!' The steward was scornful. 'After what has passed?' He reached for the poniard at his belt, and drew it from its tooled leather sheath. 'I'll ask you once more, and this time you will answer truthfully. What is in the hut?'

But Mary Pegg sagged visibly. 'Jesu . . . why can folk not leave us be?'

Barely knowing what they did, the party had drawn closer. But before they could act there came further sounds: the same shrill voice, then a muffled banging. And this time there could be no doubt whence it came.

Stainbank struggled to control his unease. He pointed his dagger at Mary Pegg. 'You will stay here . . .' He rounded on the others, gesturing them forward. And after a moment's hesitation all four, Thomas included, walked towards the hut.

But as they reached its door, which to Thomas's surprise was made of stout timber, Mary Pegg ran past them with a cry, and barred their way.

'Mercy, masters . . .' she was terrified now, ''tis not whom ye seek – I swear it!'

Stainbank snorted, feeling himself in control at last. 'You will answer for your deeds as well as your lies,' he snapped. 'Stand aside and let us do our work!'

There was a moment when it looked as if the woman would stand her ground, hopeless as her position was. But then came another shriek, from within the hut. And Thomas, Ragg and Bedell exchanged swift glances; for it was plain that whoever – or whatever – was within, it was not the man they sought.

'Stand aside!' Stainbank repeated, and made as if to pull Mary Pegg away. But instead of flinching she held up a hand. There was resignation on her face.

'Nay . . . then let me,' she said, in the saddest voice any of them had heard. 'For I see 'tis past concealment.'

They watched as she untied the piece of hempen rope with which the door was fastened. There came more banging from within. Uneasily, the men pressed forward in a body, their hands going to their daggers. Then as the door was pulled open, they peered inside.

At first, there was nothing to see. The hut was barely two yards square, windowless and dusty. A stack of firewood stood against one wall, and there were indeed herbs hanging from a crude frame at eye level. But then their eyes dropped, for there was more banging; and it came from their feet . . .

They watched as Mary Pegg lifted a heavy plank, and stood it on its end. Involuntarily each man stepped back, as a dark space was revealed beneath. But Mary had begun speaking – or rather, making the kind of soothing noises a mother might make . . . she lifted another plank aside, then a third. And every man gasped, as a dirty hand appeared . . . and finally Mary stooped, and helped the occupant to climb out.

They stared; at a filthy, naked child – if a girl of little more than twelve or thirteen years could be so named, who reached as tall as a man. There she stood, blinking in the sunshine before them, until finally her eyes widened as she saw the men clearly. Whereupon she gave a blood-curdling shriek and span round, throwing herself upon her mother's shoulder with such force that the woman staggered. Yet all the while Mary Pegg comforted her, smoothing her thick matted hair and murmuring gently.

'Soft, child . . . they shall not harm ye . . . they will go soon, and we shall be alone again . . .'

'I named her Linnet,' Mary Pegg told them. 'For when she was little, she did sing so sweetly.'

They stood subdued and silent outside her door, as the afternoon sun waned. Some way off, the horses grazed. The child? Since for the present none could think what else to do, they had allowed Mary Pegg to shut her up again, in the hole beneath the hut where she lived most of the time. Indeed, it seemed this was where she had lived since she grew too big for her mother to control her.

'I could not heal her,' the woman told them, the sadness in her voice almost more than a man could bear. 'Though I've healed many creatures, folk and beasts . . . I knew from the time she could walk she was beyond my powers.'

97

She faced them, and now there was defiance in her gaze. 'What ought I to've done? Seen her taken away bound like a felon, to be thrown in some dungeon, or worse – clapped up in that terrible place they got in London?'

Thomas almost shuddered. Alone of these men, he had been inside the hospital of St Mary of Bethlehem, in Bishopsgate outside the London walls, and knew of what she spoke. He had seen the gallants come from the taverns and pay their penny to the hard-faced porter, so they might walk the long gallery and gawp, poking fun and laughing at the wretched, chained inmates seated on their piles of straw . . .

'None but the hardest of folk could deny you,' he said.

The others remained silent.

'Yet to confine her like a beast, and in the dark . . .' Thomas went on, with a shake of his head. 'How could you do such?'

Mary Pegg turned to him, and her face was bitter. 'She is not confined the whole time,' she answered. 'It is the likes of you coming here, that forces me to it . . . some days she is calm – she even helps me work the garden.' She threw a hard look at Stainbank. 'You scoff, Master Steward, in your fine livery . . . ye know not how the likes of me must shift, when a child be born out of wedlock, and turns out so wild none can tame her. The whores men like you use freely in the towns have their own remedies – and I speak not of willow tea, nor such purges!' Her voice rose now in anger. 'I speak of what is done with the unwanted child that is carried all the way to its birth! Strangled, or drowned in a ditch – or mayhap even sold to some childless woman of another stamp, who might raise her as her own – that is what ye would wish!'

'Silence!' Stainbank almost shouted. It seemed Mary Pegg had touched a nerve in the man, for there was anger as well as contempt in his gaze.

'You think I care for your foul tales, or the feeble excuses for your wanton life?' he cried. 'That creature – your savage child, that you chose to conceal in this fashion – has struck fear into the folk about these Downs. And answer this: how do I know it has not done worse?'

Thomas drew breath, and glanced at Will Ragg, who had remained silent. Now the blacksmith spoke.

'Nay – I will not believe such.'

The others turned to him, but before Stainbank could speak, Ragg cut him short. 'I was in the party, that heard the wild girl that night,' he said. 'Had I know what it . . . what she was, mayhap I would have been less afeared, and so would the other men. For all her madness, she looks not to me like any murderess . . . nor, had she the strength of three of her sex, could she have hanged Sam Hubbard in a tree!'

He turned to Mary Pegg. 'She has run away sometimes, is that not so? Which is why you were in Lambourn that night, seeking her.' When after a moment the woman nodded, he went on: 'Who else knows of her being here?'

Then suddenly he gasped, and looked away; for inwardly he had answered his own question.

'Sarah Caldwell does,' Mary Pegg replied quietly. 'She did help at Linnet's birth.'

She turned to Stainbank. 'Now ye know the truth. What then will you do?'

Stainbank saw all eyes were upon him. He seemed to be struggling with a deep loathing. And if he expected help from Hugh Bedell he was disappointed, for the burly servant merely stared at the ground. Finally, the steward faced Mary Pegg again with a sour look.

'I will inform my master, and await his pleasure,' he said thickly. 'In the meantime . . .' He made a quick, disdainful gesture, but his meaning was clear. Inwardly Thomas relaxed, and sensed that the other men felt as he did.

Without waiting for instruction, he turned and walked towards his horse.

They were back in Lambourn by evening. Little had been said on the return journey. But as they prepared to go their own ways, Stainbank had a last word for Will Ragg.

'The search for Howes must continue,' he announced. 'Since you have assumed the acting post of constable, my master will look to you to carry it out.'

Ragg looked tired and dispirited. Ignoring the man, he dismounted stiffly and made ready to lead his horse away. Then, as if determined to have the last word himself, he looked over his shoulder. 'If that must be, I will lead a party of Lambourn men, for it is one of our own we seek. We need none such as you to guide us.'

And before Stainbank could reply, he tugged at the rein and led his mount off towards the forge.

Thomas bade the Bickington men a curt farewell. But as they wheeled their mounts to ride off towards the bridge, he started – then wondered how he had failed to notice it sooner.

On the back of Hugh Bedell's left hand was a semi-circular wound; seemingly deep and still raw and swollen. And though he caught barely a glimpse before the man rode away, he was certain that the marks of teeth were visible.

And from the size, they suggested a dog-bite.

Wanting nothing more than to ride home to Petbury, he nevertheless decided to seek Jonas Crouch. To his relief the clerk was seated in the garden before his little table, which was scattered with papers. To any callers, he might have seemed busy with church accounts, but Thomas knew better.

'She looks hungry,' he murmured, with a nod towards Crouch's goshawk. The big hawk had fixed Thomas with an unblinking yellow eye, as if to let him know he was fair game himself.

Crouch looked up, and eagerly gestured Thomas to the seat beside him, then poured wine from the jug. 'I am glad you came,' he said. 'Now we can trade news.'

Thomas told him all that had happened. By the time he had finished the sun was low, and Crouch was looking sombre.

'Then we are no nearer to finding out what happened to Hubbard – nor Henry Howes.'

'Nor to Will Stubbs,' Thomas added. For if recent events had somewhat overshadowed the churchwarden's death, he was reminded of it whenever he rode into Lambourn and saw the tower of St Michael's looming over the square. Now, recalling his last conversation here in Crouch's garden, he turned the matter over once again.

'At least we know who was in the wood the night he was killed,' he went on. 'And that poor child, I am certain, could not have done such a deed. Hence, there was someone else . . .'

'Even if that were so, what link can there be with the death of Hubbard?' Crouch asked, and shook his head. 'I confess, I cannot see any.' He refilled Thomas's cup before pouring the remaining contents of the jug into his own, and took a generous pull.

'There is one thing that could help me,' Thomas said. 'Might I be permitted to examine Hubbard's body?'

Crouch looked uneasy. 'I do not know . . . the rector can be an obstinate man.' He eyed Thomas. 'And I fear he does not think of you as an ally.'

Thomas frowned. 'I wish him no ill, and never have.'

But Crouch's mind was on another track. 'This mark you saw, on the hand of Elyot's servant . . .'

'It was a dog-bite,' Thomas nodded. 'When I recall it now, I am more certain than ever.'

'Yet you cannot be certain it came from Howes's dog . . . ?'

'It seems a timely coincidence, does it not? Like Howes disappearing right after Hubbard was killed . . .'

Crouch looked uncomfortable. 'Mayhap you should speak of it with Ragg.'

Thomas nodded. 'I will . . . I should go now and seek him before I ride homeward.'

Crouch stood up suddenly – perhaps too quickly, for he seemed to grow dizzy. 'My Lord . . .' he muttered, 'I have drunk too much on an empty stomach. I was about to invite you to supper . . .' He steadied himself, and thought for a moment. 'I have a better idea. We will feed Clement, then you will be my guest at the Horns. Nightingale keeps a goodly table – plain fare, but plenty of it.'

Thomas too stood up. 'I thank you, Jonas,' he began, 'but I should ride back to Petbury . . .'

'Oh, pish!' For some reason, the little clerk was in an odd mood. 'That wife of yours can wait . . . you should go to the Horns in any case, for Ragg will likely be there. Blacksmiths always have a powerful thirst to slake.' He tapped the side of his nose in conspiratorial fashion. 'Then we may review matters, over another mug.' Without waiting, he hurried off.

Thomas considered briefly before deciding to accept his

friend's offer. He stretched his tired limbs, watching the sun sinking behind the hills, and sighed. It would be dark before he reached home once again.

Eleven

The melodious sound of the blind harper's singing rose above the hubbub as Thomas and Crouch pushed their way into the crowded inn. The clerk was hailed on all sides, though there were fewer greetings for the falconer. He wondered whether, since this morning, some resented his being included in private talks in the vestry when they were not. Nightingale the landlord, for one, barely acknowledged his presence, but sent Nicholas the drawer over to serve them. Having ordered a supper, Crouch called for two mugs, then found a bench near the door that was not too full. As they squeezed themselves into their seats, Thomas surveyed the room but saw no sign of Ragg.

'He will be here,' Crouch said, then lowered his mug. His eyes had narrowed suddenly. 'For it seems everyone else is.'

Thomas peered through the haze of smoke and saw the portly churchwarden John Wilmott, sitting across the room and eyeing them both. Then he stiffened: for beside Wilmott sat Peter Hare, puffing on a pipe of weed. And by the way the man pointedly looked elsewhere, he knew that Hare had seen him.

'There's one knows more than he gives out,' Thomas murmured, with a nod towards the shepherd. 'The better I know him, the less I trust him.'

Crouch took another drink. 'Always was a sour fellow,' he said, then belched and quickly tried to cover it. 'Though no worse than the one next to him . . .' He glared suddenly at Wilmott. 'By the Lord, I am heartily sick of him and his ways!'

Thomas glanced at his friend. 'I confess I never saw you in this humour, Jonas,' he said.

Crouch snorted and took yet another drink, prompting

103

Thomas to suggest that it might be best to save the rest of his mug to wash down his supper. But the other merely snorted again.

'Save your advice for your 'prentice, Master Thomas,' he answered. 'I'm clerk of this parish . . .' He lowered his gaze suddenly. 'Not that it's aught but a humble post – and poorly paid at that.'

Only now did Thomas realize that his friend was already drunk. He was about to suggest that they went into the parlour to await their meal when his eye fell upon another familiar face. In the far corner, nursing a mug by himself, was the bellfounder's son, Edmund Goodchild.

The young man's face bore little trace of the slight wounds he had received two days before, when Thomas had last seen him. He seemed preoccupied, and uninterested in his surroundings. As Thomas watched he drained his mug, then looked up and waved it at the drawer for a refill.

Then Thomas felt a jolt, and turned quickly to see that Crouch had got to his feet. 'I'm tired of all the secrets!' the little clerk said loudly, prompting the nearest drinkers to look at him in surprise. 'I should stand up for myself more . . . Am I not as well-born as any of them? Not that there's many of us left, with Henry gone and Will dead . . . poor old Will,' he mumbled.

Thomas stood up. 'You need a supper inside you,' he said. 'Then I will walk home with you, before I ride back.'

'Yes . . . you can ride back,' Crouch said in a muddled voice. 'To your fine manor of Petbury, and your fair wife . . . the woman I loved died long ago, and all I do is work to blot out her memory. I'm a slave to this parish!'

Then he stiffened from head to foot, as did Thomas; for John Wilmott had risen, and was making his way towards them.

'Friend Jonas!' The man's tone was scathing. 'Is this how church officials behave, like common drunkards? You dishonour Saint Michael's, as you do our rector!'

Thinking to excuse his friend, Thomas opened his mouth, but he was too late. For immediately Crouch dropped his mug and raised his fist, waving it in Wilmott's face. 'Dishonour!'

104

he cried. 'You talk to me of that? When you whisper and plot behind my back, shutting me out of your discourse . . . I was a man of substance here, once . . . before the one you speak of came here with his harsh ways, and began treating me like a servant—'

'Enough!' Wilmott's face had reddened, though more with embarrassment than with anger. His bald head gleamed in the light of a lantern swinging from the beam above. 'You shame us all – get you home and sleep it off, before—'

'Before what?' Crouch shouted, now equally red-faced. 'You are not my master, John Wilmott! You're but a church-warden, who fawns upon Starling and puffs himself up like a fat capon . . . You dare tell me to get myself home!'

Now he did swing his fist, but Thomas was ready. He caught it, and pulled his friend's arm down. The hubbub had dropped, and every head in the room turned to see what the commotion was. There were looks of surprise, and not a few grins, to see who was the cause of it.

Wilmott had taken a step back, but his fury was great. 'You little scarecrow!' he shouted. 'You think yourself so high, because you've had a sizar's education . . . aping your betters with your scrawny hawk – rector was right. He saw you for the fool you are, from the moment he took up his living here!'

Crouch gasped and struggled, but having dropped his own mug Thomas held him firmly, pinning both arms. 'We're leaving, Jonas,' he muttered, and sought to steer his friend towards the door. But Crouch was not done.

'Fool, am I?' he shot back, his eyes blazing at Wilmott. 'At least I'm not a thief, who sneaks into a dead man's cottage the moment he's gone to see what he can loot . . . What were you looking for? Something you could use to stain the memory of a saintly old servant of the church – the man you hated, because you weren't fit to wipe his arse, and never will be!'

Now he had gone too far. Voices rose on all sides, in mingled dismay and surprise. Some men had risen, prepared to quell what now looked like an unavoidable fight – or perhaps to join in. Thomas saw ugly looks, and stared about him, ready to defend his friend. Others, however, were calling out that it was unseemly for churchmen to behave so – there would be God's vengeance . . .

But Wilmott had turned pale with fury, and veins stood out on his temples. For a moment he looked as if he would forget his own remonstrations and strike Crouch with his open hand. But at last, and to general relief, a voice of authority rang out from the parlour doorway, calling for order. John Nightingale was shoving his way through the crowd.

'You?' he stared at Crouch and Wilmott in surprise and irritation. 'What d'ye think ye do, Masters?'

'Ask him!' Wilmott answered in a shaky voice, with a jerk of his head towards Crouch. 'For I've done naught but remind him of his duty!'

'Duty again, is it?' Crouch cried, and struggled to free himself from Thomas's grasp. But Thomas had had enough.

'I'll get him out,' he told Nightingale. 'He's but taken too much on an empty stomach . . .'

But Wilmott's fury had not waned: he merely controlled it better. 'Permit me to help you,' he said. And watched by all, with a man on either side, Crouch was finally removed from the inn, puffing as he went. As they cleared the doorway and stood in the gathering dusk, voices rose behind them; and Dickon the harper, heeding the calls, began another song.

But the matter was far from ended. Outside, intending to shepherd his charge towards his cottage, Thomas gave Wilmott a word of thanks. But the churchwarden seemed not to hear; instead he retained a firm hold of Crouch's arm and kept walking. Only when the three of them, somewhat awkwardly, had moved out of earshot of the inn, and were beside the turning to the old Ramsbury path, did they halt.

'I would ask you to leave us now, falconer,' Wilmott said.

But Thomas shook his head. 'Nay, Master Wilmott, I mean to take him home.'

'Let go of me!' For the first time since leaving the Horns, Crouch spoke. 'I'm not a child . . . You think because I have drunk too much I've lost my wits?'

Thomas let go of one arm, and finally Wilmott let go of the other, whereupon their charge stepped back indignantly and shook himself. But without warning Wilmott pushed himself close, and spoke in a voice of ice. 'How dare you insult me and accuse me as you did . . . I could swear out a warrant for slander.'

Crouch, his hair and clothing awry, his face red and sweaty, fumed in his turn. 'You know what I speak of—'

'You called me a thief!' Wilmott spat. 'I am a law-abiding citizen and a churchman, and I deny it!'

'You may deny it all you like,' Crouch breathed. 'Yet you went into Stubbs's house the day after he died, and left it ransacked!'

Wilmott's eyes almost popped out. 'You clown!' he cried, forgetting himself for a moment. 'I didn't seek anything to incriminate Stubbs – I went there to save his name!'

Crouch stared, as did Thomas, for the man had said more than he intended. There was a moment, then the little clerk gasped, and pointed with his finger.

'*The Book of Martyrs* . . . you found it!'

Wilmott made no reply, but bit his lip, angry with himself for blurting it out. But Thomas, sensing there was some clue that might serve him, took a step forward.

'What do you mean? You took a book from Will Stubbs's house after he died, so it would not be found there?'

Wilmott made no answer. But now there came a shout from some yards away. A man was striding towards them: Will Ragg. Behind him, hanging back, was Sarah Caldwell.

'What's this?' Ragg halted, the surprised look on his face matching those of the drinkers in the Horns. 'I thought 'twas a bout between a couple of sots . . .'

'One sot, indeed,' Wilmott snapped, flicking a hand towards Crouch. 'I leave you to deal with him.' He made as if to go, but Thomas stayed him.

'*The Book of Martyrs*,' he said. 'Why was it—'

'I do not have to tell you!' Wilmott said angrily. 'It's a church matter . . .' He drew himself away, avoiding Ragg's gaze, and took a few paces. But as he went, he turned briefly. 'Ask your fool of a friend. Even he should be able to put a few simple facts together and make something of whole cloth – once he is sober!'

Then he walked swiftly away towards the church.

107

Thomas turned to Crouch, who was suddenly calm. Indeed, his anger seemed to have drained away. Seeing his friend's gaze upon him, he drew a deep breath. 'I owe you thanks, Thomas . . . for not letting me make an even bigger fool of myself. Will you come with me now, and take that bite of supper I promised?' He glanced at Ragg. 'Mayhap Will should come too, if he pleases . . .'

Ragg hesitated. 'I have business of my own, Master Crouch.' He looked at Thomas, then added: 'Give me but a half hour, and I will join you.'

Crouch nodded, and he and Thomas watched as the black-smith walked back to where Sarah Caldwell stood waiting, and took her arm. Together they walked away towards the almshouses.

'*Actes and Monuments*,' Crouch said. 'That is what the great John Foxe called it, though folk know it better as *The Book of Martyrs* . . . He's dead these six years, yet his book will indeed be his monument, for there is now a copy in every church in the land. That, and the Geneva Bible . . .' He paused. 'Our rector, of course, was most assiduous in seeing that Foxe's book was placed in our church. A matter that caused some folk deep misgiving.'

They sat in his cottage, the remains of a hastily prepared supper on the table before them. It had grown dark, but Thomas had lit the fire and found a couple of rush lights. Having eaten and drunk a little milk, Crouch was sober enough, if some-what shame-faced. Now he sat on his stool, facing Will Ragg. Thomas was between them.

'The book tells of those brave souls who died for their faith – burned during the reign of Queen Mary,' the clerk told them. 'With terrible images, of how they suffered in the fires . . . men and women alike. Our rector wishes all to see what they endured – though there are yet many alive who remember those times well enough.'

He frowned, then looked at Ragg. 'The book was taken from the church.'

Ragg stared. 'When?'

'Some weeks back . . .' Crouch looked uneasy. 'Starling

begged us not to speak of it. None will ask where it has gone, he said, for few in the village ever look at it. He urged us to say naught, until we might discover who took it . . .' Suddenly, he banged a fist down upon the table, startling the other two. 'I will not think Stubbs a thief! How can it be that the book was in his house? It makes no sense – Wilmott lied!'

Thomas glanced at Ragg, then said: 'I do not think so, Jonas. As soon as he had spoken, he regretted his words – you saw that too.'

Crouch shook his head sadly. 'I will not think Will a thief,' he repeated lamely.

Thomas thought for a moment. 'Let us suppose for a moment he were,' he began. 'Why would he wish to take such a book, and conceal it?' He eyed Crouch. 'The chest that was forced open. It could have been in there . . .'

'But how did Wilmott know?' Ragg objected. 'And if he suspected Stubbs, why did he not report him to the rector?'

Crouch looked up suddenly. 'He did!' When the other two turned to him, he went on: 'Now I see things somewhat clearer. Wilmott accused Stubbs, yet Starling refused to believe him. It would explain the many secret words I have seen pass between them . . .' he started. 'Mayhap Henry Howes knew something, too . . .'

'Nay – draw rein, Jonas . . .' Thomas held up a hand, his forehead creasing. 'You leap ahead too fast . . . let us untangle this, that we might come at the nub of it.'

Ragg looked uncomfortable. 'The matter should be put before Sir Robert,' he said. 'And Elyot too . . .'

'My master went away early this morning,' Thomas told him. He hesitated, then: 'And as for Master Elyot . . . need we tell him? I mean, just yet?'

Crouch frowned in his turn. 'You have a conspirator's air about you, Thomas.'

'I believe I'm among friends,' Thomas answered, with a glance at Ragg. 'Hence, let me say I do not quite trust the Master of Bickington, any more than I like the company of his steward.'

There was a short silence. Ragg picked up his cup and took a drink. 'We are of the same mind there, at least.'

'Then will you indulge me?' Thomas persisted. 'If between us we can find how these matters hang together, my master will be pleased when he returns. He will speak for us all to the High Sheriff – have no fear of that.'

Ragg nodded slowly. 'Well enough . . . but what can we do?'

Thomas turned to Crouch. 'Wilmott knows his secret's out now,' he said. 'Hence we may approach the rector, and ask him. If there has been concealment, he would surely wish to explain himself . . .' He paused. 'And mayhap he will let me look at Hubbard's body after all.'

Ragg stared. 'What do you hope to discover by that? He was hanged in that apple-tree . . .'

Thomas nodded. 'Yet indulge me, Master Will. And when we all see the whole picture, we may try and decipher it together.'

Ragg raised an eyebrow at Crouch, who glanced at them both, and sighed. 'What a triumvirate we make,' he said finally, 'to uphold the law here, and seek out murderers, and heaven knows what else. A falconer, a blacksmith and a scrivener – how shall that fadge?'

The other two eyed each other, and kept silent.

Two hours later, in the owlhoot time, Thomas let himself into his dark cottage, to find Nell in the sleeping loft, snoring like a heifer. With a sigh, he sat down on the bed and began undressing – whereupon there came an eerie shriek from somewhere outside, making Nell turn uneasily in her sleep. He started, then cursed silently to himself: Sir Robert's peacocks again. For a moment he wondered uncharitably whether it might be worth risking the wrath of Martin the steward and letting another falcon loose in the park.

In the morning he rose early and went to the mews, seeing that Ned had, as always, tended the birds well. By the time he returned to the cottage Nell was up and waiting for him. It seemed that again they would have only a moment together.

'A servant came from Bickington at sunset yesternight, with a message,' she told him. 'Master Elyot asks you to attend him this morning, with all haste.'

110

He frowned, standing by the door as the sun rose above the beeches beyond the Wantage road. 'Had the fellow known I was still in Lambourn trying to prevent a brawl,' he said ruefully, 'he could have saved himself the ride.'

She leaned forward to kiss him. 'Then you'd best stay out of trouble today – for I expect you to supper.'

And she was gone, in her grey workaday gown, walking downhill towards the house. He watched from a distance as she stopped by the archway leading to the kitchen plot and spoke with a gardener – no doubt about pulling vegetables. With a sigh he closed the door and went off to the stables.

Within the hour he had ridden into the yard at Bickington Manor. But before he could dismount, a groom who was forking hay called to him that Master Elyot was out hawking. If he climbed the hill above the house, he might find him in the west field, bordering Howes's grazing.

With a nod, Thomas wheeled the gelding and rode out into the paddock, then made his way at a steady pace north-westward in the direction of Howes's acres. Elyot's own large flock of sheep grazed in the distance. Idly he wondered whether anyone had thought what to do with the sexton's livestock, assuming the man was still a fugitive. He recalled those events of two days ago, when he and Crouch had found the farm-stead deserted; it occurred to him now to ask himself whether he had been somewhat hasty in thinking so badly of the man. Could Henry Howes truly have killed Hubbard? And one thing was certain: he could not have thrust him into the tree's fork without help.

Something floated into his field of vision, high above. Shading his eyes, he made out a soaring falcon. The next moment, having urged the horse up a slope, he saw two horsemen in the long grass a hundred yards away: Elyot, with a servant in attendance. As he rode towards them, he found himself hoping it was not Ralph Stainbank.

It was not Stainbank, but Hugh Bedell; the heavy man recognized Thomas from a distance, and raised a hand briefly. As he drew near, Elyot himself called a greeting, wheeled his fine roan horse and rode forward.

'Falconer . . . you received my message?' Thomas inclined

his head, but quickly the other man went on: 'I am displeased at the way the search for Howes is being conducted.'

Thomas made no reply. Some yards away, Bedell was sitting his horse, eyes averted.

'My steward has given me a full account of what occurred yesterday on the Downs . . .' Elyot wrinkled his nose in distaste. 'The woman Pegg I will not concern myself about – her child should be a charge upon the parish. Master Starling must attend to the matter . . . Meanwhile, the fugitive is still at large. And I hear that Master Ragg, without proper authority, is appointing himself to lead any future forays to seek him out!'

Thomas met the man's eye. 'Few men know the country better than he, sir,' he began, but the other's face darkened.

'There's small need to remind me of that!' he retorted. 'Nor is it your place to do so!'

Thomas remained impassive. The change in Elyot's demeanour towards him he found striking, recalling the relaxed way he had been when together they doctored the man's falcon. As if to remind him of it, he glanced pointedly upwards, beyond Elyot's shoulder.

'Your bird has stooped, sir,' he said.

Elyot looked round to see his Artemis dropping like a stone into the grass. All three men watched as, with a beating of wings, the falcon rose again, her prey hanging limply from her talons.

'Indeed . . .' Elyot's attention had wavered, but quickly he resumed his officious tone. 'Yet it seems I must remind you of your duty to your master. And Sir Robert, as you know, has ordered you to render me whatever aid I wish.'

Sitting erect in the saddle, Thomas made a slight bow, then could not help letting his eyes stray towards Bedell. He glanced at the man's hands and saw that he wore riding gloves.

He faced Elyot. 'I will do what I can, sir,' he replied. 'And I have a mind to come at the matter by other ways. If I could look further into Sam Hubbard's death, then perhaps we might learn something . . .'

'Look into his death?' Elyot was frowning. 'He was hanged, was he not? What else is there to uncover?'

Thomas shrugged. 'I cannot think that the sexton had the strength to place a man of Hubbard's weight in that tree . . .' He trailed off, for Elyot's frown had cleared, to be replaced by a look of something like satisfaction.

'I see how your mind moves, falconer! Mayhap he had an accomplice – if robbery was their motive, the man's purse will have been cut . . . or perhaps there may be other signs one of your keen eye can discern.' He nodded slowly. 'I was hasty . . . your reputation as a finder of what is lost is of course well known.'

Thomas acknowledged the transparent flattery; and as was his strategy at such times, he sought to turn it to good use.

'Well, sir,' he said, with a glance at Bedell. 'It seems to me now there were signs I may have missed at Howes's farm. The way his dog had been slain, for one . . .'

But before either man could react their attention was diverted, for Elyot's falcon had flown to him and dropped her prey in the grass. At once Bedell dismounted and busied himself bagging up the bird in his pouch. And soon after, having agreed to keep the Master of Bickington informed of all developments, Thomas was dismissed. But he had discerned an edginess about Hugh Bedell, and it was enough: there was little doubt in his mind now that this man had been party to the killing of Howes's dog, and suffered a bite in the process.

Though why that should be, he had not the least idea.

Twelve

He left Bickington and rode upriver to Lambourn. Dismounting in the square, he tethered the gelding and went directly to the church. And the first person he saw was Crouch.

Somewhat distracted, the clerk drew him inside the porch. There seemed to be no one about, but sounds of activity were audible from the bell-yard.

'I have spoken with the rector,' Crouch said. 'I think he may be willing to let you examine Hubbard's body after all. It lies in St Katherine's chapel . . . but first, you must speak with him.' He lowered his voice. 'He is not himself . . . I cannot fathom it. Though I know Wilmott has been at him already . . .' He drew a long breath. 'I no longer know what goes on here, Thomas. I believe I am more shut out than ever.'

Thomas looked with sympathy upon his friend, who without further word conducted him through the south transept into the vestry. Sunlight lanced through the windows and shone upon the head of Richard Starling, who stood at a small lectern, poring over what Thomas first assumed was a bible. But as he drew closer, he saw it was a heavy book bound in oxblood leather, open at a page of wood-cut illustrations. A glance told him all he needed: *The Book of Martyrs . . .*

Starling looked up, and levelled a gaze at him.

'Well, Thomas Finbow . . . I hear you have a request to make of me. Yet first let me ask you something: do you believe our sexton, Henry Howes, is a murderer?'

Though the man's expression was as severe as ever, there was a weariness behind his eyes that Thomas had never seen before. He met his gaze. 'No, rector, I do not.'

Behind him, he heard Crouch draw breath. When Starling

114

merely waited, he went on: 'It's true I believed – and still do – that his flight from the farm followed too hard upon Hubbard's death to be coincidence. And despite the search there's no sign of him anywhere . . . yet it seems to me now there's more to the matter than I first thought. Hence I would ask your leave to look over the constable's body. I know not what I may find; maybe naught, but . . .'

'You deem it worth the trouble.' Starling's gaze strayed towards Crouch. 'Our parish clerk has already spoken of your skill in uncovering what others overlook.'

Thomas said nothing, but his glance strayed to the book, whereupon Starling's face darkened.

'Do you see this?' he asked abruptly, and jabbed a finger at the illustration. 'I was there . . . in the last years of the reign of Mary Tudor . . . I stood in Smithfield, a mere boy of fifteen, and watched those blessed martyrs perish in the fire! Sometimes three burning at once – men and women both, chained to the same stake, with sticks and straw round their feet, praying for deliverance while the flames licked at them . . . and all the while the crowd gawping, and some bloody-handed priest standing by, reading from his papist tract . . . claiming this was God's work he did, while their bodies began to burn, and their screams echoed across London!'

He looked up from the book, and his eyes blazed as if the fires of vengeance burned within. 'You cannot know,' Starling continued, controlling his feelings with an effort. 'Unless you saw for yourself the manifestation of such ignorance turned to savagery, you cannot know.' He shook his head. 'Those martyrs lucky enough to have friends, who bribed a guard to place a little bag of gunpowder round their necks, died quicker. So did those who aroused the sympathy of the crowd with their piety and courage, so that folk ran forward to fling oil and brush-wood on the flames, and hasten their work. But many . . .' He screwed his face up, as if unable to bear the memory. 'Many died a slow and agonizing death, as their persecutors intended.'

He fell silent. Finally Crouch stepped forward, and Starling looked up and met his gaze. But if a spark of understanding passed between the two men, it was quickly extinguished, for the rector turned suddenly upon Thomas.

115

'So you see, Thomas Finbow the falconer, that I am not a man who is afraid to face the truth.'

Thomas met the man's eye again. 'I do, sir,' he answered. 'And I will uncover it, if I can.'

There was a moment, before Starling finally lowered his gaze. 'Do your investigations, then,' he said. 'And let me know what you find.' He glanced at Crouch, and to the clerk's surprise added: 'There has been enough deception.'

After a moment Crouch nodded. And without further word he gestured to Thomas to follow him out, through the chancel and into the chapel of St Katherine.

The body of Samuel Hubbard was lying on boards upon the old tomb that stood at the eastern end of the little chapel, covered with a sheet of black drugget. Thomas approached it, and without preamble uncovered the face.

Crouch had hung back. Now he took a timid step forward, and stared at the constable's pale visage. Hubbard had been washed, and his hair dressed neatly. The forehead was smooth and unlined, the habitual put-upon expression gone; as was the man inside the lifeless case.

'Like a statue,' he murmured. But he was disconcerted when Thomas turned and asked him to help move the corpse.

'How might we do such?' he asked.

But Thomas was impatient. 'I wish to roll it over, is all. If you haven't the stomach, find me someone who has.'

The clerk blanched, but he walked round to the other side of the stone tomb and took hold of the rigid body. And with a considerable effort, between them they managed to turn it on its side. But when Thomas pulled the white shift up to reveal the torso beneath, Crouch swallowed and looked sick.

'This shows scant respect for the dead,' he began, but Thomas paid him no attention. Instead, to Crouch's growing discomfort, he peeled the winding cloth back and began examining the heavy body closely, on every side. And quickly he found what he sought.

'There!' Without looking round, he gestured Crouch forward. Gingerly the clerk approached, and saw for himself the black marks of bruises, under the arms and along the ribs.

116

'As I thought – he was lifted up,' Thomas said. 'And by someone I wouldn't like to tangle with . . . I'll wager Hubbard weighed twenty stones, if an ounce.'

He looked round, and Crouch saw the look on his face.

'By the Lord, Thomas,' he muttered. 'You seem like a man who enjoys this kind of work.'

Thomas raised an eyebrow. 'I like to find a theory of mine proved – what man doesn't?'

The other shook his head slowly, and watched as Thomas carried out other unpleasant-looking tasks: peering into the man's mouth, examining his neck and scalp. Finally he straightened, and turned again to his friend.

'I think he was unconscious when he was stuck in that tree. Otherwise, being the size he was, the task would have been nigh impossible. There's a swelling on the head, and a few other marks I don't like . . .'

Crouch swallowed. 'So as you said, it's murder. I doubt any man would wish to prove otherwise; by this means, anyway.'

'He's welcome to try,' Thomas replied.

'You have done well, though,' Crouch said. 'For assuming the rector takes your word, and accepts Hubbard did not take his own life, he may be buried here in the church after all.'

Thomas nodded, somewhat absently, then fixed his friend with a grim look. 'But the question remains – if Howes didn't kill him, who did? And why?'

Crouch had no answer.

At midday Thomas went to the forge to seek Will Ragg. The place was not only uncomfortably hot, but on first entering he could see nothing for clouds of steam. A loud hissing came from one side, prompting him to call out. There was an answering cry and the blacksmith appeared, a pair of heavy tongs in his hand. A horseshoe was gripped between them, and the steam came from the tub of water into which it had just been plunged.

'Thomas . . . I thought you might come.' The man wiped the sweat from his brow with his free arm. 'There's a matter I would speak about.'

Thomas waited while he put aside the tongs. In the back,

the blacksmith's boy was busy at the bellows. He looked up, but gave no greeting. 'Mayhap more than one matter . . .' Ragg had taken up his jerkin and motioned Thomas to step outside, away from the heat. As they left the forge, he said: 'I can't spare time to lead any more search parties.

'I know what Elyot will say,' he went on quickly, 'not to mention Stainbank – well, let them rant. I've already neglected my work long enough.' He sighed. 'The truth is, Thomas, I can find none willing to ride with me. No one has the time for it, or the stomach. And I confess I cannot blame them.'

Thomas nodded. 'Nor can I.'

'Besides . . .' Ragg's gaze wandered towards the church. 'It's a momentous time, for I hear they will break out the new bell.'

It had occurred to Thomas that the square seemed unusually empty. 'I'll go and take a look,' he said, then saw Ragg was busy pulling on his jerkin.

'I've some business at the almshouses,' he said briskly. 'So it's best we both go.' At once he walked off towards the churchyard. Somewhat surprised, Thomas followed.

Once again there was a small crowd in what people were now calling the casting-yard. But this time there was a sense of awe among the villagers present. Thomas sensed it as he and Ragg drew close, and found a circle of folk of all ages standing round the bell-pit, gazing down. The covering of earth had been removed from the bell-mould, revealing the dome of hard, dry clay. But there was no sign of the bell-founder. Instead young Edmund Goodchild stood beside the pit, explaining with some exasperation that he could do nothing until his father instructed him. The breaking of the mould was such an important matter, he must not attempt it on his own.

'We do not even know if it has cooled enough,' he said to one onlooker who was more curious than the rest. 'There may be naught for ye to see today . . .'

Ragg caught Thomas's sleeve. 'Are you coming?'

Thomas raised his brows. 'I thought you had business with a certain Mistress Caldwell . . .'

Ragg eyed him. 'It's she I would have you speak with.'

So together they walked away from the crowd and skirted

the yard. And a short time later Thomas found himself in the garden where three days earlier he had held a conversation he well remembered with the woman who now opened the door.

Today Sarah Caldwell wore a modest beige-coloured gown over her kirtle, though the garish periwig was still in place atop her head. She smiled on seeing Will Ragg, then started at the sight of Thomas behind.

'So . . . you have brought him.'

'Had you forgot?' Ragg glanced about, seemingly eager to get himself out of sight of prying eyes. This was not lost on Mistress Sarah, who gave him a wry look before bidding them both enter the house.

There were two small downstairs rooms. The door to the other was closed, and Thomas guessed that was where she conducted business. The other was a comfortable enough parlour with a table and stools and a few homely touches. The side window gave on to the churchyard, from where they could see Will Stubbs's newly made grave.

'Well, my duck . . .' Sarah fixed her wide eyes upon Ragg, before sitting down and gesturing to the men to do the same.

'I hide naught from Sarah,' Ragg said to Thomas, somewhat gruffly. 'And since you've dealt straight with me, there's things I would have you know, from her lips.' Taking Thomas's silence for embarrassment, he went on: 'You might guess that Sarah is party to many a secret.'

Thomas looked at Sarah Caldwell. 'One of them at least is a secret no longer,' he murmured. 'That of Mary Pegg's child.'

Sarah's face clouded. 'That poor creature . . . Mary ought to've given her up when she was little – before she grew too much for her to handle. I warned her . . .' She broke off, then fixed Thomas with a harder look.

'Nature has some terrible ways, falconer. A child is made from the mix of male and female seed, in the chambers of the womb. And it's said if the male seed be not human, a monster can be conceived . . . like those women that have given birth to cats, or worse!' She paused, then said somewhat absently: 'The one who fathered Linnet was no monster . . . yet he wasn't much of a man, either.'

Thomas drew breath. 'You know who the father is?'

She made no reply. Then, meeting Will Ragg's gaze, she grew suddenly defensive. 'I swore I would never tell that,' she said. 'And you promised not to press me.'

Ragg looked away.

'Mary will never give up her secrets,' Sarah said. 'Any more than she would give up her daughter . . .' She faced Ragg again. 'I thought you wished to speak of another matter.'

'I do,' he nodded. 'Tell Thomas what you know.'

Sarah turned to Thomas, and met his eye. 'Henry Howes is no murderer – nor has he fled. I believe he was taken.'

There was a silence. From outside, the murmur of the crowd in the bell-yard was audible, but Thomas barely heard it. He stared at Sarah Caldwell, then frowned. 'If you know this, why have you not spoken?'

Ragg looked uncomfortable. 'Sarah has her reasons,' he muttered. 'Stainbank, for one . . .'

Sarah flushed, and looked as if she would silence him. But Thomas caught her eye. 'Even so, there has been murder done. I looked over Hubbard's body myself.'

Ragg looked at him sharply, and quickly Thomas told him of his examination of the corpse. By the time he had finished, the blacksmith was looking more confused than ever. 'Then they must have been more than one, like you said . . . but who, and why did they do it? The house was not broken into, nor was Hubbard robbed . . .'

'We must look elsewhere for reasons,' Thomas said, and turned to Sarah Caldwell again. 'I must ask how you know of this.'

Ragg opened his mouth, but at a glance from Sarah closed it again.

'I have never broken a confidence, master,' she said quietly. 'That's how I've managed to stay out of the lock-up these past years, and earn my keep.'

'Yet still I ask it,' Thomas countered. 'Else Henry Howes, if he is found, may be hanged for another's crime, though he be innocent.'

She paused. 'I hear you are a skilled finder of what lies hidden,' she said, with a hint of the smile she had worn when Thomas first saw her. 'Hence ye must seek it out. Yet this much I can say: if he is not found before Michaelmas, he loses all he has.'

Thomas stared. 'How do you know that?'

She made no reply, and at once he berated himself for his foolishness. Henry Howes, long a widower, had been a customer of Sarah's; like Stainbank, and a host of other men . . . the woman must indeed be the keeper of many secrets.

He glanced at Ragg, who merely said: 'This is between us, Thomas. I trust you as I do Sarah – who will be my wife before long, if we can bring it about.' He and Sarah exchanged looks, before he went on: 'But even then . . .'

'Even then,' Sarah Caldwell finished, 'I will not spill those things I was bidden to keep safe – even to you.'

Ragg said nothing, but threw a look at Thomas, the meaning of which was clear enough. With a nod to them both, he rose. Sarah rose too and made to conduct him out, but with a smile he shook his head and walked to the door.

Out in the sunshine, he paused beside the bush where he had tied his horse three days ago. From the riverbank some yards away came the splashing of moorhens and the cries of mallards – and something else. He turned to look in the other direction, upriver, and through the willows and alders along the bank made out what looked like a small tent. Out of curiosity he began walking towards it, emerging in a flat clearing beside the river. Here was the tent, and a cart, and an untidy assortment of belongings – and at once he knew what had made the sound: an old horse was feeding greedily from a nosebag. And before he even saw the man standing beside it, he knew he was in the bell-founder's encampment.

Simon Goodchild looked up and gave no sign of recognition, but Thomas knew better. Knowing some explanation was called for, he walked towards the man with his hand raised.

'Forgive me, Master Founder . . . I did not know you were camped so close by the church.'

Goodchild made no response.

'Your son was hard pressed to keep the crowd at bay, when I passed through the yard,' Thomas continued with a smile. 'They are eager to see the new bell.'

Goodchild gave a shrug. 'Then they must wait a while longer – he is slow to cool, this one.'

Thomas nodded and met the man's eye, but could discern nothing, save perhaps a wariness. Once again he was left in little doubt that his presence was an intrusion.

'Mayhap tomorrow, then?' he enquired in a conversational tone. But the founder gave a slight movement, and his attention wavered. Glancing towards the tent, Thomas saw Alice Goodchild emerge, and stop in her tracks as soon as she saw him. When Thomas gave her good-day, she merely flinched.

As before, he found himself gazing at the couple, aware of their closeness and their strangeness. They seemed like people of some old, forgotten tribe who mixed little with ordinary folk, and seemed to dislike company. And though Thomas had met moon-men and other wanderers over the years, he had known none like these. Briefly he thought of Sarah Caldwell and the conversation that had just passed: Simon was a keeper of secrets that no man would ever fathom.

The founder had taken a few steps towards him. 'Is there aught else I can tell ye?' he asked.

Thomas hesitated, then surprised himself by letting a half-formed notion leap to his mouth. 'You know there have been two deaths in this village since you arrived here,' he said. 'I wonder whether you have spared any time to ponder the matter?'

What can you be thinking of? he asked himself, though at once the answer came: because sometimes a sudden shake of the tree produces more than mere fruit . . . Half-prepared for some indignant rebuke, he waited, his eyes darting from Goodchild to his wife and back. But there was no reaction; and that in itself he found strange. Though Alice Goodchild's nervousness was obvious, he was beginning to see that this was her normal demeanour. The woman was tense as a wand, yet she kept silent. And now he wondered whether he had been mistaken yesterday, in deciding her dumbness was a sham . . .

But Goodchild took another step forward, assuming the sage-like expression he had worn when Thomas first heard him. And despite the man's dignified air, he read a warning in the eyes that was as stark as any he had received.

'Ponder the matter?' he echoed. 'What is it to do with me and mine?' A touch of contempt showed. 'Are you one of those who blames outsiders for every misfortune – from famine and plague to robbery and murder?'

Thomas met his gaze. 'I spoke neither of robbery nor of murder.'

The bell-founder gave a little smile. 'The churchmen do,' he answered. 'I hear their discourse every day, even when I do not wish to. I ask you again: what is it to do with me?'

Thomas shrugged. 'Naught, I guess. I ask your pardon.'

But Goodchild was not satisfied. 'Your words are empty, for you harbour suspicion still. Look at us, and think harder. Can we who travel the country to make bells, who carry no licence and have no home but what you see here – can we truly afford to bring trouble upon ourselves?'

Thomas shook his head. 'I did not accuse you, Master Founder. And I will not stay, when you clearly wish me gone.' He turned to go, but the other suddenly held up a hand.

'Come tomorrow, and watch the birth of the maiden bell,' he said, his composure intact once again. 'Then ye shall judge the Goodchilds for yourself, and see the folly of your words.'

Thomas looked the man in the eye, but could read nothing. With a nod, he walked away through the trees, thinking it was high time he was tending his falcons.

Leaving the churchyard, where a few persistent onlookers still stood about, he made his way across the square, meaning to retrieve the gelding and ride home. But his glance strayed towards the end cottage, nearest the river: Will Stubbs's old house. A movement caught his eye, and he tensed.

A cart with two horses stood outside. More, the door was open, and sounds of activity came from within. As he watched, a familiar figure emerged from the house, and stopped when he saw Thomas.

'Falconer!' Ralph Stainbank called cheerfully. 'Still hanging about while others are at their business?'

Curbing his feelings, Thomas started towards him.

Thirteen

Stainbank waited for Thomas's approach, a condescending smile upon his lips. As he neared the door, two labourers emerged from the cottage carrying Stubbs's old oak chest between them; the one Thomas had examined three days earlier. He watched as they loaded it on to the cart, then went back inside.

'Master Elyot told me that Will Stubbs's property would revert to him, since he was the man's creditor,' Thomas said, with a hard look at the steward. 'Yet to seize all his goods when he is barely in his grave seems somewhat hasty.'

'The goods?' Stainbank snorted. 'Their total value is but a few shillings. The man owed my master considerably more than that.'

'Ten pounds, wasn't it?' Thomas replied, recalling his conversation with Elyot the previous Friday. The impression that gentleman had given then was of a generous landowner helping out a poor neighbour, and in no hurry to collect on the debt. Now the matter looked somewhat different; for he saw that the true prize was the man's house.

Stainbank was turning to go inside. 'Ten pounds seems a good price for this hovel, falconer,' he said. 'Besides, the fellow had no family to bequeath it to. I cannot see the cause of your displeasure.'

'The village might have made use of it,' Thomas answered. 'This is but a poor parish . . .'

Stainbank's impatience was growing. 'Then they should petition my master, and ask his pleasure,' he retorted.

Thomas strove to contain his dislike for the man. 'I looked inside that old chest myself, on the day of Stubbs's funeral,'

124

he said casually, with a nod towards the cart. 'Though it seemed to me someone had already rifled through it.'

Stainbank's air of impatience merely increased. 'You had no business being here,' he said. 'But look inside again, by all means. The man had nothing worth stealing, if that's the way your mind moves.'

He went inside, and Thomas heard him instructing the two servants to hurry themselves in clearing the house. For a moment he considered looking in the chest, before dismissing the idea. If he wished to learn more, he knew he would have to seek elsewhere.

He retrieved the gelding and led it away, across the Lambourn bridge. And it was here, standing in the warm afternoon sun, that a notion suddenly struck him, with such force that he dropped the reins.

What was the term Elyot had used? The Statute Merchant . . . which meant if the debtor failed to pay up, not just the debt but all his property was forfeit. Thomas had small legal knowledge, but he recalled hearing of something called a Statute Staple . . . He groped for the memory: the debtor had to settle by a fixed time, or all his wealth went to his creditor – and immediately Sarah Caldwell's words sprang to mind: if Henry Howes is not found before Michaelmas, he loses all he has . . .

He cursed silently, berating himself for not asking the question he should have asked sooner: who had most to gain from Howes's disappearance? The answer came swiftly: Elyot, whose lands bordered Howes's; Elyot, who had in all likelihood loaned him money – if it were on the same terms as Stubbs's, and the debt was not repaid, he would garner everything: livestock, house and farm. He would increase his holdings by perhaps fifty acres of the best grazing land in the valley.

He sat in the grass, deep in thought, and let the horse wander away to browse; for now other matters were beginning to fit together. Crouch had told him that Howes was afraid – as well any man might be who stood to lose everything he had built up in a lifetime's work. But later on he had seemed more cheerful, as if his troubles were surmountable after all. Could he have raised the money to pay off his debt?

125

Then he saw it. The last thing the creditor – Elyot – wished was for the debt to be settled: he wanted the agreed date to expire – Michaelmas – so that he could claim Howes's property. Hence, if it looked as though Howes was ready to clear his debt, one solution would be to have him disappear until the date had passed.

He had been kidnapped. Hugh Bedell and probably others, under orders, had come to his farm and taken him by force. The dog . . . the dog had tried to defend his master. Or mayhap it had merely got in the way, so they had killed it; but not before it had inflicted a wound on one of them. Somehow Thomas had not thought Bedell such a cruel man as to run the creature through.

He got to his feet, his mind working fast. It seemed that Howes's disappearance on the same night Hubbard was killed was mere coincidence after all – for he now guessed why Stainbank had seized upon the matter so eagerly when he and Crouch had taken the news to Bickington. Howes a fugitive, wanted for murder: it was perfect! Unwittingly, they had helped Elyot further his scheme. Again he cursed, audibly this time, as he saw how he, Ragg and the rest had been used: all the while, the search for Howes was a sham. For there was small doubt in his mind who would have been ordered to see to the details of the kidnapping: Ralph Stainbank.

But then, where had they taken the sexton? Or was he already dead? And still, the unresolved question – who had killed Hubbard?

He looked into the distance, towards the empty Downs where larks and swifts fluttered and swooped. His master was gone; Sir John Norris too. The High Sheriff was out of reach . . . and the only remaining landowner in the area was William Elyot.

Thomas was alone. With a heavy heart he got to his feet, walked to the gelding, mounted and would have ridden homewards. Then he thought of Crouch and of Richard Starling, and their conversation that morning. From a sense of duty, though with little hope, he turned towards the bridge and rode back into Lambourn.

*   *   *

126

He found the clerk at the church door, dealing with some disgruntled bystanders. It seemed there was general disappointment that the new bell would not be broken out today. But, seeing the look on Thomas's face, his friend bade the villagers a hasty farewell and drew him inside the porch.

There and then, Thomas told him everything. When he had finished, Crouch sat down in the little seat by the doorway, staring down at his old, scuffed shoes.

'By the Christ . . . had anyone else spun me such a tale, I would call him a madman.' He looked up. 'Yet it crossed my mind, at yesterday's gathering in the Horns, to wonder how Elyot had managed to search his lands so quickly – to the borders, he said.'

Thomas nodded. 'I would guess that's the first place to look.' He sighed. 'Yet Ragg won't lead any more search parties, at least not for the present . . .'

Crouch looked excited. 'Then you and I will go alone.'

Thomas showed his gratitude, but said: 'I'm better mounted, and can cover the ground quicker. You would aid me more by putting the matter before the rector. I promised that whatever I found out, I would tell him.'

Crouch hesitated. 'Do you truly think Elyot capable of having Henry killed?'

Thomas shook his head. 'I do not know.'

And soon after, they parted; Crouch went to seek out Richard Starling, while Thomas mounted the gelding and rode out of Lambourn once again. But instead of heading homewards, he turned downriver, towards Howes's farmstead.

The place was even more empty than when he had last been here, since the chickens had seemingly wandered off. Dismounting, he led the horse through the gateway, scanning the yard, house and byre. Nothing caught his attention. After putting the gelding in the byre, he walked uphill past the house, to Howes's pasture. To the east was the border with Bickington; on the north and west, empty Downlands. Shading his eyes against the sun, he gazed southwards across the valley. Below him was the ford; on the other side of the river, Elyot's lands stretched away to Cleeve Hill, and further west to

Coppington Hill above Lambourn wood. The tops of the trees were visible through the late-afternoon haze.

He stared absently at the distant hills. As good a view as any from up here, he thought, save that of a soaring bird. Somewhere in this valley, he sensed, lay the answers to all his questions: not only the matter of who killed Hubbard, but what had happened to Will Stubbs. He winced, trying to avoid the unpleasant thought that if Elyot were capable of having Howes abducted to seize his land, could he also have ordered the killing of poor Stubbs – merely for the sake of the man's tiny tumbledown cottage? Much as he distrusted Elyot, it seemed an unlikely, not to say a desperate course of action.

Mentally he shook himself; he was accomplishing nothing. He looked across the valley again, and tried to reason: if he was ordered to seize Henry Howes and spirit him away, where would he take him?

Absently he had been watching the birds . . . there was a moment when they seemed to veer suddenly away. And it was then that a movement from below caught his eye: a figure was walking along the path from Bickington, towards the ford.

The man had a small pack slung over his shoulder, and his gait was familiar. Unsure why he did so, Thomas moved to put the farmhouse between himself and the other, so as not to be seen. Then he made his way swiftly downhill, skirted the house and emerged near the gate, with a good view of the path.

It was Peter Hare the shepherd. Unaware that he was being observed, he trudged towards the ford, then splashed his way across. The river was so low at this time of year, the water barely covered his ankles. As Thomas watched, he began walking up the other side of the valley, slowly climbing Cleeve Hill.

Still Thomas watched, his eyes narrowing. The flocks Hare tended were all to the north and east of Howes's farm . . . to his knowledge there were no sheep on the other side of the river. Though there had been, in years past . . . keeping his eyes fixed on the shepherd, he saw him veer to the left, and finally halt not far from the hill's summit. And squinting into the sun, Thomas saw a tiny shape, hardly more than a slightly darker patch against the grass. There was some indistinct movement, before Hare disappeared.

But Thomas ran to the byre, caught up the gelding's reins and led the startled animal outside. The next moment he had swung himself into the saddle and was galloping through the gateway, down the path and across the ford, the horse's hooves throwing up a curtain of spray. He urged the spirited animal uphill, and in a very few minutes had reached what he guessed was an abandoned shepherd's hut, its roof sagging but walls intact . . . and even as he dismounted, Peter Hare came hurrying out, and saw that it was too late.

Hare stopped, tense with alarm, seemingly struggling to make some explanation. But his expression gave him away; and without a word Thomas strode past him, stooped low and peered inside the entrance to the hut. There was a muffled cry, and a sharp movement . . . and the next moment Thomas was on his knees, untying the blindfold and taking it from the face of Henry Howes, who lay on his back beside the wall, his hands and feet bound. Thomas tore at the clout with which the man was gagged and pulled it away . . . whereupon Howes shouted hoarsely – and just in time Thomas heeded the warning, and ducked. The costrel Hare had swung at him missed, but he was given no time for a second try. Thomas's fist shot upwards and cracked against his jaw, sending him staggering back from the doorway to sit heavily in the grass.

They stood in the sunshine, Howes stiff and sore, rubbing his tired limbs. There was a dark bruise on his lip, and another above his eye. He drank greedily from the costrel Thomas had taken from Hare – who was sitting on the ground nursing his jaw, looking up at them with mingled fear and anger. But the sexton turned away from him, and faced Thomas with a look of gratitude.

'I don't know what would've happened to me if you hadn't come along . . . I thought I should die.'

Thomas was rummaging inside Hare's pack, and found half a loaf of rye bread. He handed it to Howes, who grabbed it and took a bite. And thereafter, he told his story in between alternate mouthfuls of bread and pulls from the costrel.

129

'Saturday night it would've been . . . I never saw them; they must have waited till I went out to see to the beasts, and come at me from behind. Though I caught one a blow, I think . . . after that I was hooded and trussed, and slung over a mule . . .' He broke off suddenly, swinging round to face the man whom he now knew had been his jailer.

'You and I never liked each other,' he said, 'but this . . . How could you do such?'

Hare made no reply. For a moment he looked as if he would try to rise, but Thomas took a step forward. 'You stay down there, else I'll break your arm.'

He turned to Howes. 'He was following orders,' he said, and swung his gaze back to the shepherd. 'And what orders were they, precisely? To hold him here, bringing him enough to keep him alive, then release him? Let me guess when that might be: say – the day after Michaelmas?'

Hare drew a sharp breath, but his silence was enough. 'It was a goodly time for a kidnap, was it not?' Thomas went on, looking hard at the man. 'With the bell-making going on, and folk distracted with talk of plague – not to mention Will Stubbs's death. By Michaelmas, folk would have thought the sexton far away, or even dead . . . who would believe him, if he turned up and said he'd been held prisoner all the while – by men he couldn't even identify?' He shook his head. 'And by then it would be too late – for his lands would have been forfeit!'

He turned, for Howes too had taken a step towards the shepherd. 'You've guessed well, Master Finbow,' he breathed. 'Has someone spoken to you of a Statute Merchant? A clever lawyer's device for stripping a fellow of all he has – for helping a rich man get richer?'

Thomas nodded. 'There'll be time enough to tell of it,' he said. 'Meanwhile, can you walk down to Lambourn, or would you like to ride my horse?'

Howes shook his head. 'To feel the ground under my feet again would be a pleasure,' he replied. He jerked his head towards Hare. 'But what of him?'

'He's coming too,' Thomas told him. 'I guess Will Ragg will be interested in his tale.'

Howes frowned. 'Shouldn't we take him to Sam Hubbard?'

Thomas looked down at Peter Hare, but the man avoided his eye. He seemed to have lapsed into the kind of sullen silence that only an inquisitor could break. But Thomas's heart lifted in relief as he faced Howes again.

'Hubbard is dead,' he said. 'And some have been quick to accuse you of his murder, since your disappearance followed hard upon it. I confess at first I was one of them, and I ask your pardon.'

Howes gasped. 'Murder?' His jaw fell. 'And they suspect me . . . ?'

'Not for much longer,' Thomas assured him, and placed a hand upon his shoulder. 'Come, let's truss this one as he trussed you. I'll tie him to the saddle, and lead him down the hill. Then, if you'll let me stand you a mug, we can talk further . . .'

Howes hesitated, and his face clouded. 'Nay, I should get to the farm – I must see what's become of my beasts . . .'

Thomas took a breath, and prepared to tell him what was left to tell.

The gathering that evening did not take place in the Horns, but in Jonas Crouch's house. When he heard the news of Henry Howes's rescue, the clerk was so pleased he at once sent out for beer and a pint of sack. Now they crowded about his small table: Thomas, Henry Howes and Will Ragg. Word of what had happened had been taken to Richard Starling, who sent answer that he would come to the clerk's house after even-song.

There had been quite a stir in Lambourn when the reappearance of the sexton became known. At first, thinking of Hubbard's death, some assumed he had been arrested; when this turned out not to be the case, they called for his imprisonment. But Jonas Crouch had been quick in spreading the truth, especially to those he knew would go speedily to the Horns and spread it further. Satisfied, he had then gone home, to find that his back room was being used as a temporary lock-up. For there was Peter Hare, securely bound and seated on the floor, staring morosely down at it.

131

Now, Crouch faced Ragg anxiously across the table. 'He can't stay here,' he said for the third time. 'You must get word to the High Sheriff . . .'

Ragg shrugged. 'If he will come . . . in the meantime, I'll think of somewhere to hold our prisoner.' He turned to Thomas. 'You've been busy, have you not? Would you like to be acting constable?'

Thomas made a wry face and shook his head. 'But I'd like to help put an end to the puzzle we've all been caught up in . . .' he looked at Howes. 'Mayhap Henry can shed more light on it.'

Howes, having washed and put on borrowed clothes, was looking a deal better than when Thomas had found him. Though tired, and somewhat disoriented to discover that he had been a captive for almost three days, he was ready to tell his tale.

He admitted his debts had grown, until William Elyot offered to buy them all up. As a result Howes found he owed what was to him a huge sum: fifty-five pounds, to be repaid by Michaelmas, or his property would be forfeit. But from friends and a few relations he had been able to scrape enough together to repay much of it . . . His mistake, he now saw, had been to let Elyot know it.

'He never wanted the loan repaid,' the sexton said with a shake of his head. 'He wanted my land. What a fool I was, to think him a fine gentleman – it seems to me now he's been seeking to increase his borders all along . . . him and that grasping cove of a steward.'

He looked hard at Ragg. 'Is there no justice here?' he cried. 'Kidnap's a felony. Peter Hare should be made to talk, and name his accomplice – not to mention his paymaster . . .'

'Soft, Master Sexton . . .' Thomas half-raised a hand, and the others turned at once to him. 'Will you hear me, before you act?' Taking the silence for approval, he went on: 'Assuming the Statute stands, your property is safe until Michaelmas – another month. By then my master will have returned. When he hears of the matter I am sure he will help you; he is generous, and a respected knight of the shire – and well known to the High Sheriff.'

Howes nodded slowly. 'Yet, why wait?' he asked, where-upon Crouch, who had been doing some thinking of his own, spoke up.

'Some of us suspect that Hare and John Nightingale were bribed to say Will Stubbs's death was an accident,' he said. 'Yet it seems likely he was murdered.'

Howes gasped. 'And Hare was a party to it? You mean there is some link between that and Hubbard's death?'

'If there is, I haven't been able to find it.' Thomas was frowning to himself. 'Yet if we scare the shepherd a little, mayhap he will spill his tale.'

Ragg's expression was grim. 'Why not let me persuade him?' he asked, prompting a shocked exclamation from Jonas Crouch.

'That would never do, Master Will! We are a law-abiding parish, and we will act accordingly . . .'

Then he started, as the door flew open. All turned to see Richard Starling enter abruptly, wearing a plain cape over his black clothes. Behind him came his churchwarden, John Wilmott.

There was a tense silence, before the men rose to make room. Wilmott indicated at once that he would remain on his feet, and stood with a frosty expression, seemingly as unwilling to be under Crouch's roof as the clerk was to be his host. But Starling surprised everyone by going quickly to Henry Howes and taking him by the shoulders.

'God be praised – you are returned to us safe and sound . . .' there was a pained look on his face. 'Could you not have told me of your plight?'

The sexton was embarrassed. 'Indeed, sir,' he began. 'Mayhap I should have . . .'

But Starling shook his head. 'I have been remiss, in ignoring the needs of those closest to me.' There was a moment, before he seemed to collect himself.

'Well, masters,' he said with an effort. 'Are we to speak plainly with each other now, and see what must be done?'

Fourteen

Peter Hare was brought unceremoniously into the room by Will Ragg, who shoved a stool forward and bade him sit. The man's hands were still tied, but now they shook visibly as he faced what looked like an interrogation – and one sanctioned by God. For as Richard Starling fixed him with his fierce, unblinking eye the man quailed visibly, and his composure broke at once.

'I'm but a poor shepherd, sir . . .' he muttered, 'who has no choice but to do as he's bid . . . in a few years I'll be too old to work! I'll be one of they that sit like a row of cracked pots outside the Horns every day—'

'Silence!' Starling's tone held no sympathy. 'You rogue – you have committed a grave felony against a loyal servant of my church. You will be handed over to the proper authorities as soon as occasion permits, but meanwhile you may redeem yourself by a mote – and no more – in telling all you know!'

Hare gulped and looked around. Howes and Crouch stood to one side in silence, Thomas and Will Ragg closer. John Wilmott was staring imperiously at him, seemingly intent upon matching the rector's angry gaze.

'All I know . . . ?' The shepherd paused. ''Tis very little, sir. Ralph Stainbank ordered me and another to take the sexton . . .' He skilfully avoided Howes's gaze. 'To seize him after dark, and bind him and hood him, and conceal him somewhere, he cared not where so long as none would find him before Michaelmas . . .'

'This we know already,' Starling snapped. 'These men have told me the sorry tale – I look to you to add something new.'

'What can I add, sir?' Hare threw back in a tone of desperation. 'We but did as we were told . . . no man denies

134

Stainbank, who knows him as well as I do!'

Thomas caught the rector's eye. 'May I put a few questions, sir?' he asked. The others stirred, but somewhat to their surprise Starling nodded. To Hare's discomfort Thomas picked up another stool, plonked it directly in front of him and sat so that there was barely a yard between them.

'Who killed the dog?' he asked. 'You or Bedell?'

Hare saw the look on Henry Howes's face, and drew a quick breath. 'Bedell,' he answered. 'He's a cruel man!'

Thomas shook his head. 'I warned you when we last spoke,' he said quietly, 'about giving false testimony.'

Hare blinked, but the colour was rising to his face. 'If you know so much, then why ask?' he cried.

'Yet I do ask,' Thomas told him, and waited.

Hare swallowed. 'The dog was making a foul racket,' he said after a moment. 'Bedell tried to kick it away, and it jumped up and bit him. I had a poniard . . .'

Henry Howes stiffened, but kept his control. After a moment he moved aside and sat down heavily.

Thomas kept his eyes on Peter Hare. 'There's a question I asked you, up on the hill above Betterdown,' he said quietly. 'I'll ask it again: who came to you the morning after you found Will Stubbs's body, and bade you change your tale?'

Hare was silent, but the other men saw his fear now – indeed, they could smell it. The man swallowed audibly. 'I know not what you speak of . . .'

Thomas leaned closer. 'Was it merely a bribe – or were you threatened?'

Sweat stood on Hare's brow. 'I found Stubbs's body lying on the ground, with his head split,' he began, but Thomas leaned closer still.

'You told William Elyot the old man was bound to a tree with a rope – yet within a matter of hours you were denying the rope existed.'

Hare met his eye. The silence in the room was so profound, the sound of blind Dickon's harp could be heard from the inn. Finally Hare's mouth twisted, and his spirits seemed to drop even as his body sagged. 'There was a rope, and he was sitting up against a tree, bound to it,' he admitted. 'That's all I know . . .'

'It is not.' Starling had started forward. 'You have not told who made you change your tale!'

'John Nightingale did,' Hare said in a dull voice. 'He gave me a gold sovereign to say Stubbs was on the ground, and had likely cracked his head on a root, or some such.'

There was a collective exhalation of breath from the watchers. 'Why would he do that?' Thomas asked sharply, but the other merely shook his head.

'I didn't ask! Is it not best that the churchwarden be buried like he was – dead from an accident? He was even older than I . . . What man wants folk raking over his death with inquests and such . . . ?'

But Starling was furious. 'Wretch!' he shouted, and for a moment it looked as if he would strike the man. 'To lie in such a manner, and conceal the gravest of crimes – you will hang for what you have done, and not a soul will weep!' He turned to Thomas. 'It seems I should ask your pardon,' he said stiffly. 'You have been ploughing a lonely furrow indeed.'

Thomas met his gaze. 'Truth will out, sir,' he replied, then glanced at Will Ragg. 'You'd best get hold of Nightingale.'

Ragg nodded grimly. 'I will – and for now, we will use Hubbard's empty house for a lock-up!' He turned to Starling. 'The High Sheriff must be told, sir . . .'

Starling gestured impatiently. 'Do what you must.'

Ragg went out quickly, and suddenly the rector grew brisk. Watching him, Thomas sensed some emotion that did not sit with his earlier manner. Catching the man's eye, he spoke up.

'I would like to question this fellow further, sir,' he said, indicating Hare. And without waiting for approval, he faced the prisoner once again. 'Stubbs's isn't the only murder Lambourn has seen in the past week,' he said. 'Samuel Hubbard's was the other.'

Crouch and Howes exchanged glances. But Wilmott, who had kept silent from the moment he arrived, now spoke.

'Is the falconer to act as inquisitor all night?'

The other men tensed, but Thomas turned and met the man's eye. 'I would be glad to turn the matter over to you, Master

Churchwarden,' he said. 'Though I would guess the questioning might take a different turn.'

Wilmott stared. 'What do you mean?'

'I mean there are a lot of things still puzzling me concerning Will Stubbs's death,' Thomas began, then saw the look on Starling's face.

'Enough . . .' The rector appeared agitated. 'We leap from one matter to another. Let us wait until Nightingale is brought to answer for his deeds. Then—' He broke off suddenly, for Peter Hare let out a cry, somewhere between a sob and a shout of laughter. As all eyes turned upon him, he raised his head and fixed Thomas with a baleful look.

'Puzzle away, falconer!' he cried bitterly. 'For ye were always one to meddle . . . Have ye not uncovered enough to sate yourself?'

Thomas frowned. 'Now you voice it, I don't believe I have.' He threw a glance at Starling, who made no response, then looked hard at Hare. 'What do you know of Hubbard's death?'

Hare snorted; and it seemed that Starling's mention of his impending fate had now sunk home. He would hang, and he no longer cared. He merely fixed Thomas with a look of hatred.

'I know naught of it!' he shouted. 'There were plenty who'd cause to vent their spleen on the constable . . . that fat-bellied sot – go look in his muster-book!'

And with that, he let fly an oath and spat directly at Thomas – a gob of spittle that mercifully fell short, and landed on his jerkin. Stifling an oath of his own, Thomas stood up abruptly and turned to the others.

'Who'll help me take him away?' he asked.

Crouch and Howes stepped forward. But at that moment the door opened and Ragg appeared, somewhat out of breath. He looked at each in turn, then blurted the news.

'Nightingale . . . he's gone, and none knows where.'

Dusk was falling as Will Ragg marched Peter Hare to the constable's empty house, bound him and left him in the lean-to among the flagons of cider. He would look in on the prisoner at first light. Then he, Thomas and Crouch hunted through Hubbard's belongings for the Lambourn Muster Book.

Fortunately it was easy to find, being the only volume in the house apart from an old prayer-book which looked as if it had been unopened since the constable's boyhood. Standing close together, they leafed through the ancient, leather-bound register by the light of a stub of candle. Outside they could hear voices from the square, where folk were gathering to talk over the events. Some had gone to the church to see the rescued sexton, but Henry Howes was not there. Weary from his ordeal, as well as from the telling of it, he had begged leave from the rector to go back to his farm.

The disappearance of John Nightingale had gone unnoticed until Ragg went to seek him. The landlord had been at the Horns earlier, though none could recall exactly when they had last seen him. But Thomas guessed that soon after Peter Hare was brought in tied behind a horse the man had vanished. For the present, however, he and Ragg agreed there were more pressing matters to deal with than attempting to hunt for Nightingale in the gathering dark.

'There.' Crouch jabbed a finger at the last page of the book on which entries had been made. It referred to the August muster, called for last Sunday – the one Hubbard had never conducted. Peering down the short list of names, which remained unchecked, the clerk's brow creased.

'We saw these men in the square on the Sabbath,' he muttered. 'I cannot believe any of them knew Hubbard was already dead, any more than we did. Though it's no secret some cursed him for pressing them into service with Norris . . .'

Suddenly he started. 'Nay – he wouldn't . . .'

'Wouldn't what?' Thomas peered at the book's dog-eared page, and saw the last name on the list:

John Tolworthy, miller.

He glanced up at the others, and saw Crouch had turned pale. 'By the Lord . . .' he breathed, 'that old enmity . . .'

Thomas looked at Ragg, who was grim-faced.

'The two of them had a falling out, long ago,' he said, gazing down at the miller's name. 'Sam Hubbard could be a hard fellow at times. When he'd taken too much drink, he'd often threaten to put Tolworthy on the muster roll. Though

138

surely the parish would have excused him – there's no other mill within five miles.'

But Thomas's mind was racing. 'His family: they could not thrive if he was sent away to fight, likely to return maimed or sick – if he returned at all . . .'

Crouch was appalled. 'You made haste to accuse Henry, and you were wrong!' he cried. 'Now you leap to point the finger at the miller! He has his faults, none would deny it – but to murder the constable?' He shook his head fiercely.

Thomas glanced at him, then at Ragg. 'We'd best go, anyway . . .'

After a moment, the blacksmith nodded.

It was almost dark by the time the two of them had ridden the mile to Uplambourn. The mill's sails showed stark against the skyline, and a light burned within. Quickly they dismounted, and Ragg called John Tolworthy's name. Startled night-birds shrieked and flew away.

There were muffled sounds from inside the mill, but no one appeared. Ragg walked closer to the heavy door, and called again. 'John – it's Will Ragg. Come out!'

Another moment; then the door creaked open, but it was not the miller who appeared. Instead the tall figure of his wife emerged, carrying a lantern. 'What can you want at this hour, Will?' she asked, coming forward. Raising the lantern, she peered at Thomas. 'And why is he here?'

'We must speak with your husband, mistress,' Thomas said.

But Ann Tolworthy avoided his eye. 'Will . . . ?'

Ragg had looked increasingly uncomfortable on the ride upstream from Lambourn; the miller was a friend. 'Why won't he come forth, Ann?' he asked. 'Is it not better he answers to me than face a party of sheriff's men?'

She started. 'Nay, Will – do not say such . . .'

There was a muffled shout from inside the mill, followed by a cry. Ann Tolworthy's hand went to her mouth, but at once the door flew wide and a large figure appeared. Thomas and Ragg tensed, but the man lumbered away towards the dark bulk of the storehouse. There was the sound of a door being wrenched open, then slammed.

It had taken only seconds. Thomas looked towards the store-house as Ragg wavered, unsure which way to turn – but there came another sound. All of them looked to the mill as John Tolworthy himself came out.

His wife moved towards him, but the miller stayed her. Taking her arm, he drew her aside, then walked forward heavily to face Will Ragg. 'Well,' he said, 'I would guess you're not here for a night's bat-fowling.'

Ragg wore a sombre look. 'I wish to God I wasn't here at all, John.'

Tolworthy gave a sigh, and both men saw the pain he bore. With a swift glance at Thomas, Ragg spoke again.

'Is there something you would tell us? About Sam Hubbard's death?'

Ann Tolworthy gave a sob and started forward, but with sudden anger her husband flicked his hand, as if to drive her back. He eyed Ragg grimly. 'Do you accuse me?' he asked.

Thomas took a step. 'If I accused you, would that help?'

The miller's face was gaunt in the flickering light of the lantern. 'There was bad blood between me and Hubbard,' he said finally. 'I'd put up with his scorn long enough . . .' He broke off, feeling Thomas's gaze upon him.

'You're lying,' Thomas said.

The man drew breath sharply, as did Will Ragg.

Now Ann Tolworthy darted forward, weeping. 'God's mercy,' she implored, 'can't you men ride off and leave us be?'

But Ragg was looking from Thomas to the miller and back. 'What do you mean?' he asked harshly.

Thomas met the miller's eye, but there was sympathy in his gaze. 'A man will do anything to protect his child, will he not?' he asked quietly. 'Even go to the gallows for him . . .'

Tolworthy stepped forward in agitation. 'Nay – you're mistaken! It's me you seek . . . I killed Hubbard, and I'll make full confession of it! That's all you need!'

Then he glanced aside, as did the others. For the miller's wife had sunk to her knees in the grass. As the men watched she bowed her head, weeping softly to herself.

'Think, master . . .' Thomas urged, coming close enough to

feel Tolworthy's breath on his face. 'What good will that do your wife, and your other children? Had you been pressed into service and sent to France you might have returned – but none returns from the gibbet.'

Tolworthy heaved a great sigh, as if his heart would burst. 'Falconer . . . talk no more of it . . .'

But Ann Tolworthy cried out. 'He's right! You think you're the only one to say what will be? The devil take the boy – for has he not done so already?'

And she was on her feet, the lantern swinging wildly as she pushed between her husband and the other two.

'Take him if you must – but be careful.' She pointed towards the storehouse. 'For when he's angry, he has the strength of four men . . .' She swung her gaze towards her husband. 'Let him be our sacrifice!' she shouted. 'For I'll not see you hang in his place! Tell them now, how it was . . .' She had mastered herself, and was gripping his arm – but the miller's head had drooped on to his broad chest, and he made no sound.

Ann Tolworthy swung round to face Ragg. 'Edward's terrified every time his father goes away,' she said. 'It's why John seldom leaves the mill . . . We feared he would be sent to fight for Norris. Hubbard was waiting for the chance to get John on the muster roll . . . He always hated him, since John refused him a loan all those years back . . .' She paused. 'Edward was beside himself . . . When we found him gone on Saturday night, we knew. John followed him, all the way to Hubbard's . . .'

'Nay!' Her husband took her roughly by the shoulders. 'You need not tell . . .' He broke off and faced Will Ragg. 'It was not murder!' he cried. 'Hubbard was drunk, sitting in his orchard . . . Edward took hold of him, started beating him . . . He wanted only to make him release me from that damned muster roll!'

He paused, his head moving helplessly from side to side. 'I tried to stop him, but he's too strong . . . has been since he was full grown. By the time I got him by the neck and dragged him away, Hubbard was sore hurt, but he was still alive – and sober. He even got to his feet . . . then he fell over. Mayhap his heart gave out . . .'

141

'So he was dead before you lifted him into the tree,' Thomas finished.

After a moment, the miller gave a nod. 'I made Edward help me . . . I thought to make it seem as if Hubbard hanged himself. God knows, there's few will mourn him.' He threw an anxious glance at the storehouse. 'What will you do?'

Ragg wore a helpless look. 'What choice have I? Some know where we are gone . . .'

He gestured to Thomas, who glanced towards the storehouse. But Ann Tolworthy came forward and spoke in a voice so low, he could barely hear.

'Nay – let me go.'

They rode downstream in silence. To their surprise, once his mother had gone into the storehouse and spoken with him, Edward Tolworthy offered no resistance, but came as meekly as a lamb. He rode Will Ragg's horse, a huge hunched figure in the saddle, his big hands bound before him. Ragg walked alongside his prisoner while Thomas rode in front, with as heavy a heart as the rest. Though Samuel Hubbard's killer was found, neither took any satisfaction in what they had accomplished. Nor were they cheered by the discovery that Hubbard's death had no connection after all with that of Will Stubbs.

John Tolworthy had insisted on accompanying them, and sat solidly upon his old horse at the rear. He had said nothing as they rode away from the mill, nor had he looked back at his wife, or the younger children crowded about the doorway. But Thomas had looked, and his spirits sank to see the children, silent and forlorn, watching their brother being taken away.

They passed the dim lights of Uplambourn, and darkness closed in as they followed the stream on their left, a mere trickle in the moonlight. On their right, the Downs rose. Nightbirds called, and once a great long-eared owl flew overhead, but no one noticed. The minds of Thomas and Will Ragg were bent on the unpleasant future that awaited their charge when he eventually came to trial; no less unpleasant was Ragg's knowledge that in the meantime he would be expected to be the boy's jailer – if this hulking youth who had beaten a man to death could indeed be called a boy . . .

142

There was a scampering in the grass ahead, and Thomas looked up to see rabbits leaping away into the dark. Briefly he thought of Mary Pegg in the old warrener's hut, miles away to the west . . . The next moment he jerked on the rein, drawing the startled gelding to a halt and looking round.

He had heard a grunt of pain, followed by a shriek of fear. The first sound came from Ragg: he was on his knees, dizzy from the blow he had received. Standing over him was John Tolworthy, who unheard by the others had dismounted, then run forward and cracked the blacksmith over the head. But even as Thomas jumped from the stirrup, he saw Tolworthy grab the reins of Edward's mount. It was the boy who had cried out in fear, and he did so again as the knife flashed in the moonlight. But his father sliced through Edward's bonds, then with enormous strength shoved him out of the saddle. The boy fell on his back in the grass.

John Tolworthy whirled round as Thomas approached, the cold light of determination in his eyes. 'Let him go, falconer,' he muttered. 'Or I'll crush the life from you.'

Thomas faced him, hearing Ragg behind grunting with pain as he tried to stand. Then he was aware of Edward Tolworthy scrambling to his feet a few yards away, whimpering.

'Faither! Don't 'ee leave me here!'

'Get you gone!' The miller's shout was harsh. 'Run west, to the border, else they mean to hang you!'

The boy yelped in fear. 'Nay – they shall not!'

Thomas met Tolworthy's gaze, even as he felt the man's anguish. 'How far would he get?' he asked. 'How would he live, on his own . . .'

'Don't waste your words!' The miller crouched, his barrel chest heaving. 'You try and stop him, I will down you, falconer – and you will not rise again!'

It was no idle boast. What would he not do, Thomas asked himself, if his own child's life were at stake . . . ?

There came a voice from behind. Will Ragg had got painfully to his feet. 'Let the boy go,' he said.

Thomas looked round. Ragg had a hand to his head, and blood showed in the moonlight. But there was no rancour in his gaze; only weariness, and understanding.

143

'Do you wish to see him hang?' he asked.

Thomas hesitated, then shook his head. There was a moment, as all three men eyed each other.

'Then let it be as I told you back there.' Tolworthy jerked a thumb over his shoulder. 'Say that I killed Hubbard . . .'

'Nay.' Ragg shook his head. 'I will not see you hang either, John, for you have hurt no one. Save me, that is.'

He managed a grim smile. There was a moment, before slowly the miller straightened up. He turned to his son, who stood watching wide-eyed, lank hair falling across his face.

'You must go, Edward,' he said hoarsely. 'Travel west, and follow the first river you find . . . follow it downstream until you come to a mill, and find a mill family that will give you a home.'

He glanced at the other men, who saw his anguish. Then, seeing Edward still motionless and staring, he grew angry.

'Go, you . . .' Shoving Ragg's horse out of the way, he stumbled towards his son. The boy eyed him, whimpering.

'I don't want you!' Tolworthy shouted. 'You have no family here! Walk till sunrise and keep walking, and never return!'

And as the other two watched, he raised his hand as if to strike the terrified boy. But Edward backed away, tears welling from his eyes. For a moment he looked as if he would plead with his father; but at last he turned, then without looking back lurched away. Briefly they saw his huge body disappearing uphill, before the night swallowed him.

Fifteen

The Wednesday morning dawned warm and sunny, and a small crowd drifted towards the churchyard of St Michael's to witness the appearance of the new tenor bell. But the talk was muted; and glances strayed towards Samuel Hubbard's house, where the shepherd Peter Hare was held prisoner. Word of John Nightingale's disappearance was also on everyone's lips. Yet though Lambourn remained mercifully free of the plague that stalked southern England this summer, the fear of infection was such that none seemed willing to ride out and take word to the sheriff. Hence Will Ragg, only too readily accepted as rightful constable, was left to uphold the law. His only ally seemed to be Thomas Finbow, the falconer from Petbury.

Thomas had spent the night at Jonas Crouch's house on a pallet on the floor, after he and Ragg returned empty-handed from their excursion upriver. In the morning they met in Crouch's garden, where the little clerk tended his goshawk, and agreed that since Richard Starling was the only man with any authority, albeit of the ecclesiastical kind, they would put the matter before him.

Responsibility weighed heavy upon Will Ragg's round shoulders as he stood in the sunshine, watching Crouch take the hawk upon his wrist. 'Nightingale's not my concern,' he muttered. 'Whatever he's done, I've said I'll lead no more search parties. Let Lord Norris decide how to act – if word ever gets to him.'

Thomas said nothing. The two of them had spoken little about the events of last night; yet the shared knowledge of what had happened had brought them closer. Their report was that Edward Tolworthy, wanted for the suspected murder of

145

Samuel Hubbard, had escaped across the border into Wiltshire, where Ragg had no powers to pursue him. John Tolworthy had been allowed to return home. Neither Thomas nor Ragg spoke of the miller's being with them on the path from Uplambourn; nor was Ragg inclined to mention the man's involvement in his son's crime. And as far as the blacksmith was concerned, that was the end of the matter.

'I've a forge to see to,' he told Thomas, not for the first time. 'Mayhap you and our friend – ' this with a jerk of his head towards Crouch – 'will go to the rector.' He hesitated, then added somewhat sourly: 'For my part, I've seen enough of Master Starling for the present.'

Thomas nodded absently, his thoughts elsewhere. Not only was he neglecting his own work, leaving all to young Ned, but there was the matter of Howes's kidnapping, and William Elyot's part in it. But what preyed on his mind most was that, despite all that had happened, he seemed no nearer to finding out who killed William Stubbs, or why. Was that not what he had been charged with, in the first instance?

He waited for Crouch to finish fussing over his hawk, then the two of them walked to the church. From the bell-yard came voices and sounds of activity. But as they neared the door someone called out; John Wilmott, at his most brusque, was striding towards them.

'I expected you sooner,' he snapped. 'What have you been about?'

Crouch bristled at once. 'We do not all have time to gawp at the bell-making,' he retorted. 'There are matters of import to relate . . .'

But Wilmott was gesturing impatiently. 'The rector awaits you by the bell-pit . . .' He stopped. 'What matters of import?'

Thomas had never understood the causes of the church-warden's hostility; but now he caught a look of anxiety in the man's eyes. Not for the first time, he sensed that Wilmott knew more about recent events than he chose to tell.

'Mayhap there are some *you* have yet to relate,' he said.

Wilmott frowned at him. 'If that were so, falconer, I would not share my confidence with you!'

146

Crouch threw him a look, and stalked off towards the bell-yard.

Richard Starling was standing by the chancel wall, watching the founders at work. As the others approached, he nodded a greeting. 'This is a momentous day for St Michael's,' he said. 'Behold, our new bell.'

They looked upon the focus of all the excitement. The bell-pit itself was now empty. But beside it, on trestles, lay the new tenor bell, almost five feet long. Its core of clay and loam had been broken out to reveal the dull-yellow metal of the interior; now what remained of its outer cope was being chipped away. Gradually, the golden bell was being revealed.

The founders had been busy. Broken clay from the mould lay everywhere. The noise of hammers echoed in the warm air, as Simon Goodchild and his son, surrounded by an attentive crowd, tapped skilfully at the cope, sending shards of clay flying along with clouds of dust. Alice Goodchild worked at the bell's mouth, washing it with rags soaked in water. At the bell's crown the great moulded loops – the canons – with which it would be raised and hung in the tower had already been cleaned.

And then all at once, or so it seemed, there was nothing more to remove. A hush fell as Simon held up a hand; Edmund and Alice stopped work and stood back. The bell was ready.

The folk of Lambourn stared at the wondrous creation, its surface not yet buffed but already glinting in the sunshine. Barely a week ago, they had dug the pit and built the rude furnace. They had watched the old, cracked bell broken up, and its shards fed to the fire along with flattened mugs and broken cooking pots. They had seen the river of smoking, glittering metal channelled along the ground and into the mould; had helped to choke off the flow and tamp down the earth. And in the days since, the metal had cooled and hardened to form the shape that now lay before them. It seemed almost a miracle.

Thomas gazed in silence, as moved as the rest. Finally Richard Starling walked forward, and the crowd parted to let him approach the bell-founder. Crouch, Thomas and Wilmott followed.

'You have worked well.' The rector was subdued. He met the gaze of Simon Goodchild, impassive as always, who merely inclined his head gravely. 'The inscription,' Starling added. 'We must speak of that next . . .'

Again the founder nodded. 'We will clean the bell thoroughly,' he said, 'and ready him for it.' He turned to indicate a structure that loomed overhead: a jib crane fashioned from heavy beams, and rigged to a winch. By this means the bell would be raised up to the tower.

'First we will lift him off the trestles, and ye shall hear the note he makes,' Goodchild said. 'Will you wait a while, Master Rector?'

Starling hesitated, and caught Crouch's eye. 'I must speak with my fellows,' he replied. 'But I will return soon, and hear it for myself.' Then, as the founder indicated his agreement, he turned and led the way to the church.

A short time later they stood in the vestry, Starling and Wilmott listening in silence as Thomas gave a fairly full account of what happened at Uplambourn – and a somewhat less full account of what had followed on the return journey. When he had finished there came a muttered exclamation from John Wilmott, whose face had darkened as the tale unfolded. But seeing the look on Starling's face, he held his peace.

'May God have mercy on the miller's boy,' Starling intoned. Thomas and Crouch, having expected him to be angry, exchanged looks. But their surprise was soon to increase, on hearing the pronouncement that followed.

'I have spent a long night in prayer and contemplation,' the rector told them. 'Since I cannot get word to my bishop, I have sought guidance from a higher authority – the one above all others. And He has given me the answer I sought.'

The others waited. Thomas caught Wilmott's eye, and thought he detected a hint of satisfaction. But he had no time to ponder it.

'My place is here, and my duty is to the church,' Starling continued. 'I have strayed too far already into secular affairs, these past days . . . The sins of all my parishioners must be addressed, not merely those that transgress the law.'

Beside him, Thomas felt rather than heard Crouch suppress a gasp of dismay. Wilmott remained silent.

'Hence, I will oversee the raising of the new bell, and the consecration of it,' Starling said. 'Then when the sexton has returned to his work, and a second churchwarden has been appointed – another matter which has been neglected – we may return to something approaching our normal round of duties.'

Sensing that Thomas was about to speak, he stayed him with a faint look of disapproval. 'The constable must deal with the crimes that have been perpetrated here,' he said. 'You may inform your master and the High Sheriff when you are able. Let the proper authorities order the fate of men like Hare, and the fugitive Tolworthy . . .' He paused. 'You did well to uncover the matter, Master Finbow, and I am as relieved as any to let poor Hubbard be buried in our church. But meantime . . .'

'Meantime, there's the matter of the kidnapping of your sexton,' Thomas put in, controlling his anger. 'Not to say the murder of Will Stubbs . . .'

'No!' Starling was rapidly assuming his imperious manner. 'You will not speak thus, without evidence . . .'

'You heard Hare's evidence yourself, of how he was bribed by John Nightingale,' Thomas persisted. 'Who has promptly fled – does that not seem a mite strange to you?'

'I have given my judgement!' Starling shouted, his patience gone. 'Pursue these matters if you will – but I warn you, you have no authority here in Lambourn. And any breach of the peace in my parish will not be tolerated.'

Thomas drew a breath and held back his response; something that he found doubly difficult when he saw the smug expression on Wilmott's face. But then, meeting his eye, the rector was disconcerted to see Thomas relax suddenly. Watched by all of them, he even gave a smile of compliance.

'Well, sir,' he said at last, 'you have given your judgement. Mayhap I should not have expected you to soil your hands further with worldly matters.'

Starling's eyes flashed, but Thomas was already leaving. 'That lonely furrow you spoke of . . . I will plough it yet,' he said. 'Else I too may suffer from sleepless nights, before I reach its end.' Then he strode out of the vestry, his boots ringing on the flagstones.

Jonas Crouch faced Starling. 'I thought we were to have no more deception,' he said, with a look more of regret than of anger. And before the other could speak, he followed Thomas out.

In the bell-yard, Simon and Edmund Goodchild, with the help of other men, were raising the bell upright by means of the crane. Thomas had paused to watch, but as Crouch drew near he saw that his friend's mind was elsewhere.

'Whatever you decide to do, I'm with you,' he said.

Thomas favoured him with a smile. 'You have plenty to busy you here . . . I had best ride out alone.'

Crouch frowned. 'Ride where?'

'To Bickington – where else?'

'And do what?' The little clerk's brow had creased. 'Accuse the principal landowner hereabouts of kidnap—'

'Not to mention deception,' Thomas added. 'And mayhap more . . .'

Crouch shook his head. 'Leave it until Sir Robert returns,' he urged. 'Or you are likely to find yourself at the mercy of Elyot's lawyers yourself.'

'You forget we've got a witness,' Thomas replied. 'The kidnap victim.'

'Even so . . .' Crouch trailed off, watching the great tenor bell rising off its trestles. Onlookers murmured their approval as the massive object, which must have weighed half a ton, swung free. Since there was as yet no clapper fixed, however, it made no clang. So there was a further flurry of excitement among the watchers as Simon Goodchild stepped forward and with a grand gesture hit the bell's sound-bow with his hammer.

The strike-note rang out, deep and melodious; and the effect was both instantaneous and remarkable. Birds squawked and flew from the treetops. Across the village and at their work upon the Downs, folk stopped in their tracks as the sound carried; as far, some might have said, as the mill at Uplambourn. The tenor bell of St Michael's, newly born, had spoken for the first time.

There was a look of awe on Crouch's face. 'Indeed,' he murmured, 'it is a maiden bell.'

From the corner of his eye Thomas saw the narrow priest's door open, and glanced round to see Starling appear to gaze upon the bell. Then without further ado he went off to saddle the gelding. Within a short time he was clattering over the Lambourn bridge.

The sun was still climbing, and the Downs rose at his left, with Petbury a mere three miles away eastwards. But Thomas had no time to dwell on thoughts of home, of Nell and of his work. Instead he let his mount have free rein to gallop down-river, its mane flying, both horse and rider glad to feel the breeze in their faces. Soon he had reached the ford, and was slowing as he neared Howes's farmstead.

He reined in, uncertain whether to speak with the sexton before riding on to Bickington. Since the meeting with Starling, and the earlier conversation with Will Ragg, Thomas had formed a resolve to act alone, and report only to Sir Robert upon his return. His master and Sir John Norris would know what to do. He was about to touch heels to the gelding when there came a distant shout. He looked up to see Howes waving, striding down from his yard towards the gate. He waved in return and dismounted.

The sexton looked a different man from when Thomas had last seen him. His smile was warm as he opened the gate. 'I don't believe I've yet thanked you fully for what you did,' he began, then, seeing Thomas's face, frowned slightly. 'You're troubled . . . Will you walk up to the house, and take a little breakfast with me?'

Thomas shook his head. 'I have business that will not wait,' he answered.

Howes's frown deepened. 'You're riding to Bickington? And before Thomas could answer, he stepped forward. 'I would not have you steep yourself further in the troubles between me and Elyot,' he said. 'I mean to speak with the rector today, and ask him to call upon the bishop. I will have justice!'

Thomas made a wry face. 'I fear the rector may disappoint you, Master Henry,' he said. 'Henceforth he intends to spend all his efforts on the church, and leave the law to others.'

151

Howes started. 'He said this to you?'

Thomas nodded. 'It seems to me that justice has taken a leave of absence from the West Downs this summer. I know not how you will get redress for what was done . . . indeed, what is to stop the same thing happening to you again – or worse?'

The sexton drew a deep breath. 'That thought has occurred to me,' he muttered. 'I sleep with a sharp billhook close to my pallet . . .' He broke off suddenly. 'May I ask what you thought to accomplish, by going alone?'

Thomas shrugged. 'It was Elyot who drew me here in the first place,' he said. 'He wished to solve the business of Will Stubbs's death, or so he told my master. I will tell him that not only have I failed to come near to the nub of that, but I will be giving my master a full account of all that has happened. That ought to shake his feathers.' He paused. 'Or, let us say I merely want to see the sneer wiped from Stainbank's face.'

Howes nodded grimly. 'I too would like to see that.'

'Then let me ride on,' Thomas said. 'And if you wish to help, when you go into Lambourn tell Will Ragg what I do.'

But Howes surprised him by reaching out and taking the gelding's bridle. 'Will you not reflect, Master Thomas? You have seen what Elyot is capable of . . . He could have you seized and held on some pretext or other. Stainbank would have no difficulty concocting a charge. You have no powers . . .'

To his surprise, Thomas's composure broke. 'If I'm moved to reflect on anything,' he said sharply, 'it's the way folk of every station have been telling me for the past week that I've no authority! I am grown heartily sick of it – now pray let go my horse!'

Howes dropped his hand, but met his eye. 'Then at the least you will need a witness,' he said.

Slowly, Thomas relaxed. 'And what would you hope to accomplish by coming with me?'

Howes managed a grim smile. 'I intend to claim compensation for the killing of my dog.'

The sexton owned no horse of his own, so they walked the short mile together, Thomas leading the gelding. As they passed through the imposing gates of the manor a servant in livery hurried from the paddock to challenge them, before recognizing the Petbury falconer.

'We have business with Master Elyot,' Thomas told him, 'and it will not wait.' After a moment the man nodded and came forward to take the gelding's rein, but Thomas waved him away. 'I'll walk him to the stables,' he said. Then a thought struck him. 'Is Hugh Bedell close by?'

The man stiffened, then shook his head and made as if to go. Whereupon Henry Howes took a step towards him.

'I wish to see him too,' he said. 'Where might I find him?'

The servant would have ignored him; then he saw the look in the sexton's eye. 'Bedell's no longer here,' he said quickly. 'He has left my master's service.'

Thomas threw a wry look at Howes. 'Somewhat convenient . . .'

The servant hurried off and disappeared round the wall of the stable yard. The wide grey bulk of the house was before them. But some minutes later, having tethered the horse, they found their way to the door blocked by none other than Ralph Stainbank. Behind him two or three liveried men loitered, as if ready for trouble.

'Falconer . . . ?' Today the steward was dressed in a smart cherry-red doublet and hat; and his smile was very thin indeed. 'What do you want here?'

Thomas indicated Henry Howes. 'I think you already know . . .' he began, but the other returned his gaze with a bland stare.

'Let me save you a deal of waiting,' he said. 'Master Elyot has gone to Newbury on business . . . Further, he has let it be known he has no further need of you. His hawk is healed, and you were well paid for your services.'

Thomas kept expression from his face. 'You know my visit has naught to do with falcons,' he said.

As if to affirm it Howes took a step towards Stainbank, so abruptly that the other flinched. 'There's a matter of a kidnapping to be addressed,' he began, but at once the steward raised a warning hand, and his face was filled with contempt.

153

'Have a care, Master Howes, else you may find yourself in even deeper water than you are already.'

Howes bridled, but Thomas threw him a warning look before facing Stainbank again. 'Your master is within,' he said. 'His horses are all in the stable – and more, I do not think he has the courage to ride as far as Newbury while the infection rages downriver . . .'

Stainbank drew a sharp breath, and made a quick gesture with his hand. At once the Bickington servants stepped forward. Each looked to Thomas to be of similar stamp to Hugh Bedell – presumably the toughest men Elyot had at his call.

But to their surprise, Thomas smiled at them.

'Well, masters,' he said, 'shall we have a bout here, and spill blood within sight of the house? Mistress Jane would have a fine view from her chamber.'

The men started, and looked uncertainly at Stainbank. But the steward's face had taken on a sickly expression. Along with Howes, he followed Thomas's gaze upwards to the nearest first-floor window. There indeed was the lady of Bickington, staring down at them with a look of fury. At once she vanished from sight, but Thomas knew his point had struck home. Seizing the moment, he leaned close to Stainbank, so that the man must summon all his nerve not to back away.

'Conduct me to your master,' he said quietly. 'Else, plague or no, I'll take word to Rycote myself of all that has been done here.'

Stainbank's face was a mask of anger. But finally, with an impatient gesture to the servants to give way, he span on his heel and led the way inside the house.

Sixteen

They stood on the rush-strewn floor of the great hall in silence. The room was warm, but the chill emanating from William Elyot, who sat on the other side of the table in a walnut-brown doublet trimmed with silver, would have been enough to quell the spirits of most men.

'You dare to come to my house in this manner?' he said at last. 'Do you not realize the consequences you face?'

Thomas let his eyes rove quickly round the room. Stainbank was standing near his master, eyes averted. The same burly servants who had been at his back earlier were close at hand, along with others. Thomas and Henry Howes, who stood stiffly at his side, were not only surrounded – their position looked very weak indeed. For his part, Thomas felt an odd surge of excitement: he would flout convention and hang the consequences. Whatever he had done, had it not been but to try and uncover the truth? Surely Sir Robert would understand, and support him?

But Sir Robert was far away; as was any other means of help. Once again he had only his wits, and they were as sharp this morning as they had ever been.

'Well?' Elyot was glaring impatiently at him. Taking a long breath, he met the man's eye and answered.

'You should know, sir, that Peter Hare has made a full confession.'

But Elyot merely raised an eyebrow. 'The shepherd? What on earth has he confessed to?'

Thomas hesitated. 'Taking the sexton here, against his will, and holding him until his debt to you shall expire—'

He broke off, for Elyot had given a shout of laughter. 'What nonsense!' He glanced about the room, and taking the cue his

155

servants grinned too, at the absurdity of the charge. Stainbank in particular made a show of being highly amused. As if to emphasize his position, he picked up a silver jug and poured wine for his master, then for himself.

With a nod of approval, Elyot took his cup and drank.

'Has it truly not occurred to you, Finbow,' he said at last, 'that no court in England would take the word of a drunken shepherd against that of a gentleman?'

'Which gentleman do you mean, sir?' Thomas asked. 'Surely not this bully of a steward, who is rough-handed when dealing with women, yet cannot even control your servants?'

There was a collective intake of breath at Thomas's brazen impudence. Stainbank froze, but Elyot banged down his cup, eyes blazing. 'I could have you arrested, and cast out of Sir Robert's service!' he snapped.

Thomas eyed him. 'As you know my master is at Cowdray attending the Queen,' he said. 'But I mean to get word to him soon of all that has happened here—'

'All that has happened?' Elyot echoed. 'And what precisely is that? Did Master Howes here even see the men who waylaid him – if indeed he was waylaid as he claims? How then could he identify them – where is the evidence?'

Howes's voice was shaky, as he now spoke in turn. 'My dog was killed, stabbed by Hare, on his own admission,' he said. 'The man with him was your servant Bedell, whom you have sent away. There lies the evidence—'

'God's heart!' Elyot almost spat the words at him. 'You think anyone will believe Hare – a drunken misanthrope, who has neglected his work so badly that sheep have strayed halfway to Chaddleworth? The Betterdown flock is now so mixed with my own, I have already had to hire men to undo the mess . . .' He paused, then: 'I need not remind you, Master Howes, how vulnerable is your position. Had you come to me sooner, as a neighbour, and asked my help, mayhap we could have reached some arrangement that satisfies us both—'

'That satisfies you, you mean!' Howes, a man slow to anger, had begun to boil at last. 'I know what you do, sir, and how you have plotted to seize my land to increase your own. You will serve no purpose by spinning further lies—'

'Lies? That is a most serious accusation, not to say a slanderous one.'

Every man started and looked to the door, for the voice was that of Jane Elyot. And though soft and melodious, it bore a coating of ice.

Elyot was on his feet, gesturing irritably to his servants, who scurried about bringing a chair for the lady of the house and stools for the maids that accompanied her. But Jane remained standing, fixing Thomas and Henry Howes with cold stares as she approached the high table.

'Falconer . . .' she favoured Thomas with a vague smile, as if she had all but forgotten who he was, 'I meant to enquire after your mistress last time you were here. How fares the good Lady Margaret?'

'She is safe at Stanbury, my lady,' Thomas answered. 'Yet we look forward to her return, as well as Sir Robert's. I have a great deal to tell them.'

Jane Elyot met his eye. Her authority so outdid that of her husband, it was almost possible to feel sympathy for the man, who still stood wearing a forced smile. Watching them closely, Thomas saw a look of distaste flit briefly across the face of the man's wife. Then, so rapidly that he thought he had been mistaken, a flicker of understanding passed – not between the two of them, but between Jane Elyot and Ralph Stainbank.

He drew breath, feeling the tensions in the room. Henry Howes seemed to feel them too, and was now silent, his eyes on the floor. But Thomas had been present at many such encounters, at Petbury and elsewhere; his work brought him closer to the gentry and the nobles than most men. And having read the signs, his imagination did the rest. It was the Lady of Bickington who had laid the plans to enlarge the manor; perhaps she had even ordered the kidnapping of Howes. Despite her beauty and her intelligence, she was no different to any of those he had met who wished to entertain on a grander scale like Sir Robert or the Norrises, and widen their circle of influence. Perhaps she saw a knighthood for William Elyot . . . perhaps her hopes soared even higher. And hence, Thomas saw the danger he now faced; for these people would not let their ambitions be thwarted by such as he or Henry Howes, or anyone else.

But Jane Elyot had looked away, and raised an eyebrow at her husband. 'I fail to see why these men have not been dealt with elsewhere, as befits their station,' she said coolly. And now she looked at Stainbank, who winced as if struck. The brief, bungled confrontation outside would not be overlooked.

Stainbank opened his mouth, but William Elyot intervened at last. With a sour look at Howes, he said: 'You have laid grave accusations here, Master Sexton. Mayhap you should withdraw now and ponder your actions. I would advise you to seek the services of a good lawyer at the earliest opportunity. If your purse allows it, that is . . .' He trailed off, taking satisfaction from the look that came over Howes's face.

There was a silence now, all eyes on Thomas and Howes, who were clearly expected to make a swift withdrawal. But Thomas looked Elyot in the eye.

'I intend to put the sexton's plight before my master, as soon as I may, sir,' he said. 'I believe he may wish to help him over his present difficulty – before Michaelmas, I mean.'

Then, without waiting for any reactions that would follow, he made his bow quickly and turned to go, catching Howes's sleeve as he did so. The sexton hesitated for a second, before following him out without another word.

They walked rapidly down a passage and through a side door into the noon sunshine. As Howes caught up with him in the yard outside, Thomas said: 'I will retrieve the horse, and ride through the paddock. You should cut across the gardens now, and meet me at the gates.'

Howes showed his alarm. 'You think we'll be pursued?'

'I cannot say,' Thomas told him. 'But I don't intend to press my luck any further.'

The other hurried off. Thomas reached the stable, found the gelding and led it quickly outside. As he did so a door banged, and boots sounded in the yard. Without looking behind, he swung himself into the saddle and urged the horse away. There may have been voices at his back, but he paid them no mind;

merely galloped down the lane to the gates, where Henry Howes, somewhat breathless, was running to meet him. Thomas reined in and reached down a hand, then helped the sexton mount up behind him. Then they were away, thundering upriver towards the ford, with Bickington disappearing behind them.

They were in Lambourn within a quarter hour, and dismounting in the square. Howes would go to seek out Richard Starling. But first, he gave Thomas his thanks. 'Were it not for you . . .' He shook his head, but Thomas put a hand on his shoulder.

'We do what we can. And you know Jonas Crouch is your friend, and would have been sooner, had you confided in him.'

After a moment, Howes nodded. 'I will speak with him.' He frowned suddenly. 'The new bell . . . is it ready yet?'

Thomas nodded, and watched the man hurry off towards the church. Having intended to go straight to Will Ragg, he was leading the horse past Samuel Hubbard's old house when someone hailed him. Crouch was standing by the door, an anxious look on his face. As Thomas walked over, the little clerk hurried to meet him.

'Ragg's been looking for you. It seems our friend Hare wants to make some sort of confession!'

Will Ragg had brought Peter Hare out of the cramped lock-up into the orchard. Having spent a miserable night with the smell of fermenting applejohn in his nostrils, the man was looking pale and sick, and considerably less defiant then he had been yesterday. He begged to be allowed to take some fresh air, along with the loaf and mug of watered beer Ragg brought him. But more importantly, he wished to speak to his jailers. Now he sat on the grass beneath a tree, his legs bound and stretched out before him. The rope around his hands had been loosened enough for him to take his meal.

At first, he tried to gain sympathy. 'I'm a poor man,' he whined, looking up at the three of them. 'I've none to speak for me. I've likely lost my place, and my home too . . .'

Thomas nodded. Glancing at Ragg, he sensed an opportunity, and gave the shepherd a hard look. 'I hear your flock has got mingled with Elyot's, who's had to hire men to sort them. I guess you're none too popular with Giles Ingle, either.'

Hare tilted his mug and downed the last of his ration. As he did so the others saw his hand shake.

'As for the other matter . . .' Thomas shook his head slowly. 'Elyot means to disown you. He denies you and Hugh Bedell were ever employed by his steward. And Bedell is gone – no doubt with a purse to speed him on his way.'

Hare gasped. 'The whoreson runagate . . .' He tugged suddenly at his bonds, but the knots Ragg had tied held firm. 'I should never have listened . . . it was Bickington men made me do it – now they'll have me shoulder the blame!'

He threw an imploring look at each of them. 'For the good Lord's sake, masters, show mercy. What purpose will it serve to see me hang? I'm a neighbour!'

Ragg was scornful. 'Since when were you ever a good neighbour to anyone, Peter?' he enquired. 'Even when you work with others, as for the bat-fowling, it's all you can do to keep a civil tongue – and you've oft-times took more than your rightful share, if I recall correctly.'

Hare squinted into the sun, wiping the sweat from his face. The others could smell the man's rank clothing. Even as he squirmed, they sensed he was calculating. But what could a man in his position have to bargain with?

Jonas Crouch, who had stood aside with a look of distaste, spoke up. 'You told Will you had matters to confess. Is it not time to air them?'

Hare hesitated. He had but the one card to play, and he had held it back. Now he looked up again.

'I'm a papist,' he said.

But Crouch and Will Ragg merely snorted.

'You think no one knew that?' Ragg demanded. He threw Thomas an impatient look. 'As if he's the only surly old shepherd on the Downs who cleaves to the faith of his fathers . . .'

'Hear me!' Hare looked up, blinking at them. 'I'm a papist, and yes – there are others I could name.' There was a glint in his eye that made Thomas wary. 'One in particular, for he is dead now and cannot be harmed. Yet it might help ye seek for his killer

Thomas stared, feeling a prickling at the nape of his neck. Then something slid softly into place, in a corner of his mind that he had left dark of late. Now he understood why.

'Will Stubbs,' he said.

Crouch gasped, and started forward. 'What!'

But Thomas was watching Hare, whose face fell; as if he had played his card, only to find it was not the ace after all.

'That sweet, kindly old man . . .' Thomas spoke almost to himself. 'Devoted to the church, and to God's work . . . the rock on which Master Starling could lean as he drove home his changes, no matter how hard they are for folk to stomach.'

He faced Crouch, who had turned white. 'It never sat squarely with me, Jonas,' he said. 'A man of Stubbs's age, born under old King Henry . . . embracing all that Starling wished to do here with never a word of dissent, nor of complaint.' He gave a wry smile. 'I told you, I find it harder than you to think any man could be such a saint.'

Crouch had no reply. But Will Ragg, with a look of mingled wonder and alarm, was looking at Thomas. 'How does it fadge?' he asked. 'Stubbs was not Berkshire-born – why come here, and live in a far-flung village like this, and work for the church . . . ?' He shook his head. 'I doubt there's a priest within ten miles where he could have heard mass and made his confession.'

'What if he was in hiding?' Thomas asked.

Ragg took a breath, and looked quickly down at Hare.

'I think you'll have to do a mite better, Peter,' he said.

Hare had been watching the exchange between the three men. Now, as if he had been given a ghost of a chance, he shook his grizzled head and spoke rapidly.

'Did you search his house well?' he asked. 'For there was evidence within . . . he showed me once, long ago. We were closer then, when we thought our prayers might be answered . . . when there was hope of the rightful religion restored . . .'

Bur Ragg took a step forward, and his voice was harsh. 'If you mean the Spanish plots against our Queen, they're the chaff of history! I care not for your lost hopes – we speak of what happened to Stubbs that night, in the wood, remember?'

He pointed. 'You claim the man was a secret Catholic, then you'd better offer some proof . . .'

'That's what I do!' Hare shouted. He threw a look of hatred at Thomas. 'But the falconer knows it all, don't he? Let him puzzle away, and find the answers . . .' He broke off, his mouth twisting. 'What does it matter anyway . . . you'll all broil in the fires, and Lord help me, I will likely broil along with ye!'

But then he gulped, as Ragg leaned down and gripped his bonds, twisting the rope so that his wrists were pressed hard together. 'I've had enough,' he said. 'You start spilling something new, or you won't see the gallows. I'll take you out in the woods myself and split your head like someone split Stubbs's. Come to that, how do I know it wasn't you?'

Hare's jaw dropped. 'You were there! You know how me and Nightingale found him!' he cried. But Ragg twisted the rope harder, making him cry out.

'Nightingale's gone, and there's none to attest to anything you say. When you hang I'll make sure there's a man of Starling's persuasion there, to give Protestant rites. Then you'll truly burn in torment, will you not?'

'You damned Lutheran . . .' Hare tried to wrench his hands free, knowing it was useless. 'Jesu – let me go!'

He cried out, then went limp suddenly, all his strength gone. 'Proof, is it . . . then I'll give you proof!' He gazed up at Ragg with a bleak look. Finally the blacksmith released him, straightened up and waited.

'There's some relics, in a pouch.' Hare's voice was sour, but his eyes flicked towards Thomas.

'Holy relics . . .' Hare went on. Then his eyes dropped, and his voice with it. 'A lock of the blessed virgin's hair is one, tied up with silk. A drop of Christ's blood is another, in a little phial . . . and there's also a white rock, from Golgotha.'

The others were silent. Crouch had turned aside, and was staring distractedly at the grass, shaking his head in disbelief. Only yards way, the midday sounds of the village floated by them, but none heard. They had ears only for Hare, as he told the last remnants of his tale.

'That enough evidence for you?' he asked bitterly. 'A lock

162

of hair, a drop of blood, a stone – and a fragment of the true cross.'

Thomas started. 'That chip of wood . . .' he turned to Crouch, 'in the chest, in that old pouch . . . I paid it no mind, yet I thought the timber was not from these shores . . .'

Crouch met his gaze. 'All fake, most likely,' he said at last. 'There's many engaged in making such trifles, and passing them off as holy relics—'

'Liar!' Hare jerked at his bonds, pointing a shaky finger at him. 'You know naught of what you speak! And you will suffer for it – make no mistake, Jonas Crouch: the Lord will smite you, and you will beg His forgiveness at the last, and it will be too late!'

Crouch's face showed only anguish. He ignored Hare and looked to the others. 'Assuming he speaks the truth,' he said, 'what in heaven's name is to be done?'

Ragg drew breath. 'I've one suggestion,' he said. 'Our friend has given us his testimony, in return for which he expects mercy. So instead of sending him for trial, I will offer him an alternative.'

He bent and brought his face close to Hare's, making him flinch. 'I have charge of the muster-book, until such time as there be a new constable,' he said. 'I will put your name on it, and send you to Norris as a recruit. Then you may go to France and fight for our Queen against the papists. How would that suit you?'

Hare said nothing for a long time. Then finally he raised his eyes, and there was nothing but a blankness within.

'I would rather hang,' he said.

Seventeen

Late in the afternoon, Thomas and Will Ragg met at Crouch's house. For the present, Peter Hare remained in the lock-up. Ragg was still uneasy about his role as acting constable and now jailer; and events had taken such an unexpected turn, he was at a loss how to proceed. The summer would soon be waning, he said, and with luck the risk of infection with it. Then surely someone could ride at last to the sheriff and turn the whole matter over to him?

Thomas had ridden back to Petbury briefly, long enough to reassure himself that all was quiet. Seeing how preoccupied he was, Ned Hawes refrained from asking when he would return to his work. Having agreed to take a message to Nell, he stood outside the mews and watched Thomas wheel the gelding away, to canter off across the Downs again. The boy sighed, and went to do his grumbling to the falcons.

In Crouch's parlour Thomas sat down to take a mug of beer, determined to piece together the scattered fragments of some picture that, he felt certain, was almost complete. On the ride across the Downs he had turned it about, and found himself somewhat elated – he was on the scent, and he knew it. But before he and Ragg could share their views, it was Crouch, still shaken by Hare's revelation, who pointed out what now seemed obvious.

'Wilmott,' he said. 'He knew. The more I dwell on it, the more certain I am.'

Thomas nodded. 'That might account for some of his behaviour . . . he admitted taking the *Book of Martyrs* from Stubbs's cottage. He could have taken the relics too.'

Ragg frowned. 'Then why not take the pouch and all – including the fragment of the true cross?'

164

'Likely he didn't know what it was – or what it purported to be,' Thomas replied. 'He thought as I did, that it was but an old chip of wood.'

Crouch had been taking a long pull from his mug. 'But if Wilmott knew of Stubbs's secret,' he asked unhappily, 'then why did he not use it? I have told you how he grew to hate Will . . . was not this a heaven-sent opportunity?'

'For blackmail, you mean?' Ragg frowned at him. 'But to what end? Stubbs had nothing . . . Wilmott could only have gone to Starling and told him. Then Stubbs would have lost his place—'

'Precisely!' Crouch was nodding fiercely. 'To see Stubbs unmasked as a secret papist, disgraced and reviled – a plaster saint fallen from his pedestal. That would have been more than enough for John Wilmott.'

'Then the matter seems clear to me,' Thomas said. 'Someone killed Stubbs before Wilmott could act upon what he'd found out.'

'Then why has he not spoken since?' Ragg asked.

Crouch ventured an explanation: 'Guilt?'

Thomas was nodding. 'We'll go to Wilmott and have it out,' he said. 'Then we'll put it all before Starling. Let him try and avoid his responsibilities this time.'

Crouch sighed. 'The rector's wrath will be great,' he muttered. 'You have but seen a part of it as yet . . .'

They did not go to the church, but waited until sunset before walking across the square to John Wilmott's house. A widower, the churchwarden lived in the last cottage beyond the forge, across from the inn, with his young daughter and son-in-law. The lad was drinking in the Horns, but Wilmott's daughter opened the door, and seeing Crouch on the threshold, bade them enter. She was a plain, slight little creature, and the men exchanged uncomfortable glances, thinking of the unpleasant task ahead. But there was no time to dwell on it, for Wilmott himself was rising from his chair by the window, greatly surprised by their arrival.

'What do you want?' The man looked annoyed. Then he saw Thomas, the last to enter, and grew alarmed.

165

'We would have urgent speech with you, John.' Will Ragg had summoned all the authority his temporary position allowed, and taken the lead.

'About what?' Wilmott remained standing. Then instinctively he glanced at his daughter. 'You'd best leave us, Eliza.'

The girl hesitated. 'D'you wish me to go and fetch Tom?' she asked, but her father shook his head impatiently.

'I will call if I need you.'

She went out, leaving the men alone, filling the small room with their bulk. There was a short silence, before Ragg took a breath, and told Wilmott what Peter Hare had told them. By the time he had finished, the churchwarden had sat down heavily. Finally, he threw Jonas Crouch a bitter look.

'No doubt it will please you,' he said, 'to see me brought low.'

Crouch looked surprised. 'Why should it?'

'Don't play me for a fool,' Wilmott retorted. 'You and the falconer have been burrowing away like moles for the past week. No doubt you have come at some conclusion – now you want my confession, to sit alongside that wicked cove Hare's!'

Ragg glanced at Thomas, signalling him to add his voice.

'We mean you no harm, Master Wilmott,' Thomas said. 'If you will but tell what you know, you might help us find out who murdered Will Stubbs . . .'

'You think I did it?' Wilmott snapped, so abruptly that the others blinked. He glared at Crouch. 'Our busy little sparrow of a clerk knows well enough how I felt about the man . . . Has he accused me of that, too?'

Crouch shook his head, becoming angry in turn. 'I would accuse no one without evidence,' he answered.

Wilmott snorted. 'Evidence . . . do you mean to search my house for those relics? You think I would keep them under my roof?'

'Where did you take them?' Thomas asked.

Wilmott gave a snort of laughter, then met his eye. 'You know most of it, don't you?' he said. 'Why not set it out?'

'Very well.' Thomas was mastering his dislike of the man. 'I do not know precisely when you learned of Stubbs's true

166

faith, but I guess you meant to put your evidence before the rector, and hence see the man destroyed . . .'

'Destroyed, yes . . .' Wilmott gave a bleak smile. 'And so he was soon after, was he not? Quite brutally.' He looked at Crouch. 'You think I hated him that much?'

'I believe you did,' Crouch said quietly. 'Yet I do not think you capable of murder.'

'Well, friend Jonas – you don't know me so well as you think!' Wilmott cried, and got suddenly to his feet. He faced Crouch, who flinched. 'For I am capable of it, and had I slipped deeper into the pit I'd made for myself, I might indeed have done it!'

The others stared, seeing at last the torment that lay beneath the man's anger.

'Permit me to satisfy you on one score, Master Clerk,' he said with an effort. 'I will resign as churchwarden, for I am unfit to hold even that humble office. Then you and I will not have to wrangle as we do at our vestry meetings, month after month . . .' He trailed off, and faced Thomas again.

'I know not who killed Will Stubbs,' he said. 'Nor do I wish to – for whoever it was, they were but God's instrument.'

Crouch gasped. 'You cannot think such . . .'

'I do!' Wilmott threw back. 'And it's a relief now, to spill the whole sorry tale . . . for I have been cased and bound up, like that chest where Stubbs kept the vile tokens of his old life . . .'

He turned a haggard face to them all. 'I bided my time,' he said. 'I was building a case, as the lawyers would have it. I knew Stubbs was no saint . . . He pulled the wool over everyone's eyes, even our dear rector's, but he didn't fool me. I watched him, certain he bore some secret. When I found what it was, I gave thanks to God, for I could expose him, and all would see I was right! Then they would look to me, as a true servant of the church . . .' He shook his head, his mouth working. 'And then – when I was all but ready – it seems someone decided to kill him. Broke his head, in that wood where he went in secret to pray in his own wicked fashion, on his knees in the dirt, like a true papist . . . begging forgiveness, howling at his God for his sins . . . yes!' Seeing the other men's faces, Wilmott nodded vigorously. 'I followed him there, more than once . . . that's how I knew there was a deal more to be uncovered here than mere papistry . . .' He fixed Thomas with a hard look. 'You have not found it, have you? Any more than I could. And now it is too late, for he's in his grave and his secrets with him!'

Thomas gazed at the man, surprised to find his own anger had ebbed away. 'Master Crouch believes it was guilt made you take the relics – as do I,' he said finally. 'You wished Stubbs destroyed – and when he was you blamed yourself. I saw you at the graveside . . .'

'It was my judgement,' Wilmott cried. 'God was showing me, saying: this is what you wanted, is it not? Now he's gone, and you are still churchwarden . . .'

'Is that what you meant,' Thomas persisted, 'when you said you took the *Book of Martyrs* the morning after he died, to save him? To save his reputation?' He nodded to himself. 'Then you spoiled the house to make it look like robbery . . .'

But Wilmott merely looked away. 'You know it already . . .' He sat down suddenly in his chair. 'I know not why he hid the book, unless it be that the pictures stirred evil memories for him.' He paused. 'I took the relics to Starling.'

Ignoring the others' reactions, he went on: 'Mayhap Stubbs was no greater sinner than I, who wished to gain favour by unmasking him to the rector . . .' He gave a bitter laugh. 'Yet I see now, Richard Starling cares nothing for me, only for St Michael's – his little kingdom, and what he will make of it. And he will use any means – even to dealing with a papist!'

He looked hard at Crouch. 'You know that as well as I.'

After a moment, Crouch nodded. 'Could you not have shared your discoveries with me, or with Henry?' he asked. 'Did you truly think us your enemies?'

'If you are, I have made you such.' Wilmott stared at the floor. 'May God forgive me . . .'

Then he closed his eyes and let the tears come, as if he no longer cared who saw. Crouch looked round, and saw that Ragg and Thomas were turning away.

As they reached the door, Wilmott's daughter appeared.

'Master Jonas . . . ?' she began, then looked quickly at her father, a look of alarm on her face.

Crouch hesitated, but could find no words. He followed the others as they left the churchwarden's house and stepped into the warm night air.

But this night was far from over.

The wind rose, bringing a promise of some respite from the unrelenting summer; yet it would remain a chill night in the hearts of Lambourn folk, now and for years to come. Thomas felt it, as the three men walked away from John Wilmott's house. He was deep in thought, for Wilmott's testimony had thrown up more questions: the first one being, who else might have stumbled across Will Stubbs praying in the woods of a night-time?

The familiar sound of voices and of blind Dickon's harp rose from the Horns as they passed . . . then there came a shout, and Thomas halted. It had come from somewhere beyond the inn, near the almshouses. Ragg heard it too, and looked round. The next moment there was a scream, and with a glance at each other all three men began to run.

They rounded the wall of the almshouses to see a dancing light – someone was holding a torch. Quickening their pace, they ran towards it, and several figures materialized out of the gloom. Others had emerged from the doors to see what the commotion was. The first one was Sarah Caldwell. She turned at their approach, saw Ragg and showed her relief. 'Will – thank the Lord! There's been some devilry here . . .'

She pointed to where three or four folk stood, apparently staring down at something in the bushes beyond the path. One of them, a poor fellow in patched clothes, held the torch. As Thomas hurried forward the man turned, his face pale and anxious in the torchlight.

'It looks like this man's dead . . .'

Thomas bent down to look, bidding the ragged fellow bring the light closer. He did so – to reveal the limp figure of a fairly tall man, fully dressed, his hair and clothes streaked with mud, lying on his face.

Thomas reached out slowly and turned the body over . . . then sat back. Above him, there were gasps of horror. One

169

came from Crouch, who now knelt down beside Thomas . . . to gaze upon the hatchet face of the innkeeper, John Nightingale.

They stood huddled together by Sarah Caldwell's door: Thomas, Ragg, Crouch and the widow herself, wrapped in a woollen cloak against the wind. Her neighbour Elias Fitch, the man in ragged clothing, stood nearby holding the torch. He had been told to keep back curious folk who had wandered over from the Horns. The news, spreading swiftly, brought cries of amazement and alarm.

'If folk will help, we'll get him to the inn,' Ragg said, somewhat shakily. 'Then it must be closed – we'd best lay him out on a table or some such . . .'

To the others' surprise, Crouch seemed to have got over the shock of the discovery and was determined to restore some kind of order. 'I will call Henry Howes – he's likely still at the church or nearby. And the rector will be told . . .' He broke off, glancing suddenly at Thomas. 'I can guess what you're about to say,' he said. 'You will wish to examine the body!'

Thomas eyed him. Since the discovery, his mind had been whirling. The condition of the corpse, its location . . . something tugged at his senses, urging them to a realization that still eluded him.

'I do wish it,' he replied. 'Yet I would make one guess already: that Nightingale didn't die where he lies. That's river mud on his clothes. He was dragged here and thrust in the bushes – a hasty concealment.'

'You speak of murder once again.' Ragg drew a deep breath, and looked away. There was a silence, and the others could almost feel the weight that pressed upon him.

'You're not alone . . .' Thomas gripped his shoulder. 'We'll puzzle this out – with or without Starling's help. And when we do a picture will form . . .'

Ragg frowned at him. 'You mean that John's death sits with the others – how?' He shook his head helplessly.

'This isn't the time,' Crouch said, and turned to Thomas. 'You organize a party to carry the body . . .' He hesitated. 'We need something to cover him.'

170

Sarah Caldwell pulled off her cloak and held it out. 'Use this,' she said. As the others looked at her in surprise she added: 'He was not a bad man . . . He liked to seek out folk's secrets, it's true – but he never used what he knew to harm anyone. There is much he could have told . . .' She glanced at Ragg. 'Don't think harshly of him.'

Ragg said nothing. But Thomas took the cloak from her with a kindly look, and went to cover the corpse.

Thereafter, throughout the night and the morning that followed, the folk of Lambourn found themselves caught up in more excitement than the little community had known for years. For a moment, even the imminent raising of the new bell was forgotten, as people who had slept through the events gathered outside the Horns to find out what was happening. And initial alarm at finding the inn closed until further notice gave way to dismay when the news of the landlord's death was told.

Within there was sadness, if not despair. Nicholas the drawer, who had struggled to keep the inn going since John Nightingale's disappearance two days ago, was shattered by the discovery. He sat alone in the front parlour, and would speak to none save blind Dickon, who, having nowhere else to go, stayed nearby and played mournful airs on his harp.

In the back room there was a different atmosphere – subdued but businesslike. Thomas the falconer had got his way, and examined the body, which was stretched upon a board laid on kegs covered with a cloth. Having finished his examination, Thomas had gone outside to wash and walk a little in the early-morning air. Jonas Crouch and Henry Howes, who had been here most of the night, sat awaiting his return.

Howes had talked long with Crouch, the two of them alone in a corner, until there seemed no aspect of recent events that had not been turned about to the point of exhaustion. But by the end, the two men, the only remaining servants of the church of St Michael's, were resolved to act as one: to stand up to their ebullient rector and demand he take action.

They looked up quickly as Thomas came in the back door and bolted it behind him, then sat down heavily.

171

'I would guess he was killed in similar manner to Stubbs,' he said. 'Not one blow to the head, but two. If there was a lot of blood, most of it's been wiped away. Both blows came from the front . . .' He paused. 'Whoever Nightingale's killer was, he likely saw him before he died.' He frowned to himself. 'Mayhap he was even facing him.'

'The weapon . . . ?' Crouch began.

'Was the same, I believe,' Thomas answered. 'Thereafter he fell and was taken to where he lay. If he was killed the same night he disappeared, then I guess he was moved later on, else someone would have found him sooner.'

'You say there's river mud on his clothes.' Crouch again.

Thomas nodded. 'I'm going to go and look, now it's daylight. There ought to be marks . . .'

Howes spoke up. 'You have reasoned well, Master Thomas. We will aid you, if we can.'

Thomas barely heard him. The sight of the deep gashes in John Nightingale's skull had stirred memories he disliked; of his brief time of soldiering, those long years ago in the Low Countries . . . yet he was puzzled. He had seen men killed and maimed in many ways, and by a variety of weapons. But no sword or club, nor pike or halberd, would make the shape of the wound he had found; not even an old-fashioned mace. The top of the skull was stoven in by some assailant who was either very strong, or perhaps wild with rage . . .

He glanced up to see the other two looking at him. 'Will you find Ragg, and ask him to meet me at the place where the body was found?'

Howes gave a wry smile. 'He's likely close by already,' he murmured. 'If mistress Caldwell had aught to say in the matter . . .'

A short time later Thomas indeed encountered Will Ragg, emerging sleepily from Sarah Caldwell's door. There was no sign of the widow. Without preamble they conferred, and Thomas quickly acquainted the other with his discoveries.

Ragg was irritable this morning. 'What in the Lord's name are we looking for?' he asked. 'A murderer, who hated both Stubbs and Nightingale? The two had naught in common that

I know of – save that they were both in Lambourn wood that terrible night.' He grunted. 'And John was no secret Catholic, I'd stake my life on that.'

'Yet Nightingale bribed Hare to lie about how Stubbs was found,' Thomas murmured. 'Why would he do that?'

Ragg shook his head helplessly. They had taken a few paces and were now standing close to where Nightingale's body had been discovered. Some kindly soul, perhaps from the almshouses, had laid a few wild flowers near the spot.

Thomas began casting about. But there were no tell-tale drag marks, no streaks of mud in the grass or on the path. He took a few steps in both directions, peering at the ground, then walked back to Ragg.

'Looks like he was carried,' he said.

'Then he was strong, whoever he was,' Ragg observed. 'John wasn't a small man.' He glanced around, then gestured vaguely at the trees that stood between them and the river, blocking their view of it. 'This thicket's as likely a place as any to start looking, isn't it?'

Thomas was about to reply, then he froze. 'The bell-founder's camp. It's barely forty yards through there.'

Ragg stared. 'Close enough . . .' he frowned. 'You don't think he—'

'I never know what to think whenever I encounter Master Goodchild,' Thomas interrupted. 'But it wouldn't hurt to ask him if he saw or heard aught, would it?'

Eighteen

The two of them strode through the trees to the clearing by the river, to find the bell-founder's camp deserted. His horse was tethered on a long rein, grazing by the riverbank. The tent was open at the front, and a glance within revealed nothing untoward. Nor did the founder's cart, a ramshackle old vehicle with a patched cover. Thomas paused and looked around. Already the sun was climbing, and from the direction of the church came the sound of a hammer. Then he remembered.

'The inscription,' he said. 'He has to cut that in the bell before they raise it to the tower.'

Ragg nodded, and together they walked along the river, to emerge a short time later in the bell-yard.

There were no watchers today. News of John Nightingale's death was still spreading, drawing folk to the Horns and to the square. But the founder and his family worked on, seemingly unaware of village affairs – or perhaps merely unconcerned with them.

The bell, now thoroughly cleaned, had been moved: it stood mouth downwards, resting on timbers, so that the founder himself could work at the part just below the crown: the band known as the 'mully groove' in which he would place his inscription, horizontally around the bell.

Edmund Goodchild, stripped to the waist, was shovelling earth and rubble, filling in the now-redundant bell-pit. His mother stood beside Simon, though in what way she was assisting him was unclear. The man was bent over the bell, concentrating hard, skilfully cutting two-inch-high letters into its surface with a small hammer and chisel. Tiny curls of golden metal rolled away to fall at his feet.

As Thomas and Ragg approached, the founder and his wife both looked up. There was a short silence before Simon straightened and fixed both men with his habitual stare.

'Good-day, Master.' Ragg nodded to him. 'Though I wish not to disturb your work, I'd like to have speech with you.'

The bell-founder raised an eyebrow.

'A man was found dead last night – just beyond the trees, not far from your encampment.' Ragg pointed over his shoulder, trying to gauge Goodchild's response. But all he got was a blank look.

Thomas watched Alice Goodchild. But he too could discern no reaction, save what he might expect from anyone who had been told such news. The woman put a hand to her mouth, and gave a little shake of her head.

Simon Goodchild gazed at Ragg. 'You wish to know if we have knowledge of this man's death? We have none.'

Ragg shrugged. 'It's only, your being so close by,' he said.

The founder made no reply.

'Your boy,' Ragg persisted, indicating Edmund, who had stopped work and was looking towards them. 'Might he have seen anything . . . ?'

'If he had, he would surely have spoken to me of it,' the founder replied. 'But then, we took supper early and retired at sunset. We have much to do before the morrow.'

'You mean to raise the bell tomorrow?' Ragg nodded his approval. 'Should be a goodly crowd here, for market day.'

Simon acknowledged his interest politely.

'You never visited the Horns, master – unlike your son.' Thomas spoke up suddenly, catching the man slightly by surprise. 'A pity, for Master Nightingale kept a good brew on tap. I'd have thought yours thirsty work, deserving of a mug at the end of the day.'

A trace of annoyance flitted across the founder's face. 'We carry all that we need with us,' he answered. 'Though I doubt not that your unfortunate innkeeper was as capable as any in these parts.'

'You know it's he who's dead, then,' Ragg said sharply.

There was a slight pause, then Goodchild's blank stare was back. 'You said he *kept* a good brew,' he said to Thomas. 'I guessed it was he – even had I not seen the sad-looking folk gathered outside the inn since sunrise.'

Ragg drew breath. 'These are troublesome times for Lambourn,' he said. 'Murder's a rarity on the West Downs.' When Goodchild made no reply he added: 'At present folk are shocked – but soon they'll be angry. They will likely look for someone to blame . . .' He broke off, looking round.

Edmund Goodchild had downed his spade and was walking towards them. 'Is aught the matter?' he asked.

With a glance at Ragg, Thomas took it upon himself to explain. And at once he sensed an unease that the boy found difficult to conceal. It would be many years, Thomas reflected, before the young man would learn his father's rock-like composure.

'What's that to us?' Edmund demanded.

'Naught, I see,' Thomas told him. 'But two men killed in the same manner, in the space of a week . . . Do you wonder that we are bent on seeking out the cause?'

'The cause?' Goodchild eyed him. 'Surely it is the perpetrator you must seek. Doubtless the cause will then reveal itself.'

'Very likely,' Thomas said. And deliberately he allowed his gaze to slide downwards, to the small hammer in Simon Goodchild's right hand.

There was a moment's silence, before Ragg took a sharp breath. But at once Thomas spoke up, somewhat loudly, as if to prevent his friend's getting a word out.

'We should take our leave now, master,' he said, 'and not keep you longer. For I see your work will not wait.'

He pointed with approval at the letters which the founder had carved thus far: *S.G. ME FECIT*. 'I have no Latin,' he smiled. 'What will the inscription say?'

But Goodchild was not fooled by his change of tack. With an ironic smile in return, the man pointed to each letter with his chisel.

'S.G. are my initials . . . "Simon Goodchild made me," it reads. Then will follow the year, and "*LAUDATE DEUM*" – "Praise God".'

Thomas nodded. 'We will be glad to watch the raising

176

tomorrow . . .' He turned to Ragg and signalled to him with his eyes to come away. After a moment, with a last glance at the founder and his family, Ragg followed him.

They did not speak until Thomas had rounded the wall of the south transept, where he halted.

'That hammer . . .' Ragg began. 'It's—'

'Too small,' Thomas said tersely.

The other frowned. 'I speak of the weapon used to kill Stubbs and Nightingale . . .'

'So do I. I looked closely at Nightingale's skull. If a hammer was used, it had to be somewhat bigger than that.'

Ragg's face fell. 'Jesu, Thomas – you try a man's patience.'

Thomas shrugged. 'If it's hammers we seek, your forge is as good a place as any to start looking.'

The other's jaw dropped. 'What! You mean to accuse *me* now . . . ?'

'No!' Thomas shook his head, with a look of exasperation. 'I know you better than that, Master Will. We must look everywhere, try every direction, is all I—'

'Is it indeed all?' Ragg was glaring at him. 'Mayhap I should leave you alone to poke about, since it's plain I do little but hinder you.'

Thomas sighed. 'I ask your pardon.'

Ragg hesitated, breathing hard. 'And if I don't feel inclined to give it?' He paused. 'I go to my work now. But I'll come to the Horns around midday, and if Nick won't draw me a mug, you can do it yourself.'

Thomas relaxed, allowing a smile to form; then a thought occurred. 'Your tools . . .' he asked. 'If any had been stolen, would you have noticed?'

Ragg uttered an oath, and stalked off across the square.

Thomas returned to the Horns, which remained closed. But he was let in the back door by Crouch, who locked it behind them.

Nightingale's body was laid out in the rear parlour, draped in black. Keeping a vigil was Elias Fitch from the almshouses. As Thomas entered, the man looked up and nodded a greeting.

'A strange fellow, was John,' he muttered. 'Always knew

more than he cared to tell . . . but I've cause to be grateful for the times he allowed me a mug when I couldn't pay him.' He looked away. 'Why in God's name would anyone want to kill him?'

Thomas shook his head and, hearing voices from the front parlour, followed Crouch through the doorway. Here, to his surprise, was a lively enough gathering: Sarah Caldwell and another woman, Nicholas the drawer and blind Dickon, who was tuning up his harp.

'Falconer!' Mistress Caldwell rose cheerfully to welcome him. 'Come and take a sip of Rhenish. John wouldn't wish us to be melancholy.' Pouring wine from a jug, she held out the cup to him.

'It's somewhat early in the day for me,' Thomas answered with a smile. But Sarah waved a hand airily at him.

'Pah – you're as gloomy as Will.' She turned to indicate her friend, a smiling brown-haired woman in a plain hood. 'If you won't take it from me, mayhap you'll take it from Marjorie . . . she's in need of a little company.'

Thomas hesitated, then looked round in relief as Crouch came to his rescue. 'Master Finbow has matters of import to discuss with me,' the clerk said disapprovingly. As he and Thomas moved towards the window, he muttered: 'You'd think it was a wake already – and the man not even in his grave yet.'

They sat at a table with Nicholas, who appeared to have recovered somewhat since the early morning. Indeed, he now seemed eager to talk.

'I've gone over it time after time, trying to sift it . . . yet it's like a bit of earth you turn too often. It gives little in return.' He frowned. 'This I will say: I knew John's ways, and I'm certain he had matters on his mind these past days. He carried on as usual, but there was something . . . I thought it was the shock him and Hare got after the bat-fowling, finding old Will Stubbs dead like that.'

Thomas and Crouch exchanged glances. Close by, Dickon ran his fingers expertly up and down the strings, then struck a long, rolling chord.

'Did he leave the inn at all?' Thomas asked. 'I mean, before he went missing?'

178

Nicholas shook his head. 'He seldom went far . . . Folk came to him, as a rule.' He paused. 'Even yon bell-maker did.'

Thomas froze. 'When was that?'

Nicholas thought for a moment. 'Last market day it would be – early in the morning. He had speech with John at the back door, before we even opened. Don't ask me what 'twas about.'

Thomas said nothing, but Crouch was becoming excited.

'You're certain he said nothing to you?' But as the other shook his head, he went on: 'The day he disappeared . . . surely he told you he was going out? Leaving you alone, without a word . . .'

Nicholas looked uncomfortable. 'It weren't like him,' he admitted. 'I never even saw him leave . . . he went out the back, I thought to fetch something. Only I never saw him again. Till now,' he added, and lowered his eyes, as the harpist began picking out a particularly gloomy tune.

'Would you care to give us a little peace, Master Dickon?' Crouch asked testily. He turned to Thomas as if about to say something, when the harper surprised everyone by speaking up.

'You'd best look in John's ledger. For he'll not need it any more.'

There was a silence, broken only by Sarah Caldwell and Marjorie talking in animated fashion across the room.

Thomas spoke sharply. 'What ledger is that?'

Dickon plucked a few notes before answering. 'I keep it . . . always have. Ask Master Nick.'

Nicholas was nodding. 'John entrusted his book to Dickon, since he can't read it. He wasn't a trusting man – even I've never looked in it.' Seeing the expressions on the faces of Thomas and Crouch, he added: ''Tis only payments, bills of reckoning and such . . .'

'Where is it?' Crouch asked. When Dickon made no reply, he touched him on the arm and repeated the question.

Dickon flinched. ''Tis under my pallet, in the roof,' he replied. 'John bade me always keep it there, save when he asked for it.'

Thomas faced the harper. 'Will you get it for us, master?' he asked gently. 'It may be important.'

But it was a disappointment.

The harper laid down his instrument and felt his way to the narrow stairs, then climbed up to the little chamber above. Thomas had not even known that the man lived at the inn. Within minutes he had returned carrying an old leather-bound book fastened with a rusty clasp. With an air of suppressed excitement, Crouch laid it upon the table and opened it. Meanwhile Dickon took up his harp again, and began to play softly.

They pored over it, but saw only lists of figures in the landlord's spindly handwriting: sacks of grain, malt and hops for the brewing; foodstuffs of every kind; and purchases from candles to bed linen. There were payments made, going back twenty years: a thatcher for repairing the roof, a plasterer for newly rendering the back parlour. The last entry, made only a week ago, was to Tolworthy the miller for torches used in taking pheasants.

'A meticulous man, was John,' Crouch observed softly. 'Even the bat-fowling gets a listing.'

Thomas stared at the page. In his mind, he saw Peter Hare telling of a gold sovereign Nightingale had bribed him with . . . Hardly surprising, though, that there was no mention of that. He turned to the front of the book, then the back, and saw nothing untoward. Then he started.

'The back cover,' he said. 'It's thicker than the front . . .'

Crouch was enjoying playing the investigator. He felt the back cover, then fumbled in his doublet pocket for a penknife. Watched by Thomas and Nicholas, he began to slit the paper around the edge of the cover. In less than a minute he had pulled out a single sheet of folded vellum, yellowed with age.

The others bent forward as the little clerk opened the paper and smoothed it out, revealing a page of closely written text. He peered at it, then held it to the window to gain more light. Finally he lowered it, and turned to the others with a crestfallen look that was almost comical.

'It's his last will and testament,' he murmured.

There was silence, before Nicholas gave a sigh. 'John had no close family here,' he said. 'Likely some outsider will inherit the Horns, and want to sell it . . .' he turned to the harper and raised his voice slightly. 'Mayhap you and me will be looking for a new roof over our heads, Dick.'

'No . . .' All turned to Crouch, who was holding up the paper in surprise. 'He's left it to you.'

At midday the Horns reopened, to universal approval. And when it quickly became known that Nicholas Pearse the drawer was now landlord, there was something like celebration. This despite the fact that John Nightingale was still lying in the back parlour, and somewhere a murderer was on the loose. What next, this plague summer? folk asked, and hurried to take a mug to steady their nerves.

Thomas bought Will Ragg a dinner by way of appeasement, with beer to wash it down. Satisfied, the blacksmith sat back in his shirt sleeves to hear the others' assessment of the situation.

Jonas Crouch had been about his business in the morning, though he had been unable to speak with the rector. Instead he had talked with Henry Howes, who now sat beside him.

'Master Starling won't talk to anyone,' the sexton said. 'Since John Wilmott came this morning and spoke with him, he's shut himself up in the Trinity chapel. To pray and seek guidance, he says.'

His look was sombre. 'I collared Wilmott though,' he went on, 'and made him tell me. He's resigned as churchwarden, right enough. He thinks rector is waiting until tomorrow, when they raise the new bell. He'll likely announce Sam Hubbard's funeral . . . maybe Nightingale's too,' he added.

'I guessed as much.' Crouch looked round the table. 'I would wager my hawk he'll say he's had a sign – he'll use the market-day crowd. He likes a good audience.'

'Speeches . . .' Ragg shook his head. 'That's all well enough, but who'll help us track down John's killer?'

No one had an answer to that. And soon after, they went their own ways. But as Thomas stood outside with the blacksmith in the afternoon heat, Sarah Caldwell came up, somewhat the worse for drink, and slipped her arm through Ragg's.

'It's an ill wind, my duck,' she smiled, and kissed him on the cheek.

181

Ragg frowned in embarrassment. 'What do you mean . . . ?'

'I mean I'm to have a goodly place – here at the Horns. Work as hostess for Master Nick. Turn the spigot, and serve tables and all . . .' She was smiling broadly. 'Is't not wondrous news?'

But Ragg was not smiling. 'You call that a goodly place?' he retorted. 'Having every drunken cove putting his hands down your shift – why, it's little better than—'

'Than what?' Sarah's smile had vanished. 'No better than what?' she repeated, staring fiercely at him. 'What I am now, you mean?'

Ragg's shoulders sagged. 'Lord, Sarah . . .' he muttered. 'What is it I can say . . . what would you would have me do?'

'Do?' The widow hefted the shoulders of her low-cut gown, which had drooped so that her breasts almost fell out. 'I would have you behave like the man I know you can be!' And she was gone, holding her skirts up out of the dust.

Ragg gave a long sigh, ashamed to look at Thomas. But finally he summoned the courage to meet his eye.

'He won't marry us,' he said.

Thomas frowned slightly. 'You mean Starling . . .'

The other nodded. 'I would have taken Sarah as wife last year – then he came here, with his high and mighty ways. When I went to him he promised to consider, as he always does, and give his judgement. Then he gave it: because of what he terms Sarah's sinful life, he will not marry us in his church. Yet how else could she live, while a single woman?'

Thomas sighed. 'I'm truly sorry, Will.'

'I'm the sorry one,' Ragg said in a dull voice. 'I should have taken her away somewhere where no one knows us, and married her in another church. Then she would have my name and be a woman of note – wife to Will Ragg, blacksmith.'

Then without another word he went off towards the forge.

Somewhat heavy of heart, Thomas walked back to Crouch's house where he had left the gelding. But as he neared the corner of the old Ramsbury path he heard hooves, and turned to see a man approaching him, leading a good Barbary horse. He stopped at once, for he recognized the animal: one of those from the Bickington stables. Then he recognized the livery,

182

as well as the servant he and Howes had encountered only the day before, at the entrance to the manor; the one who had told him that Hugh Bedell was gone.

He waited until the man drew close. There was no greeting. If anything, however, the other seemed ill-at-ease rather than hostile. He halted the horse, dropped the rein and stepped forward.

'My Master, William Elyot, wishes to speak with you,' he said.

'About what?' Thomas asked, somewhat sharply.

'I cannot say,' the servant answered. 'But if you ride back to Bickington with me, you will learn . . .'

'No.' Thomas shook his head. 'I will not ride to Bickington – ever again, unless it be at the behest of my own master.'

The man gave a little sigh. 'I was told you might say as much,' he said. 'Very well – then I am instructed to say, Master Elyot's steward will come to the village tonight, and meet with you at a place of your choosing, and speak in his master's stead.'

Thomas stared. 'Why does he ask this?'

The man shrugged. 'Again, I cannot say.'

Thomas considered, then gave his reply. 'I name the rooms of Mistress Sarah Caldwell, in the almshouses.'

The man frowned. 'I do not think—'

'There, and nowhere else,' Thomas said. 'I'll be waiting at sunset, and for an hour thereafter. If no one appears, I will be gone.'

There was a moment, then the man caught up his horse's reins. 'I will convey the message,' he said. Then he turned quickly and led his mount away towards the bridge.

Thomas watched until he was out of sight. He was still there some minutes later, deep in thought, when a curious Jonas Crouch came out and asked him what he was doing.

Slowly, Thomas came out of his reverie. 'I know not,' he replied. 'But I hope it's none too rash.'

Nineteen

Will Ragg was annoyed.

'What in God's name possessed you?' he demanded. 'I'm in enough dudgeon with Sarah as it is, without you using her place for your twilight goings-on . . . and you didn't even ask her leave! Had you not thought what trouble there might be?'

They stood in the forge as the afternoon waned: Will bare to the waist, his chest running with sweat, hammering violently on his anvil in between bursts of angry speech. For his part, Thomas did not have a ready answer as to why he had named Sarah's rooms as the meeting place; indeed, he scarcely understood the reason himself. Somehow when the notion occurred it had seemed right, and over the years he had learned to trust his instincts.

He faced Will, ready for another onslaught. 'If you'll let me speak, I would tell you how I went to Sarah an hour since and explained the matter. When I said I'd pay for the use of the rooms, she was content.'

Will glowered. 'What sort of humour was she in?'

'She'd rested a little . . . slept off the Rhenish, I might say.'

The blacksmith grunted, then flipped the red-hot horseshoe expertly on the anvil, caught it with his tongs and resumed beating it. The clanging was beginning to make Thomas's ears ring.

Then Will stopped hammering and looked up. 'You say you want me there?'

Thomas nodded. 'And Henry Howes. I doubt there will be trouble – of the sort you mean. But if there is, you and Howes are the ones I'd want beside me.' He tried a wan smile. 'This is not Jonas Crouch's field of play . . .'

The other snorted. 'If that's flattery, you won't butter no parsnips with it.' He hesitated. 'But I do confess, I'd dearly like the chance to plant a fist on Stainbank's smug face . . .'

They gathered a little before sunset, having been admitted to Sarah's front parlour. After seeing them bestowed with a jug of ale for company, she retired to the back room and closed the door. She had no wish, she said, to know what went on, nor to see Ralph Stainbank. Mention of the man seemed to bring unpleasant memories. And she had made Will Ragg swear that at the first sign of trouble he and the other men would take it outside. She would then bar the door, and admit no one except him.

Howes disliked being here at all. His last encounter with Stainbank, at Bickington, had left a sour taste. But he understood Thomas's view that if Elyot wanted to deal privately with him, it could be that some sort of trade was being offered, with his steward as mediator. Thomas well knew that when his master returned and had learned all that had occurred, Elyot's position in the Downlands would be, to say the least, uncomfortable.

'Yet I'll not stay and listen to that steward huff and puff,' the sexton said. 'Else I know not what I might do.'

Dusk was falling. Ragg struck a flame and put light to two small candles. Then he poured each man a mug, and gestured to them to sit.

They had not long to wait.

Thomas was first to hear the sound of hooves. As the other two looked up, he held up a hand and counted: three horses. Naturally enough, Stainbank would not come alone. And knowing him, he would not expect Thomas to be alone either.

There were further sounds: jangling harnesses, footfalls, low voices. And before anyone could bang on the door, Thomas had opened it to find himself face to face with Stainbank, cloaked over his riding clothes. Behind him in the gloom, he made out two of the men who had stood with the steward outside the door at Bickington Manor.

Nothing was said as they entered. The tension was palpable, as Ragg and Howes rose from the table to stand on one side of the room. Stainbank and the other two remained near the door, which remained ajar behind them.

'I would prefer to speak with you alone.' Stainbank's tone was haughty – though not, it seemed, as haughty as usual.

'My friends are here as witnesses,' Thomas answered.

The other paused, then said: 'What I have to say is for your ears and no other's.'

It was Thomas's turn to hesitate. He could sense Ragg's powerful dislike of the steward, intensified by their location. Here, after all, relations had likely taken place between the steward and Sarah Caldwell, of which he had boasted so harshly on the Downs that day . . .

He glanced at Howes to see he was harbouring similar feelings of hostility, and berated himself. Things were about to turn ugly very quickly, which was not what he had intended.

'If I ask Master Ragg and Master Howes to leave us,' he asked, 'will your men follow and swear to wait apart, without making any coil?'

Stainbank frowned slightly. 'Any coil will not be caused by those in Bickington livery.'

Ragg disliked the idea. 'I prefer to stay,' he muttered.

Thomas faced him. 'Give me but a moment,' he said. 'Then I will come out to you . . . isn't that best?' He slid his eyes quickly to indicate the door to the inner room.

Ragg hesitated, and caught Howes's eye. But the sexton was nodding. 'We'll wait on the path,' he said, and made his way deliberately towards the door, causing one of the Bickington man to move aside abruptly.

There was some lessening of tension as the four men went out: Howes and Ragg first, then the two servants, who stepped away the moment they cleared the doorway. But from the warning look Stainbank gave them, Thomas did not expect the men to make trouble.

He closed the door. But no sooner had he turned round than Stainbank was fumbling at his belt. There was the chink of coins, and a leather purse appeared.

'Twenty crowns,' the steward said. 'Yours, and none will know of it except we two.'

Thomas stared. 'And your master, of course,' he added.

'Of course,' Stainbank echoed curtly.

There was a silence, which grew until the steward's expression changed to one of puzzlement.

'Take it,' he snapped. 'Or were you hoping for more?'

To his dismay, Thomas smiled slightly. How long was it, he asked himself, since he had been offered a bribe? He was trying to remember, even as other thoughts pushed the notion aside. Finally he gave voice to the most obvious one.

'And what should I do, to deserve such a handsome sum?'

Stainbank's snort suggested he was unused to dealing with such unsophisticated thinking. 'I would guess that if you employ a little imagination, you will come at the answer to that soon enough.'

Thomas nodded slowly. 'Say naught to my master of what happened to Howes—' he began, but the other interrupted, as if he did not wish to dwell on details.

'As I said, falconer, you will stoop at the answer, like one of your birds. You are nobody's fool.'

'I'm flattered you think so,' Thomas told him. 'Nor am I anybody's toy.' When the other drew a sharp breath he added: 'You can take your twenty crowns and throw them down the jakes, then jump in after them.'

Stainbank controlled himself. 'So – how much more is it you want?'

'I want naught from you,' Thomas answered, feeling his own anger rising. 'If it were twenty thousand, I'd still tell you where to shove your dirty money . . .'

'Dolt!' Stainbank cried, his composure gone. 'Can't you see that—' He broke off as Thomas stepped forward abruptly.

'Out,' he said in a hard voice that surprised the other. 'I should have listened to my friends . . .' He gripped Stainbank's wrist, the hand still holding the proffered purse, and thrust it against his chest. 'Get you gone, else there will be a coil after all – and I'll start it myself.'

The other man gasped, and there was fear in his eyes. But at that moment the door to the inner room flew open, and Sarah Caldwell appeared.

'You promised me!' she cried, her eyes going from Thomas to Stainbank and back. There was a moment, before she added:

187

'I should never have agreed to have that cove under my roof again . . .'

Stainbank flinched, and tore himself from Thomas's grasp. The purse vanished as he side-stepped towards the front door and wrenched it open. But as he went he threw a sneering look over his shoulder.

'Don't fret, Sarah,' he said. 'I've no more desire to be here than I have to lie between your flabby legs again . . .'

He put a foot through the doorway, then cried out. For Will Ragg, who was standing there, had seized him by the shoulders and yanked him outside.

Thomas groaned, and turned to the widow. 'Sarah,' he began, 'I ask your pardon—'

But from outside came the immediate sounds of scuffling, mingled with cries. With a helpless look at Mistress Caldwell, he plunged through the doorway.

There are times in a man's life, Thomas reflected briefly, when he has no choice but to fight, or run and be branded a coward. And this occasion, with his companions not only unarmed but outnumbered, was one of them. He knew it as he ran from Sarah Caldwell's door, to find Henry Howes pinned to the ground by one of Stainbank's men – then saw the man whip something sharp-looking from his belt. Without checking his stride Thomas raised his fist and banged it against the side of the fellow's head with all his strength. The man went over like a sack of grain, allowing a dishevelled Howes to scramble breathlessly to his feet.

'Where's Will . . . ?' The question was superfluous, as both of them span round, aware of cries to their left, near the wall of the almshouse. The front door stood wide, throwing a shaft of dim light on to the scene. And Sarah Caldwell stood framed in the entrance, hand to her mouth.

Stainbank was finished after a matter of seconds: he lay where Ragg had left him, semi-conscious by the wall, bleeding from nose and mouth and wherever else the blacksmith had managed to land his blows. The gasps and oaths came from the mouths of Ragg himself and the other, taller Bickington man, who were engaged in a tussle some yards off, grappling like wrestlers at the fair. But even as Thomas and Howes hurried over, the two men parted, fists whirling. Thomas caught the sexton's arm and stopped him, knowing that Will Ragg neither wanted nor needed their help. The two watched as he ducked the other man's swing and came up fast, his squat shoulders hunched. One blow caught the fellow under the chin, stunning him; the second thudded against his cheek, with a crack that must have been audible across the river. Then Lambourn's acting constable and upholder of the peace stepped back, breathing hard, and watched his opponent keel over, to lie still upon the flattened garden.

There was silence, broken finally by Mistress Sarah, who walked from her door, pulling her gown about her shoulders.

'Will . . .' She shook her head slowly, as Ragg turned to her, his face bruised and running with sweat. He said nothing, for he was still struggling to regain his breath.

Thomas looked round, and saw Henry Howes staring about with a look of disbelief on his face.

'Is that all it took?' he asked. 'I thought we were done for . . .'

'We had anger on our side,' Thomas told him, glancing back towards Ragg. The blacksmith's shoulders drooped suddenly; and both men looked away as Sarah Caldwell put her head on his chest and allowed him to wrap his arms clumsily about her.

But Thomas's head snapped round, in the direction of the churchyard. Howes did the same, for he had heard it too: a single mount, approaching at a trot.

They waited as the rider on his tall horse materialized out of the night. Slowly he drew rein and looked about, observing the battlefield in silence. Will Ragg and Sarah parted, staring at him, but the man ignored them. Finally he dismounted and walked towards Thomas, his good riding boots crunching on the loose pebbles. It was William Elyot.

'Whatever he said to you . . .' He indicated Stainbank's motionless form by the wall. 'It was not on my authority.'

Thomas stared. It may have been merely the light, but Elyot's face looked pale and taut.

'Nor was it I sent word this afternoon, bidding you come

to me,' the Master of Bickington went on, then gestured towards the open door. 'Might we talk inside?'

Thomas hesitated. Howes and Will Ragg had drawn closer, all three of them looking equally surprised at this turn of events. But then Elyot's glance strayed to Sarah Caldwell, who came up to stand beside Ragg.

Ragg was first to speak. 'Whatever you wish to say, sir,' he muttered, 'it must needs be said out here.'

Elyot opened his mouth, then stopped himself. For Sarah Caldwell had stepped forward and made a quick curtsey.

'If it please Master Elyot, we had best go in,' she said. She pointed with her chin, and the others looked round to see that all the doors were open, revealing several folk staring out with unashamed curiosity.

Elyot inclined his head, and the widow led the way inside.

'You have acted well,' the gentleman said softly to Thomas, 'while I have been a knave and a fool.'

They stood awkwardly, crowding the small parlour in the half light, scarcely believing what they heard: Ragg and Sarah close together by the table, Thomas and Henry Howes apart. Elyot had been offered a stool, but declined it.

Thomas watched, and now there was no mistaking the look of misery in the other man's gaze. Though quite what had occasioned it he could not imagine. Finally, Elyot breathed deeply and seemed to gather his strength as he turned now to Henry Howes.

'Master Sexton . . .' Howes stiffened, but the other half-raised a hand, almost in apology. 'I . . . matters of which you know nothing, have made me . . .' He broke off, unable to find the words. Nobody spoke, and the men looked away in embarrassment. None of them had ever seen William Elyot appear contrite.

'Let me reassure you,' he said at last, struggling to look Howes in the eye, 'that I've had cause to reflect upon what has been done to you. Your demand for redress shall be met.'

Howes looked stunned. He opened his mouth, then closed it. But having got this far, Elyot was determined to continue.

'Our arrangement will be extended – nay, altered . . .' he

said, with a nod which conveyed more than was said. 'If you would be good enough to come downriver tomorrow – as my guest, I would add – then we may discuss details in private.' He paused, then added somewhat hastily: 'Unless you would prefer I came to your farm instead?'

Howes swallowed. 'I believe I would prefer it,' he said.

The other nodded. 'Be assured I will come alone,' he said. 'You have naught to fear – and everything to gain.'

Howes nodded, but he was dumbstruck. And as he looked round, it seemed to the others as if the years fell away from him.

'Then if that's all, I think I'd like to go now, and take a mug,' he said quietly.

Ragg nodded. 'I'll likely join you, in a while.'

Howes threw a look at him and at Thomas, and went out.

There was another silence before Elyot spoke again. But to the men's surprise it was to Sarah Caldwell.

'Mistress Sarah . . .' with her, he appeared even more embarrassed for some reason, 'whatever harm my steward has caused you, I will make it good.'

Sarah swallowed, then shook her head. 'No harm was done me . . .'

'And I ask you to believe me,' the other went on, 'when I say he has acted outside my instruction . . .' He stopped and looked away. 'More, indeed, than I could have imagined,' he added. 'While you have done naught to warrant such treatment.'

Now Ragg spoke up, as if in all the sudden bonhomie he did not wish to miss his chance. 'Master Elyot . . . I beg pardon for the brabble – the injuries done to your servants,' he began. Then he paused, for Elyot was shaking his head.

'As far as I'm concerned, they were waylaid in the night by persons unknown,' he said quietly. 'They had no leave to be here in any case.'

Thomas and Ragg exchanged looks. But before either could speak, Elyot turned again to Sarah. 'There's another matter known to you and I,' he said, and waited. And this time Sarah's face flamed red to the edge of her periwig.

'Nay, sir,' she stammered. 'That's locked safe in my heart, where none shall see . . .'

191

'I know it,' Elyot replied. 'Yet while I am here, I may take the occasion to say that things will not remain as they were.' He lowered his eyes. 'I have let things slide far enough . . . and I do not intend to let that continue.'

Sarah stared at him, then her anxious face cleared. For a moment she looked as if she would dart forward, but she merely bobbed.

'Now I will return home,' Elyot said, 'and trouble you no further.' He paused. 'My servants can find their own way – when they have recovered.'

He gave Thomas a wry look. 'Falconer . . . I will ride to Petbury again, when Sir Robert returns. And after he has heard your account – which I doubt not will be as full as you promised – then he and I may talk, and see what must be done.'

Thomas inclined his head, as dumbfounded as everyone else at the change in the man. And without further speech Elyot took his leave, waving away Sarah's attempt to show him out and closing the door behind him.

The three of them waited until they heard his horse's hoofbeats recede in the distance. But when Ragg turned to Sarah, she shook her head quickly. 'Let's be thankful for what's come out of this,' she said. Then she found Thomas's gaze upon her, and went out to the back parlour.

But Thomas said nothing, nor would he meet Will Ragg's enquiring eye. For he had guessed who was the father of Mary Pegg's child; and he rejoiced inwardly that the man was at last prepared to take action – perhaps even some responsibility – for the welfare of poor Linnet.

He and Ragg went out then, and with a couple of folk from the almshouses, who were only too glad to satisfy their curiosity, gave the Bickington men some rudimentary aid. Though bleeding and sore, neither of the servants was badly injured, and neither needed any second instruction from Ragg to make themselves scarce – particularly since one of them had recovered in time to see William Elyot depart from Sarah's door. With many a sour look, but no further words, they got themselves mounted and rode off.

Stainbank's injuries demanded more attention. He too was conscious, and had sat himself up against the outside wall,

192

where Thomas found him. There, by the light of a harvest moon, he proceeded to bathe the man's face from a basin of river water. But after a very few minutes, finding himself strong enough to stand as well as to vent some of his rage, the steward got to his feet, brushed the dirt from his fine cloak and glared.

'I've had enough from you for one night,' he breathed.

Thomas straightened up and faced him. 'Then you'd best get yourself home,' he said.

Stainbank said nothing. Suddenly he sagged, looking sick. Before Thomas could react, he threw him a baleful look.

'Home? I have no home . . .' He gave a bitter laugh. 'Then you know, don't you? You've had more speech with Elyot . . . You've been thick with him ever since you cured his damned hawk!'

Thomas looked blank. 'I know not what you mean . . .'

'Don't try to deny it!' the other shot back. 'I saw your eyes, back in the great hall at Bickington, roving about, putting matters together . . . You know it all, don't you?'

Thomas shook his head. 'I know that something has occurred to cause a change in your master, yet—'

'He's not my master!' Stainbank cried. 'Not any more . . . I shall lose my place – I shall lose everything!' Suddenly he was in tears; a pathetic, snivelling figure, wiping his nose with his soiled sleeve.

Thomas gazed at him, barely able to digest this new turn of events. Something momentous must have occurred at Bickington in the twenty-four hours since he and Howes were there. Watching Stainbank closely, he began to voice his thoughts. 'You and Mistress Jane . . .' he began, but at once the other gave a cry, more of anguish than of anger.

'Of course it's *I and Mistress Jane*,' he hissed, then looked round quickly. 'There's no need to daub it on the wall!'

He put a hand to his head, and closed his eyes, seemingly forgetting Thomas's presence. 'He found me gone, and forced it out of her. Why else would he have come . . .'

Thomas froze. He had suspected that the whole business of kidnapping Howes in order to gain his lands had been first concocted by Jane Elyot and Stainbank. Now, he saw that there was somewhat more to the matter than that.

'Caught you both out at last, has he?' he asked bluntly.

Stainbank made no reply. Filled with shame and rage, he made an attempt to straighten his clothing, then looked about.

'Your horse is tethered over there,' Thomas said. He realized that his anger had evaporated; he felt nothing for the man now save contempt. He still recalled his behaviour that day on the Downs, and at Mary Pegg's . . .

Then he almost gasped, for he saw now that he had been wrong about something else too.

'You . . .' He caught at Stainbank's arm, just as the other was about to walk away towards his horse. 'You didn't only whore with Sarah, you went with Mary Pegg – years ago, when you and Elyot first came here . . .'

Stainbank's head whipped round, as he pulled himself quickly from Thomas's grasp. 'Let me alone!' he cried. 'I'm little better than a fugitive already – are you not yet satisfied?'

'Nay . . . I am not!' Moving swiftly, Thomas blocked his path. 'You were wrong: I knew not half of what you thought I did – but you've told me all in these last minutes.' He leaned closer. 'That poor brute of a child – she's likely yours as anyone else's!'

'No! She cannot be!' Stainbank lashed out at him viciously, and tore himself away. The next moment he was stumbling towards his horse, grabbing the reins and pulling at them with trembling hands.

Thomas started to follow, but Stainbank had freed the knot and scrambled up into the saddle. Then he jerked the rein savagely, making the animal rear in pain, and wheeled about.

'Damn your black soul, falconer!' he cried. 'May you rot in your grave!'

Then he dug his heels into the horse's sides and galloped off into the night.

Twenty

When Thomas woke, the sun was already rising. He sat up quickly, aware of a receding dream . . . something to do with a hand reaching up to him from a hole in the ground. Then he remembered, and looked quickly about: he was on the floor of Crouch's cottage. From outside came village sounds – and something much closer. He started, then relaxed as his friend appeared, carrying an earthenware dish.

'I thought it best to let you sleep,' Crouch said with a wry look. 'From what I hear, Henry Howes got himself mighty drunk at the Horns, before you and Will Ragg followed suit.'

Thomas put a hand to his head. 'It seemed right, at the time . . .' He coughed, and took the bowl gratefully. In a short time he had drunk the whey, and was feeling somewhat better.

'Have they told you . . . ?' he began, but the little clerk waved a hand impatiently at him.

'Unlike you, I've been abroad already. It's market day, or had you forgotten? The booths are already up.'

Thomas stood up unsteadily, fighting the ache in his head, and looked through the window. 'Market day . . .' He turned to the other. 'And they're raising the bell . . .'

Crouch's eyes gleamed. 'Indeed – this will be a momentous day for Lambourn.' Then his face clouded. 'Mayhap in other ways, too. Starling has sent word that Henry and I should be at the church within the hour.'

Thomas sat to pull on his boots. 'You've seen Howes?'

'I have.' Crouch wore a prim look. 'He told me all that occurred at your little party last night.'

Thomas eyed him. 'I'm in no mood to hear you pronounce judgement on me, Jonas. Though I thank you for breakfast . . .'

195

He held up the bowl. After a moment, Crouch took it and went away.

Soon after, they went out into the square, to find more than the usual air of business and bustle. The market stalls stood in their places, but few folk were buying. Instead there was a movement towards the church, to view the momentous spectacle of the raising of the new bell.

Thomas followed Crouch to the bell-yard, and found what had become a familiar sight this past week: a crowd of all ages, gathered about the bell-founder and his creation. And once again – perhaps for the last time, he reflected – Simon Goodchild was in control.

The founder and his helpers had been busy. The bell was ready, roped by its canons to the crane, which loomed over everyone's heads. A team of strong young men had already been formed to winch it up towards the bell-tower, supervised by Goodchild himself. An assortment of ropes, tools and timbers lay about. Looking up, Thomas saw that the other part of the process would be carried out by the founder's son: for the young man was visible high above in the belfry, with another helper, testing the heavy ropes which dangled from the opening. When the great bell had been raised to that height, it would be eased into place by Edmund. Then it would be secured to its headstock, and after the clapper was fixed it would be rung for the first time along with its fellows.

He glanced round, realizing Crouch had disappeared. Nearby, he saw Alice Goodchild, in a clean smock, standing apart as always. And as always there was a tenseness about her; but on this occasion it was understandable, for the excitement in the yard was such, none could avoid feeling it.

'Thomas . . .' Howes appeared at his shoulder, looking the worse for wear but thankfully sober, which was not how Thomas had left him outside the Horns last night.

Thomas was about to give greeting, then saw the man's expression.

'There's going to be mayhem,' the sexton said quietly.

Thomas frowned. 'Why's that?'

'The inscription,' he muttered. 'It's in Latin . . .'

Thomas nodded. 'I know.'

'So did everyone else, it seems – save the rector.'

And at once Thomas saw, and wondered why it had not occurred to him before. 'He wanted it in English – it will smack of popery to him—'

'That's a mild way of putting it.' Howes looked away for a moment, then said: 'If he hadn't cut himself off from everyone these past days, he'd have known it. That's what he's truly enraged about – claims everyone has kept it from him. I've had to endure his spleen already – now Jonas is getting his share.' He sighed. 'Starling will be out any moment, and call a halt to the whole business.'

But Thomas looked round sharply. Howes followed his gaze and drew breath – for the raising had begun.

'He'll be too late,' Thomas said.

A collective sigh rose from the crowd, of excitement mingled with satisfaction: at last, the mighty bell had begun its journey of ascent. Goodchild was calling out instructions in his deep voice, and the watchers heard the grunting of the lifting team as they bent their backs to the winch.

The bell was off the ground. It swayed, and the heavy beams of the A-frame crane bent slightly, but held. Goodchild himself leaned forward to steady the wondrous object, putting all his weight against it. A few feet away, his wife watched in silence.

The thick hempen ropes slid through the pulley at the crane's apex. And slowly, as the village men heaved and strained, the bell rose: its gaping mouth stood level with Goodchild's waist, then his chest, then his shoulders. He looked up and waved to Edmund, though what the signal conveyed, other than that all seemed well, nobody knew. High above, the boy gave an answering wave, both he and his helper watching intently as the bell rose steadily towards them.

Heads were now tilted upwards, squinting into the sun, which seemed to bless their endeavours, its rays reflecting off the gleaming bell-metal. Many times Thomas heard the words, from all parts of the crowd, which had thickened so that the yard was almost filled: *Our maiden bell . . .*

The bell was out of reach now, even of Simon Goodchild's long arms. Suspended in mid-air, soon it was closer to the tower than to the ground. Eagerly Edmund leaned out to admire it, his face flushed with pride. For a moment it seemed he had leaned too far, and one or two folk gasped, but his helper pulled him back by the arm. Edmund and the other young fellow grinned, and the danger was past.

Then there came the slam of a door, and a roaring voice from the back of the crowd:

'In the Lord's name, stop this blasphemy!'

There was a gasp from a hundred throats. Heads snapped round to see Richard Starling, his hair awry, holding a bible in his hand as he strode forward like the zealot he was. And at once the crowd stood back, as he made straight for the bell-founder.

A silence fell, so suddenly that birds could be heard calling from the alders by the river. Even the market folk, on the other side of the church, seemed to have heard the shout, and stopped in wonder.

Thomas stared, even as Jonas Crouch came hurrying up behind the rector, looking very anxious indeed. Howes left him and walked forward, and instinctively Thomas followed. From nowhere, Will Ragg had also appeared, as if drawn by the scent of impending trouble. For trouble there was about to be, and in prodigious quantity.

But all eyes moved from Starling to the bell-founder, who stood like a man of stone, tall and motionless, while the bell dangled a dozen feet above him.

'I order you to stop!' Starling shouted. 'For this bell will not be hung here, until the foul words writ around its crown be erased!'

Goodchild's chest swelled, as he mastered his anger. 'The inscription is as agreed,' he answered. 'My initials, and the date, and—'

'You know full well what we agreed!' the rector cried. 'But it was to be in English!'

There was a low groan from the villagers; more of dismay than of dissent. But the rector span on his heel and glared at them. 'Be silent! Unless you wish to be party to this sinful act . . .'

'Sinful?' To Thomas's surprise, it was Howes who spoke. His face flushed, he flinched as the rector turned the force of his wrath upon him, but stood his ground. 'Where's the sin, master? It is a maiden bell, cunningly made, with some words of devotion; what matter if they be in Latin—'

'What matter?' Starling's mouth twisted in contempt. 'If you do not know, then I despair of you – for you are as your fellows . . .' this with a scathing look at Crouch, who stood by trembling visibly, 'unfit for your office, like those two wardens – filled with wickedness, both of them!'

Now people gasped, and Thomas heard voices rise in amazement as well as indignation. Will Stubbs, wicked . . . ? It seemed blasphemy to say such.

For a moment people had almost forgotten the founder. But Thomas tensed as the man took a step towards Starling. From the corner of his eye, he saw Alice Goodchild also dart forward. And as Starling turned to face him, the founder made his pronouncement.

'The bell will be raised. It cannot be stopped.'

Starling's jaw dropped. 'I am master here, and I employ you – you will do as I bid!'

Goodchild was immoveable. 'I will not.'

And before Starling could reply, the founder raised a hand to the lifting team, who were standing in shocked silence.

'Again,' he intoned.

'No!' Starling raised a shaking hand, the one with the bible in it, and pointed it at them. 'You follow this man's orders, and I will cast you from my church!'

The crowd gasped again, and the hapless lifting team shrank back, some shaking their heads. One man had laid hands to the wedge which had been placed to stop the winch slipping backwards. But at Starling's words he quickly let go.

Goodchild bristled, his composure shaken at last.

'Raise the bell,' he called out. 'Else the demons I cast from the mould will return, and wreak vengeance upon you!'

Now there was more than dismay: there was real fear. It rippled outwards to the edges of the crowd, and some people moved back. Almost unnoticed, children were being shepherded away by frightened mothers. Few women remained alongside the men.

'Lower the bell!' Starling's voice had risen almost to a

scream. And Crouch's words, about the true extent of the rector's wrath, came home to Thomas with a jolt. Starling was puce with rage; veins stood out on his neck and temples. Thomas saw it then, as did others – the man was more than merely obsessive; he was mad.

Looking nervous, Will Ragg had eased himself forward to stand close to Starling. Now he dared to put out a hand.

'Master Rector: you should come away, and let the bell-maker do his work. It's dangerous to let the bell dangle like this . . .'

Starling almost choked, as he turned his terrible eye upon him. 'You too . . . you are bent on my destruction. Clods and villains all . . . I spit upon you! You are not worthy of this church!'

There were gasps, even oaths. Men glanced at each other, some angry, many aghast. Ragg caught Thomas's eye, seeming to signal that they should take the rector's arms and remove him by force.

But now, of all people, it was Jonas Crouch, tousled-haired and somewhat red of face, who stepped forward.

'Richard Starling.'

Starling looked round in outrage.

'Richard Starling . . .' Crouch repeated, struggling to master the tremor in his voice. 'There has been strife and wickedness aplenty here, these weeks . . . even months, I might say. And as one who has served this church loyally since before your arrival, I ask you to give way.'

There was a shocked silence at the little clerk's boldness. For his part, Starling merely stared at him. Then he snapped his head aside, as a movement caught his eye. Unnoticed, Edmund Goodchild had come down from the bell-tower, and now hurried to stand beside his father. Alice, too, had moved nearer. As when Thomas had first seen them, the founder's family stood together: an indivisible wall of opposition to the man who was now their enemy – if he had not been from the start.

It was become a picture: the trembling Starling, almost frothing as he faced them, one hand brandishing the new Geneva bible that was written in plain English, for all to read and understand. Against him stood a man from an earlier age – whose forefathers had indeed wrought bells for monasteries, as the rector himself had said. And around those bells had been words written often in Latin; the language of the ancients.

But what did that matter now? Folk stared, some shaking their heads, seeing no resolution. The tension was unbearable – until at last Goodchild chose to break it.

'Let me raise the bell,' he said in a harsh voice. 'Else I will denounce you to your bishop as unworthy of this diocese.'

Starling let out a cry. 'Devil – antichrist! You will burn in the fires!' He lunged forward. Goodchild reacted, raising a hand instinctively – but the rector was not concerned with him. Brushing the man aside, he almost ran at the poor souls who made up the lifting team; four or five sweating men, still standing helplessly about their winch.

'Let it down at once!' he shrieked. 'Or you will suffer such torment as you cannot imagine!'

The men backed away, plainly terrified. But from behind the rector came a sudden, blood-curdling scream that froze everyone to the spot.

'Kill him! Kill the basilisk, afore he strike ye dead with his wicked eye!'

For the second time there was complete silence, but this time it was one of amazement. Every pair of eyes settled on the bent, pointing figure of the founder's wife; the woman who was unable to speak, yet now stood shrieking venomously at their rector. It was difficult, at that moment, to decide which of them was the madder.

'You want the words struck from the bell?' She ran up to Starling, and stood yelling into his face. Her voice was shrill, like a cracked treble bell itself – perhaps because it was so seldom used . . .

'D'ye know what that will mean?' Alice Goodchild cried, even as her husband and son, faces filled with dismay, came forward to take hold of her. 'It means the bell will be ruined, for she will be scarred with the file and the chipping hammer, and lose her strike note – and then she will be no maiden bell! Mark ye not that, viper? Curse be upon thee!'

Wrenching herself free of the restraining arms of her husband, she darted to a pile of tools. And watched by every person – including Starling, who looked dumbstruck – she seized a maul with a square-pointed head, and raised it . . .

The chipping hammer.

Thomas gasped, looking swiftly at Ragg, who cried out, both of them leaping forward as one, knocking Simon Goodchild and his son aside, catching Alice and pulling from her hand the hammer now become a weapon, which she was about to bring down upon the head of Richard Starling. The weapon which would have shattered his skull and killed him, as it had killed John Nightingale; as it had killed William Stubbs . . .

Cursing under his breath, Ragg tore it away from her, as she screamed like a kite at him; and went on screaming as her husband gripped her in his strong arms, pinning her, and her son grabbed hold of her legs, and the two of them lifted her and bore her off without looking back . . . a writhing figure in a pale smock, her limp hair hanging loose, her screams fading as they hurried her away, heeding nothing except their need to get her out of sight to their camp, where they alone could deal with her. And her screams ebbed, and turned into a child-like weeping, as the trio stumbled away to the riverbank and disappeared through the trees.

In the bell-yard there was, as Howes had predicted, near mayhem. Men drew close about Ragg and Thomas, who with Howes and Crouch seemed to form a nucleus of order. Ragg raised his hands, begging for calm. But excited voices rose, along with mutterings of anger.

Thomas spoke under his breath. 'You'll have a mob here in no time, if you don't act . . .'

But as Ragg looked about in agitation, there came a cry of alarm. Both of them whirled round to see that Starling had marched to the lifting winch. Watched by the young men, who at first failed to realize what he was doing, he bent to the wedge locking the drum in place.

'Stop him!' Ragg lurched forward, but Thomas was quicker. Even as others saw the danger and began to move, he leaped towards the rector and grabbed his arm.

202

'Let go of me!' Starling cried, and lashed out at him.

Now there was a new peril – and it dangled above their heads, swaying alarmingly. Shouting to people to keep back, Ragg hurried to help Thomas restrain the struggling, shouting figure of Richard Starling, whose strength seemed that of two men. Desperately, he still clutched with a claw-like hand at the oak wedge.

Then it slipped.

With a whiplash sound the wedge flew up into the air, cracking one man on the jaw. But as he cried out, and others leaped back, there came other noises: a fearful groaning, as the winch's drum turned suddenly; and a loud creak from the crane's timbers overhead, as the rope snaked upwards.

There were screams, which lasted longer than the brief seconds it took for the bell to fall from its terrible height. And the dumbstruck crowd could only watch in horror as it descended upon the manic figure of Richard Starling, face flushed in some kind of ecstasy . . . Too late, far too late, he looked up and saw the falling bell, which dropped with all its weight upon his left shoulder, crushing him like a chicken, flattening his black-clad body into a heap, and coming to rest upon the earth again.

They rolled the bell clear, to huddle in a stunned group about the prone, broken body of the rector. Most were too shocked to make a sound. But Crouch and Howes knelt either side of him, the sexton dumbfounded, the little clerk in tears. And from somewhere appeared the hitherto missing churchman, John Wilmott: shoving his way through the watchers, his face taut with anguish, to drop to one knee beside his fellows.

'He's alive . . .' Howes bent forward, cradling the man's head; yet it was clear he was beyond all help. Blood and the ends of protruding bones showed in so many places, it was a miracle he had not died instantly.

'Lord have mercy on him . . .' Wilmott's whisper was so low, only the other two heard it.

Starling opened his eyes and peered about, his mouth working feebly. Thomas and Ragg, who had both hung back, came closer. The dying man coughed slightly, and a spray of bloody froth flew from his mouth. 'His lungs are torn . . .' Ragg dropped to his knees. 'If I'd only shoved him aside . . .'

Thomas gripped the blacksmith's shoulder hard; the man was blaming himself. But to their surprise it was Wilmott who turned swiftly to Ragg, shaking his head. 'Men make their own doom . . . He wished to bring the bell down, and he did it!'

Starling was wheezing. They leaned closer, even as he gave another cough; and it was plain the end would not be long in coming.

'Don't try to speak . . .' Crouch had taken the man's hand in his. He squeezed it, but it remained limp. Then a faint sound emerged from Starling's mouth: but so low, the words were lost. Seeing their faces, he tried again, a look of desperation in his eyes, as if he feared he would not be heard.

Howes bent his ear close to the rector's mouth, listening intently. But there came nothing more than a brief sentence, or perhaps two, before the man gave up. With a sigh his last breath escaped, and the eyes filmed over. He was gone.

The sexton sat up, and turned a haggard face to the others.

'I suppose he meant the founder,' he muttered, then drew breath sharply. 'Mayhap he meant Stubbs . . .'

'What did he say?' Crouch asked dully. He placed the man's lifeless hand on his chest.

'He said: *He hated me, because I knew what he was.*'

Twenty-One

Starling's body was laid in St Katherine's chapel in the north-east corner of the church, where the body of Samuel Hubbard still rested. John Nightingale's was yet in the inn; and now there was none to conduct one funeral service, let alone three.

But that was a matter for the churchmen: Howes and Crouch and Wilmott, who, though officially no longer churchwarden, gathered with the others in the vestry. What was said between them, none knew; but somehow the three men finally emerged the stronger from their ordeal, if sorely shaken. And that, folk would say in later years, was their salvation, as well as the beginning of a new St Michael's, that would rise from the turmoil that had been caused by the raising of the new bell. Or perhaps, some said, its causes went back a deal further: to the arrival of Richard Starling as rector.

Yet now, more immediate matters must be addressed. And a different trio assembled in the bell-yard, grim-faced and determined: Thomas, Will Ragg – and John Tolworthy. The miller, in Lambourn for market day, had come late to the bell-raising. Yet he had been in time to witness its terrible climax, and the fate of Richard Starling. Seeing him standing apart, a subdued figure, Ragg had called him over, relieved to have a friend at his side. Indeed, what had passed between them on the Downs three days ago seemed if anything to have strengthened their bond of friendship. The three men stood together, to decide how to act.

But to begin with, Ragg was at a loss for words. After a while he turned to Tolworthy, bidding him speak.

'If none will ride to the High Sheriff, then I will go,' the miller said. 'And word must be sent to Salisbury, to the bishop . . .'

Ragg nodded, seeming to gather his strength. 'First it seems I've a murderer to arrest,' he said quietly. 'Unless any man doubts what we saw?'

Tolworthy shook his head. 'Could it really be she – the founder's wife? Doubtless she's mad as a hare, but . . .'

Ragg was frowning. 'Madder than any I've seen. Yet why she did it, I know not—'

'Did what?' Thomas had been staring at the bell, still on its side in the yard. The men who had been helping to raise it stood around looking lost; though one was untying the rope from the canons.

He came out of his reverie and faced the others. 'You suppose because she attacked the rector with that hammer, she did the same to Nightingale?'

Ragg eyed him. 'You said the founder's other hammer was too small, but that one . . .' He looked round and pointed.

The chipping hammer still lay on the ground, where it had fallen after the struggle to restrain Alice Goodchild. Quickly Ragg walked over and picked it up. The others followed him.

'Well?' the blacksmith hefted it in his hand, then offered it to Thomas, who took it and examined it. After a moment he handed it back. 'If there was any blood, it's been washed away thoroughly,' he said. 'Yet, it would fit Nightingale's wound.'

'Then why wait?' Ragg was working his hands, as if eager to use them. 'Look – I'm a smith acting as constable, not a scholar,' he said, with a frown at Thomas. 'If you know better, then speak.'

'I know no more than you,' Thomas answered. 'Yet it's clear where we might find the truth.' He looked towards the river. 'Would you like our help, Master Constable?'

Ragg nodded. 'Let's not waste more time.' Glad to take some action at last, he led the way to the bell-founder's encampment.

They emerged into the clearing, to find an air of utter tranquillity. A few yards away the river trickled by musically, and moorhens splashed in its shallows. There was no sign either of Simon or of Alice Goodchild. But young Edmund rose from his seat by the open fireplace, as if he had expected them. As the three men approached, they saw clearly the anguish in his handsome face, pale under its tan.

'Masters . . .' He looked intently at them, as if trying to gauge their mood. Seeing they did not offer force, he waited.

'I would speak with your father, boy,' Ragg said.

Edmund nodded. 'He will answer you soon . . . only spare him a moment. For he needs time to quiet my mother.'

His gaze strayed to the tent, which was closed up. From within, the others fancied they could hear voices. There was a moment, then Thomas broke the silence. 'It was she gave you your bloody nose that day, was it not? There was no mysterious assailant with whom you had a bout.'

The other two looked at him sharply. Edmund did not reply, but the look on his face was affirmation enough.

'How long has she been thus?' Thomas asked, not unkindly.

Edmund sighed. 'Since before I was born,' he said.

Ragg drew a deep breath. 'You mean she has flown into such rages at other times?' When Edmund merely looked helpless, he stepped forward, angry now. 'Answer me!'

Edmund answered him unhappily. 'She cannot help herself,' he said. 'She has something inside her, like a vile spirit – her child-demon, she calls it. At times it breaks forth and she becomes . . . as you saw her.' The young man was suddenly agitated. 'Yet she seldom does harm – I beg you, treat her gently, and she will respond—'

'Respond?' Ragg's face was reddening, all the emotion of the past half hour welling up. 'She has killed a man—'

'No!'

Ragg's head snapped round, as the familiar deep voice rang out across the clearing. Simon Goodchild had emerged from the tent, pausing only to secure the flap quickly behind him. Then he strode towards the other men, who stiffened immediately.

'She has killed no one . . .' The bell-founder spoke with his usual authority, but there was a catch in his voice that none had heard before. It seemed that since his desperate argument with Starling, and what had occurred after, his control had been stretched too far.

Tolworthy stepped aside, one eye on Edmund, who had

tensed visibly. Thomas was on the other side of Ragg. But with a glance at the blacksmith, he moved forward.

'Your account belies the evidence, master,' Thomas said. 'For everyone saw how she seized your hammer, and made to attack the rector. And now he is dead . . .'

Goodchild and his son started. 'Dead . . . ? But she did not touch him!' the founder cried, eyes flicking at each of them. 'You took the weapon from her yourself!'

'The weapon, yes . . .' Ragg nodded. 'Yet in one way, it might be said the rector died at your hands. The bell fell and crushed him.'

There was a silence. Edmund sat down heavily on a log by the unlit fire, while Goodchild merely stared, as if hoping it was a lie. But he saw that it was not.

'My bell has killed him . . . ?' he muttered. 'It cannot be . . .' Suddenly he clenched his fists, and drove them hard against his sides. 'May God forgive me . . .'

Scarcely knowing what they did, the others had closed about him. But the founder made no move; merely bowed his head, and remained still.

The silence was long. Thomas's glance strayed to the tent, from which no sound emerged, then to young Edmund, who was the most visibly grief-stricken. For once, there was no current of understanding between father and son. Instead, both seemed lost in their own thoughts. Then Ragg spoke up.

'Simon Goodchild, I accuse your wife of the murder of John Nightingale, innkeeper—'

'Sweet Jesu – no, master – I beg!' Edmund Tolworthy was on his feet, staring wildly at Ragg. 'She is a poor lost soul, who scarce knows what she does—'

'Enough!' Ragg was in no mood to listen. He eyed Simon grimly. 'Bring her forth to answer the charge, else I will arrest you too, who have impeded me enough!'

'Then that is what you must do,' Goodchild said abruptly. 'For I am guilty of the murder.'

There was a moment . . . and Thomas's gaze, then Ragg's, strayed towards John Tolworthy, who almost gasped. Was the man bent on saving his wife, by false confession? The little tragedy played out between these men and poor Edward

Tolworthy, on the windy Downs above Uplambourn, was a raw memory in each man's mind. And for a moment they were at a loss.

But Goodchild, seeming to sense some advantage, was looking intently at Ragg. 'You will hear me – you must, for you trust my words.'

Ragg hesitated. 'Speak, then . . . but if there is one scrap of your account which does not tally with what I and the falconer here – ' this with a jerk of his head towards Thomas – 'with what we know, then I will place both you and your wife in chains.'

Goodchild swallowed and took a step back, as if gathering his energies. Then he gave a deep sigh.

'The innkeeper died here.'

He gestured to the edge of the camp, beside the river. 'He and I had hard words, and we fought – I seized the nearest of my tools, and struck him. Once, twice . . . on the head, thus.' He put a hand to the top of his forehead, to show them. Then he looked away, before making an effort to continue.

'When he fell, I saw what I had done . . . I dragged him under the cart, there. Later, I carried him through yon thicket, and left him by the bushes, on the path . . .' He stopped and faced them, a look of desperation in his eyes.

But Edmund groaned, his gaze fixed helplessly upon his father. 'He did not carry him alone,' he muttered. 'I helped.'

The others exchanged looks. But Tolworthy turned away, as if unwilling to witness the pain that flowed between father and son. Ragg swallowed, unsure how to respond, and glanced finally at Thomas.

But Thomas had been looking intently at Goodchild, and now spoke up. 'Why does your wife pretend she can't speak?'

The founder turned to him with a frown. 'It is easier thus,' he answered. 'She fears most folk. She cannot stand normal discourse, save with us.'

Thomas nodded slowly. 'It must have been hard to bear, all these years. For you and your children, I mean.'

The founder said nothing; but his expression was bleak.

'Forgive me, for I do not see a clear picture,' Thomas persisted. 'What were you and the innkeeper fighting about?'

Goodchild hesitated. 'A matter of payment,' he answered.

'You came to him early last market-day morn, and had words with him at his back door,' Thomas said. 'Was that also about a payment?'

Goodchild drew a breath. 'What does it matter now, why we argued? I have admitted I killed him.'

Thomas went on as if he had not heard. 'This payment you speak of – might it not better be called a bribe?'

Ragg started, and looked from one to the other. When Goodchild made no response, he stepped closer. 'Answer!'

Still Goodchild did not speak. Nearby, Edmund had turned away, and was casting about in great agitation. More than once his gaze went to the closed-up door of the tent.

'Hare was bribed by John Nightingale . . .' Ragg was working it out for himself now. But Thomas finished for him.

'Who had been already bribed by Master Goodchild here, to lie about the way Will Stubbs's body was found.' He paused, nodding slowly, for he had seen the last fragment fall into place. 'When Hare was caught, Nightingale saw it would come out, so he went to you for a pay-off, to flee the village . . . Did he threaten to tell the whole tale, if you refused?'

'Nay . . .' Goodchild was alarmed now. 'You are wrong! I fought with Nightingale and killed him. You have your murderer, by confession—'

'Let's say we have one of them,' Thomas allowed. 'Yet I still cannot imagine how you came to kill Will Stubbs – what was he to you?'

'Stubbs . . . ?' The founder was breathing faster, tugging at his thick beard. 'He was nothing – he fell! He was an old man . . .'

'He was killed by a frenzied blow to the head, from your hammer,' Thomas said. 'Then he was sat upright and bound to a tree, so that all could see it was an execution—'

'For pity's sake, stop!'

With a desperate cry, Edmund Goodchild leaped at Thomas, fists flailing. And the tension that had held all of them spellbound snapped. Ragg sprang forward and grabbed the boy, even as Thomas seized his hands and held them away, avoiding the threatened blows. But they were feeble; and the young man went limp and fell to the ground, head down, sobbing. And as Ragg and Thomas lowered their arms, breathing hard, Simon Goodchild sank to his knees beside his son, hugging him to his chest. There they stayed, the one silent, the other weeping like a child.

But there came another voice . . . high and strange, though not frenzied as before. And Thomas and the other two span round, and saw Alice Goodchild hurry from the tent, run to her family and drop to her knees beside them.

They watched helplessly as she looked up at them at last, with a face devoid of expression.

'I killed the one you know as Stubbs,' she said softly. 'For I knew him by another name . . . more than thirty years ago, in the time of Mary . . . when he sent my father to the fires. And I have no regret; for he was wicked, and has met his end at last.'

A dozen village men stood about the clearing, filling the founder's camp. They had bound both Goodchilds, husband and wife, and placed them in their own tent under guard. Then Ragg had spoken with John Tolworthy, who had gone to find his horse, to begin the long ride to take word to the High Sheriff.

Thomas talked with Howes and Crouch, who had hurried from the church when they heard what had happened. Ragg, tired but calm, had ordered someone to ride downriver to Bickington and ask William Elyot to provide a secure lock-up for the prisoners. In Thomas's opinion, the man would likely be pleased to offer his help.

Edmund Goodchild was not yet arrested; he had been allowed to remain with his parents and have some private speech with them. After a while he emerged from the tent and walked over to where Ragg and Thomas stood.

'With your leave, masters . . .' His face was pale, but there was a calmness about him now, as he faced them both.

'My father has charged me with completing our commission,' he said. 'If the folk of Lambourn wish it, and will lend their aid, I will raise the bell. Then I will clear the yard, and if you permit it, strike camp . . .'

Ragg began to voice doubts. 'You may yet face charges yourself, boy,' he said, though without anger. 'I'm loath to give permission . . .'

'I will not flee,' Edmund answered. 'I will await the sheriff's pleasure and answer all charges. It is but that my father begs you to let me finish his work.'

There was pleading in his gaze, and finally Ragg nodded, whereupon the young man went off towards the bell-yard; though his head hung low. Ragg turned to find Thomas's gaze upon him.

'If you allow, I would dearly like to hear what she has to say . . .' Thomas said.

The other nodded. 'I wouldn't think of preventing you.'

They crowded into the warm tent, its flaps open now to admit a flow of air: Thomas, Ragg, Crouch, Howes and others, facing the bound couple, who sat on pallets with their backs against the wall. Their wrists were bound, but not so tightly that they could not clasp each other's hands. More villagers were gathered about the entrance.

At first, Alice had lapsed into the apparent dumbness with which she normally faced the world. And though it would no longer serve, she seemed unwilling to utter a word. So now, her husband spoke for her.

'She was but fourteen years old when her father went to the fires,' he said quietly. 'Like many honest men and women, who would not deny their Protestant faith, but fell foul of that bloody-handed monarch, Mary Tudor . . .' He paused, glancing at his wife, who did not meet his eye.

'The man who came here, to begin a new life in this far-off place, thought he had escaped retribution; after Queen Elizabeth took the throne and turned tables upon the papists . . .' There was a bitter twist to his mouth. 'You knew him a s Stubbs – pious and devout, friend and comforter to everyone – he even became a churchwarden! But she . . .' He nodded to indicate Alice. 'She knew him as Daggett – Simon Daggett, one of those who infiltrated secret meetings of Protestants, who feigned to worship alongside them, and claimed to share their faith, then informed upon them. So it was with James

Dawberry, my wife's father – a good man, taken with the rest . . . chained to a stake with straw about his feet—'

'Enough!'

All turned to stare at Alice, who was gripping her husband's hand so tightly the knuckles showed milk-white.

'I will speak . . . I'll tell you . . .' The high voice, cracked now with grief, fell upon their ears like that of some Downland bird. She looked around, flinching at the many eyes fixed upon hers.

'I was but a maiden,' she said. 'And Daggett took my maidenhood as surely he took my father's life – as he took my mother's, for she died within a year, of naught but grief. He took it – not with his body, for we had fled far away by then – he took it with his wicked testimony: spilling his list of names, sending folk to their deaths, making widows and orphans by the score . . .' She screwed her eyes up tightly.

'We hid, in the weald of Kent, among hard men – miners with hard hands and hard bodies . . . there it was I lost my maidenhood, and became little more than a waif. Until a good man came to the village to cast bells, and took me into his family.'

Few could fail to be moved, as she closed her fingers again about her husband's. 'I grew up, and married his son. I became a bell-founder's wife, and bore a bell-founder's sons,' she said. 'And that has been my life.'

She paused, then: 'Yet the child-demon was within me, and would burst forth at times . . . This man learned to deal with it, better than any other could have done. And we have travelled since, far and wide, and all might have been well, had we not come upriver this summer to Lambourn, where the one who called himself Stubbs lived.' She glanced at Ragg, then at Thomas. 'You know what followed.'

'You recognized him?' Ragg asked, in a voice filled with wonder. 'After all this time . . . ?'

Alice nodded, and spoke so low they had to lean closer to hear. 'The year of fifteen fifty-six seems but hours ago to me . . . for I stood with my mother, and watched my father burn.'

Men averted their eyes, sobered by her testimony. But Thomas gave Alice a kind look.

213

'You followed him to the woods, where he went in secret to pray,' he said. 'We have learned that he was a Catholic . . . he hid it well, from most. But not from everyone: you and Richard Starling, to name two . . .'

There were murmurs of astonishment. But this was not the time for such matters to be aired. With a glance at Thomas, Ragg pressed the woman to continue.

'You struck him from behind, then tied him, as your father had been tied.'

Alice lowered her eyes. 'It was fitting.'

But for Thomas, another light had dawned – something that now seemed to him somewhat ridiculous, and sat poorly with the gravity of the testimony they had heard.

'*The Book of Martyrs*,' he said. 'Stubbs – Daggett – hid it, because it has pictures of the fires . . .'

Crouch, who had hitherto said nothing, gasped aloud. 'He thought he would be recognized!'

Alice gazed at him. 'He might have been,' she said. 'For he was present at many burnings, alongside the priests; aiding them, rejoicing as the martyrs burned . . .'

Then she stopped, shaking her head, and her husband took her hand again, his mouth tight with anguish.

'You have heard enough, have you not?' he said.

After a moment Ragg nodded. 'I'd say we have,' he replied. Thomas straightened up, as did the others. It was over. Leaving men with the prisoners, Ragg ushered everyone outside.

In the sharp sunlight that filtered through the trees, they walked a few yards. Crouch had followed, along with Henry Howes. The four men gazed in silence at each other.

'What will happen to them?' Howes asked finally.

Nobody spoke.

'It seems hard that she should hang for her deed, wicked though it be,' the sexton went on. 'To be condemned to death as her father was . . .'

Ragg turn to him, suddenly angry. 'A quick death, at least,' he retorted. 'What would you have me do – free them both? The man who killed John Nightingale, and the woman who killed—' He broke off, as if irritated with himself for the words

214

that would have followed. *Will Stubbs . . . ? There was no Will Stubbs . . .*

Thomas turned to him. 'You've done all you can,' he said. 'Let the law take its course.'

Then as if at some unspoken command they separated, each man drifting away, bent on his own thoughts.

Twenty-Two

Eight days later, on a mild Saturday afternoon, Sir Robert Vicary came home to Petbury, his face flushed with joy. Not only had he attended the Queen on her royal progress to Cowdray; he had waited upon her personally, and even gone hawking with her.

He lost little time in speaking of it, to any of the household who happened to be within earshot. Change was in the wind, he said. The Queen in her late years needed men she trusted near her. He would be called to Court soon, and would likely be spending more time in London. Especially now that it was September, and the plague was diminishing at last; thank heaven it had not travelled upriver after all. Meanwhile . . .

Meanwhile, it appeared that certain matters had occurred in his absence. Martin the steward was first to have discourse with him, having been given an account of the events at Lambourn by Thomas the falconer. By the time Martin had finished, Sir Robert's face wore a very different expression indeed.

'Murderers and felons clapped up at Bickington?' His brow had creased into its familiar furrow. 'What in God's name . . .' He broke off. 'Tell Thomas to ready a couple of birds, and get himself horsed within the hour.'

Thomas was waiting at the mews with Ned when Sir Robert came riding up. He reined in and muttered a greeting, then leaned down to take the hooded falcon on to his gauntlet.

'I hear you've had your hands full,' he said.

Thomas nodded. 'Indeed, sir, I've been absent more than I liked.' He turned to his helper. 'But Ned has been a more than capable deputy . . .'

Sir Robert grunted, then, seeing Ned standing like a post with his customary awkwardness, gave a wry smile.

216

'Ease up, boy. You know I won't bite . . .' He frowned suddenly. 'How fare my peacocks?'

Ned gulped, but Thomas threw Sir Robert a smile. 'They are in good fettle, sir . . . Might we talk as we ride?'

They cantered westwards on to Greenhill Down, then loosed the birds and let them soar. A few clouds drifted overhead. After a while, Sir Robert bade Thomas tell his own tale, to sit alongside Martin's somewhat terse summary. When he had finished, the knight exhaled loudly, and gave him a long look.

'I would guess the High Sheriff and I will have much to discuss, when he comes here.' He lapsed into thought for a moment. 'And Elyot's steward is flown, you say?'

Thomas nodded.

The knight wrinkled his nose. 'He's no loss to the locality . . . They say he and Mistress Jane hatched many a plot between them – and cuckolded Elyot to boot! No credit to him, for taking so long to see what was under his nose.'

He looked up. 'What of this church bell, that has caused such discord?'

'It has been raised at last, sir,' Thomas answered, 'with much rejoicing. The bishop has sent a temporary rector to St Michael's – a good man. He it was who conducted the funerals of the constable and the innkeeper . . .'

He did not add that the rector had also agreed to the posting of banns announcing the wedding of William Ragg, blacksmith, and Sarah Caldwell, serving-maid. Nor that Edmund Goodchild the founder's son, after some private speech with Will Ragg, had been allowed to slip away with his cart the night after the bell was installed. It seemed right, some said, that the boy should not suffer for the crimes of his parents, but would carry on his father's work.

'And Richard Starling?' Sir Robert asked, breaking Thomas's thoughts.

'His body was taken away,' Thomas answered. 'It seems he had a family, who never saw him . . . The church was all of his life.'

Sir Robert nodded, watching the falcons float high overhead. A light breeze ruffled the collar of his cloak.

'What of your life?' his master asked abruptly.

Thomas was taken aback. 'My life is here, sir . . .'

'I know that,' his master replied. 'I mean, does married life suit you, once again? I thought you might wish for a bigger cottage, especially if Nell falls pregnant—' He started. 'She isn't, is she?'

'She has not said so, sir,' Thomas answered, struggling with his embarrassment. If truth be told, he and Nell had had little time for speech upon any matter in recent weeks. But since his return they had settled down to something like contentment.

'The cottage, then . . .' Sir Robert repeated, looking across at him. Thomas sat a different horse today than the one he had ridden to and fro about Lambourn. The animal was unused to him, and was somewhat restless.

'The cottage suits me well enough, sir,' he answered. 'As it has always done.'

'Then you wish no reward?' Sir Robert asked, raising his eyebrows. 'From what Martin tells me, the folk of Lambourn were profuse in their gratitude after the aid you rendered them. Doubtless there will always be a welcome for you in that far-flung little parish.'

Thomas inclined his head. 'I have good friends there,' he agreed. His thoughts flew briefly to the farewells he had taken, almost a week ago: from Crouch and Henry Howes; from Will Ragg and Sarah. But what came to his mind now was the report that Mary Pegg had been offered a home in the almshouses, but declined it. She preferred to remain where she was, in the old warrener's hut on the Downs.

'Sir John Norris will return soon, as my guest,' Sir Robert was saying. 'When he hears all, he would expect me to give you some token of appreciation.'

Thomas shook his head. 'Nay, sir . . . I need naught—' He stopped himself. 'Save perhaps one thing.' Taking the knight's nod for encouragement, he went on: 'It's as much for the contentment of the whole manor as mine; and I believe it would please Lady Margaret mightily, when she returns home . . .'

Sir Robert was frowning. 'You fill me with alarm. Out with it, man!'

Thomas took a breath. 'It concerns the peacocks . . .'